Ishmael

By M. Ward Leon

For information, or to order additional copies, please contact:

Beacon Publishing Group
P.O. Box 41573 Charleston, S.C. 29423
800.817.8480| beaconpublishinggroup.com

Publisher's catalog available by request.

ISBN-13: 978-1-961504-00-4

ISBN-10: 1-961504-00-4

Published in 2023. New York, NY 10001.

First Edition. Printed in the USA.

For my Joanie, Meghan, Auggie Doodle
And for all my homies in Bruges

Ishmael

They call me Ishmael. I and I alone am the only living survivor of the *Pequod,* a once-mighty whaling ship whose Captain Ahab and her entire crew were lost, 'cept one, after being attacked by the great white whale, Moby Dick.

I, too, would hath been lost if it were not for my friend Queequeg's coffin that he had built prior to our deadly encounter with the behemoth leviathan. It was my lifebuoy for one whole day and night. I clung to it as a baby clings to its mother for dear life. It sustained me on that soft and dirge-like main until a sail appeared off on the horizon.

It was the whaling ship, the *Rachel,* that also had a deadly encounter with Moby Dick. It found not the child they had been searching for but another orphan, me.

One would think that's where my story would end, but ye would be wrong, my friend.

"What be ye name?" Captain Gardiner of the *Rachel* asked.

"Call me Ishmael," I answered.

"How do you come to be here?"

"I was crew on the *Pequod.*"

"The devil, you say."

"Aye."

"Were you swept overboard, man?"

"Nay."

"Where be the *Pequod*?"

"She went down with all hands."

"How is that possible?"

"Moby Dick," I answered.

"All lost? Are ye sure?"

"Aye."

"Even Ahab?"

"Aye. Just as the prophecy predicted." Says I.

"Prophecy? What Prophecy?"

"Just before setting sail, I was told that one day, I would smell land where thar be no land. And on that day, Ahab will go to his grave, but he would rise again within the hour. And when he rises, he shall beckon. Then all, save one, shall follow."

Gardiner and the others all looked pale and scared.

"Was it as it was prophesied?" Gardiner asked.

"Aye." Says I.

"How can that be?"

"Once Moby Dick had been spotted. We launched all the whaleboats; even Ahab captained one. As we waited for the breach, thar came the smell of land, like an island, like a coral reef with green moss and shells. The devil Moby Dick be an island unto himself, that be for sure. Then someone yelled, "Thar she blows!"

He rose up from the depths and swam right towards the Captain, staring directly at him with its blue/black eye. Ahab thrust the lance deep into the whale's back as it neared, but the whale did not flinch. Several more harpoons were plunged into the monster, yet it did not acknowledge them. Finally, it dove deep down into the sea, taking one of the whaleboats and its crew down with him.

We waited for the breach; we waited for what seemed to be an eternity. Overhead thar were hundreds of gulls circling above us. Ahab shouted, "Watch the birds!" Then the birds took flight as the great behemoth breached out of the sea, crashing down upon Ahab's boat. It dragged Ahab and everyone else down into that watery Hell.

When Moby Dick rose again from the depths, Ahab was caught up in the lashings from all the harpoons the monster had inherited over the years. Ahab be dead, yet as the whale swam by us, Ahab seemed to beckon us to follow him as his free arm was gesturing.

We were all chilled to the bone with fright, and the men were wailing and crying out to abandon such folly and head back to the safety of the *Pequod*. And we would hath, too. If it were not for Chief mate Starbuck, who rallied us all to his call, "We are whaling men. We do not turn from whales. We kill them! Death to Moby Dick!"

So, after the monstrous whale, we chased. Each time Moby Dick breached, he blighted another and another of the boats until thar were no more. As it smashed a boat with its breach, it would bring its mighty fluke down upon the poor souls with a vengeance. And after all the whaleboats had been destroyed, he turned his wrath to the mothership, ramming her head-on into the starboard side, sending the *Pequod* down to Davey Jones's locker, with all souls on board.

I soon realized that I was the only survivor. Thar was nothing and no one as far as the eye could see. Then, just as Moby Dick had breached the surface, so did my friend Queequeg's coffin that you found me holding fast when you saved me." Said I.

Nary, a soul spoke. They all looked at me as if I were some sort of a Jonah. I sensed their fear. I beseeched them, saying, "Fear me not, brothers. For I am but the messenger of this tale, not the creator."

Thar were many of the crew that cursed me, calling me a Jonah and even a few that mumbled of casting me overboard, thinking that I be bad luck.

Captain Gardiner quickly came to my defense, "Let it be, lads. He be the victim, not the villain, here. I will hear no more about it."

Once I had rested, Captain Gardiner came to see me in the crew's quarters and informed me that the crew had come to peace with my plight. And that we are to sail on down to the tip of South America to Patagonia before they would be sailing back to England. He kindly offered me the opportunity to join his crew or disembark when they stopped in Kingston, Jamacia, for supplies and stores so that I could make my way back to New Bedford.

"You do not hath to decide at the moment. I know that ye be tried and are in no mind to decide. So, give some thought and let me know." Gardiner said.

For the following weeks, I was the subject of much curiosity, as all of the crew members and officers wanted me to retell the story of Ahab and Moby Dick. At night I would be awakened by terrible dreams. I would scream out in terror, waking the others and be soaked to the bone from my own sweat, shaking in fear. It was clear to me then that I needed to go back to New Bedford, back to the land and away from the sea.

"Captain Gardiner. I thank ye for all that you hath done for me. But I think it best that I make my way back home." I said, slightly ashamed.

"I understand, lad. Thar be not any shame for your decision, for ye hath lived through a nightmare that I cannot even imagine. By my calculations, we shall be in Kingston Harbor in six weeks. Thar should be plenty of ships bound for the states that will be looking for able-bodied men. But first, we must stop in Havana, Cuba, to unload some of our bounty."

"I thank ye for my life, Captain Gardiner. I owe you a debt that I fear I will never be able to repay you, sir."

"You owe me nothing, lad. I did but what any Christian man would hath done for his fellow man."

I thanked him again and then made my way back to my seaman's duties. Today was the cleaning of the decks, and tonight I begin standing watch on the larboard side. I feel it's the least I can do to help earn my keep.

Over the following weeks, I hath a sense of melancholy and shame. Why were I the only one to survive whilst so many others, equally good men, perish? The young mate, Starbuck, a thoughtful Quaker, married with a son. Stubbs, the second mate, always with a pipe in his mouth and a smile on his face. And then thar was Queequeg, my bosom friend. The son of a South Sea cannibal chieftain who left home to explore the world. It were his vision of death that ultimately saved my life.

I am but a shell of my former self. I feel dead inside. I find myself percolating the idea of ending me life so I may attain some peace and solitude. I fear my life has lost all meaning. I do not know what will become of me.

"Land Ho!" Jack Morgan, the lookout, hollered from above in the crow's nest.

As we approached the island of Cuba, we saw hundreds of humpback whales returning to their breeding grounds. But they concerned us no more as our oil casks were full. Since the *Rachel's* belly was full of liquid gold and whale oil, the crew were able to watch as the behemoths played and courted each other for the mating rights.

At four bells, we dropped anchor in Havana harbor; the sky was a brilliant azure without a single cloud above. Thar were many a ship moored as far as the eye could see, merchant ships, man-o'-warships, frigates, whaling, and even slave ships; they flew flags from countries from around the world, England, France, Spain, Dutch, Sweden, Italy, and America. A few flew no flag at all, meaning they were either pirates or privateers looking to hire out to the highest bidder.

We were moored not far from the slave ship *Esmeralda*, out of Charleston. She was carrying a full load of human cargo. We could hear the crying of babies and the wails and moans of the men and women. The crack of whips, the hollering of the slave guardians, and the constant beatings day and night.

I could not imagine the sheer terror and horror of being torn away from everything and everyone I had known all my life to be cruelly transported halfway around the world in horrific conditions. To be beaten, tortured, raped, and then sold off as if they be nothing more than a piece of livestock.

Thinking back on it, on all sailing vessels that had a negro cabin boy, they were a sort of a slave. Onboard the *Pequod,* Pip be our cabin boy. After several unfortunate incidents in the whaling boats, some sailors believed that Pip became an idiot or mad. But I found Pip's madness to be full of poetry and passion. Captain Ahab sympathized with Pip and took him under his wing.

Tom Thumb be the cabin boy here on the *Rachel;* he is small of stature and slight of build, just like Pip was. I took a shine to him right off. He was intelligent, quick, and eager to learn. Whenever I had the time, I would help him with his schooling.

On our first day in Cuba, being that I was the newest man, I was to be one of the men who had to stand the first dog watch from sixteen hundred hours to twenty-two hundred hours so that the rest of the crew could hath the first crack at going ashore for leave. By the time the men of my watch and I got to shore for leave, Havana was still thriving, with thousands of people out in the streets. Unbeknownst to me, members of the *Rachel's* crew had gotten drunk and had begun to spread the tale of Moby Dick, the *Pequod,* and me.

I walked into a British pub named The White Lion Inn that sat across from the *Iglesia de San Francisco de Paula* (Church of San Francisco de Paula) when I heard Smitty, our first harpooner, say, "And all hands perished, 'cept one. It be a white whale named Moby Dick."

"I hath heard of such a beast." A Norwegian sailor said.

"Ah, ye be daft man. No whale could do such a thing! Kill every man and sink a ship. Nay, it cannot be." Said a sailor who had the look of a scurvy dog.

"I swear it to be the truth. Hast I ever lied to ye?" Smitty said, appealing to the barkeeper.

"Never." The barkeeper said.

"And what say ye bout the sailor, be him a Jonah?" The scallywag sailor asked.

"He be a good man. I wrong him not." Smitty said defiantly.

"Then I say, he be jackin' ye about, or he be full of bilge water."

"Are ye calling me a liar!" I says to the sailor as I enter the smoked filled room. I made my way to the bar and said to the keeper, "Ale."

"And who might ye be?"

"Ishmael," I announce as I sidled up to the bloke.

He appeared to me in his fifties; he bore many a scar, some from sailing and some from fighting. His face, so dried from too many years in the sun, looked like an old, weathered boot. The man wore a black patch over his left eye. He dressed like a buccaneer and carried a cutlass and a dagger. Not a man to be trifled with.

"So, you be the teller of tall tales?" He says.

"Ye ever been a whaling?" I asked.

"Can't say that I hath."

I took one step back from the man, looked him up and down, and said, "Aye, I can see that ye hadn't the metal for it."

Thar were many a mariner and seafarers gathered around the bar who began to snicker and taunt the old buccaneer, getting his ire up.

"What say thee!" He barked as he began to draw his

rapier.

Since I was not carrying a weapon, I threw my ale in his face throwing him off, and then I smashed my pewter tankard upside his head with all me might, knocking him down to the floor, unconscious.

Several of his mates started to draw their weapons and advance toward me. They were quickly aborted when the barkeeper pulled an Avery Double Barrel Shotgun from behind the bar.

"Avast ye sons of a biscuit eater. I'll be having none of that in my establishment." He announced as he pulled the hammers on both barrels.

CLICK CLICK

"Smitty and the rest of your mates, best take your leave. Ye others shall be staying for another round of rum on the house. Now go!" The barkeep barked.

A roar of delight arose, the crowd rushed the bar, and the scuffle were soon forgotten. The poor sod lying unconscious on the floor got trampled on, puked on, and unintentionally pissed upon.

Thar were much frivolity and flummery about my encounter with the gruff sea rover that night on the *Rachel*. Smitty produced a bottle of Cuban rum from his bunk that he had hidden away.

Holding the rum bottle up in the air, he said, laughing, "Ahoy, me hearties! Here's to Ishmael, a bold rapscallion who tried to tie a bowline in the devil's tail tonight."

A thunderous roaring cheer of 'yo heave ho' echoed from within the crew's quarters.

I feel a fire in my belly that I had not felt in a long time.

James Young "Smitty" Smith had been a whaler since the age of seventeen. Born and raised in New Bedford, Massachusetts: he were a third-generation whaler. He would turn thirty-four this year, half of those years spent out at sea hunting and killing whales. He were a tall, sturdy, stout man and as solid as an American Sycamore.

Smitty was always good-humored, easy-going, and careless. Although he was an educated man, he were articulate, quizzical, and yet a bit of a nihilist. He be an extremely skillful harpooneer who, when whaling, hunted as if he were trying to avenge some sinister offense that the whale had done him.

Smitty and me became fast mates after the Cuban altercation. Thar be nothing like a melee to sort out whose one's friends are from those who quietly back away. Smitty stood by me when things got onerous. I felt a kinship like I had with Queequeg. I looked upon Smitty as I would an older brother.

The following day after the fracas, we set sail for Kingston Bay. Late in the afternoon, we hear from above in the crow's nest; the watchman hollered, "Ship ahoy! Off the portside."

Captain Gardiner was called up to the poop deck where the helmsman stood by the wheel. First Officer

Wilkes was already peering through his looking glass. Gardiner held an enormous spyglass to his eye when he had brought it down; his expression was one of fear.

"All hands hoay!" Gardiner shouted.

The command was bellowed throughout the ship from stem to stern. All the crew members rushed topside to assemble on the main deck, attentively facing the Captain.

"Men, thar be a ship flying the Jolly Roger. She be fast approaching. All hands, prepare yourselves. Master of Arms distribute cutlasses and small arms to all hands. Cannon crews prepare to your stations and listen for my commands. Now away with ye." Gardiner gruffly ordered.

As the Man-of-War got closer, it struck the Jolly Roger flag and replaced it with an all-black flag, the internationally recognized symbol for offering to parley. When the two ships were approximately fifty yards apart, the Man-of-War lowered one of its longboats with half a dozen men and made way towards the *Rachel.*

"Ahoy, me hearties. Permission to come aboard." Shouted the captain of the pirate vessel.

The Captain be a striking figure of a man. He stood over six feet tall with a black beard and a mane of braided black hair tied off at the ends with bright calico cloth ribbons. He sported a black Tricorne hat decorated with exotic bird feathers, a bright blood-red velvet frock coat with gold buttons and trim, a fine leather baldric to sheathe his cutlass, and a white colonial shirt with matching knee breeches that fed into knee-high black cavalier boots.

"Aye. Come aboard." Gardiner hollered down to the boarding party.

He turned to us and said, "Be wary, lads."

The entire crew of the *Rachel* stood ready with cutlass and pistols in hand. The Captain was the first to step onto the main deck, followed by six of the saltiest seadogs that I ever did see.

"I be Captain Calico Jack, and this be me first mate, One-Eyed Willie! We be buccaneers, and we sail the skull and crossed bones on the *Flying Dragon*." He bellowed proudly.

Thar, to everyone's surprise, stood the one-eyed scallywag that I had run a rig on the old salt and waylaid him, embarrassing him to all his mates.

Gardiner stepped forward and announced, "I am Captain Gardiner of the whaling vessel the *Rachel*. What is it that I can do you, Captain Jack?" Gardiner asked.

"I come in peace to make ye an offer."

"And what pray tell might that be?"

"My lads are weary from our most recent skirmish, and although we hath scored much booty and treasures, alas, we lost a few souls in doing so. I've come to make ye a proposition."

"And what might that be?"

"Well, as Willie and I spied ye vessel, at first I was all for pillaging and plundering, but One-Eyed Willie says to me, Captain Jack let us not be hasty. The men are tiresome, and we be needing several new mates for the crew. These stout fellows might be interested in a parley, says Willie. Shiver me timbers, says I. That be a grand thought, and besides, we don't be trading in Whale oil.

Now, I could hath blown your ship out of the sea, but that would not solve me problem and be a tremendous waste of shot and powder. Nay, what I want is six able-bodied men and your cabin boy in exchange for not sinking the *Rachel* and all who sail upon her. And to show ye no ill will, I shall pay ye twenty-five gold doubloons for each man and five for the boy. What say ye to that?" Jack queried.

I could see that Gardiner was mulling over his options. It was true that the *Rachel* could put up a reasonable fight but looking at the cannons that the *Flying Dragon* carried, it would be a futile one. He weighed the consequences of doing the right thing versus the practical thing.

"For how long will ye conscript these men for?" Gardiner asked.

Calico Jack puffed out his chest with pride and crowed, "Any man that volunteers to sail with me and the *Flying Dragon*, thar be no wages lads, but we operate by pirate law, no prey, no pay. Ye shall receive a full share in all booty and treasure taken. And if after one year of service ye decide that this be not your desire, I promise ye a safe passage to a neutral harbor, so as ye may go thy own way.

But let it be known that ye must carry thy full load, for be thar any man that thinks he can run a rig on me shall soon find himself severely punished. I be a fair master, but a strict one. What say ye to that One-Eyed Willie?"

"Aye, Captain Jack. Listen up me buckos, Calico Jack he speaks the truth. We live by Captain Calico

Jack and Company's Articles of the Pirate's Code."

Captain Gardiner turned to his men and asked, "I shall not force any man to go pirating, but be thar any of ye that hear the call of adventure?"

My mate from last night's skirmish and our lead harpooner out from Boston, Smitty raised his hand and hollered, "I be of a mind."

"Thar be a good lad." Captain Jack said with a smile.

Then came Henry Roberts, Jack Morgan, Francis Bonnet, and Bartholomew Davis, who walked out from our body of shipmates and sauntered over to join Captain Calico Jack.

"Come on, me hearties. Thar got to be another who longs for more than just the tedium of a whaler's life." Calico Jack said invitingly.

I thought to myself that this just might be me calling—a life of adventure. To be living on the knife's edge, and so, before I knew it, I also was walking toward the Captain and One-Eyed Wille. Not just for myself but for the sake of Tom Thumb, the little negra cabin boy that would be forced to go. Maybe I could keep an eye out for him. At least that's what part of me wanted it to be. Besides Me, best mate Smitty has the adventurous calling as well.

"And what be your name, matey?" Calico Jack asked.

"Ishmael." One-Eyed Willie said.

"Ye know each other?" Captain Jack asked.

"Aye, me and Ishmael met last night in The White Lion Inn. He bested me at a challenge, and for that, I say he be a man worthy of sailing on the *Flying Dragon*."

"Aye, I hath heard of thee. If you be the Ishmael of

Moby Dick legend."

"Aye, that be me."

"Well, blow me down! It be an honor to sail with ye, lad. Any man who can best a beast and One-Eyed Willie is welcome to crew on the *Flying Dragon*."

"Thank ye, Captain." Says I.

"Hath any of ye lads been buccaneering before?" Captain Jack asked.

Nary, a one of us, replied, aye. Calico Jack smiled and said, laughing, "Not to worry, lads. It's as easy as walking the plank."

Captain Gardiner brings along wee Tom Thumb, the cabin boy who looks a bit scared with trepidation.

"Captain Jack, this be Tom Thumb," Gardiner says.

So, to ease the lad's fears, I say, "Tom, me boy. Fear not, ye are amongst friends. Ain't that right, Captain Jack?"

"Aye, that be a fact, young Master Thumb. And if any man aboard me ship mistreats ye, I shall hath him flogged within an inch of his scurvy life."

I walk Tom over to where the volunteers be standing to join the men of the *Flying Dragon*. Whilst we're waiting, Captain Jack says, "Willie pay the good Captain. We be men of our word."

"Aye, Captain," Willie replies whilst counting out one hundred and fifty-five gold doubloons, the bounty for his reward of six men and wee Tom Thumb.

"Well, we be off now, Captain Gardiner. So, it's fare thee well me hearties. And may the wind be always at your back." Captain Calico Jack barked as we climbed down the Jacob's ladder to the longboat that awaited us to take us to our new life.

THE BEGINNING

"All hands hoay! Thar be a black squall a brewing. Willie, batten down the hatches. All hands, tend sails!" Calico Jack ordered.

"Aye, aye, sir." One-Eyed Willie replied.

The man with one eye turned to the crew and relayed the orders given by the Captain. Then he quickly began shouting, "Aloft with ye! Aloft! Weather mainbrace! Haul away! Lay on your backs and haul, men!"

It be a sight to see fifty men scrambling up the shrouds aloft to set the sails. Smitty and I climbed to the top of the foremast, first to stow the foretop gallant sail. We then worked our way down to the foretopsail, and finally, we stowed away the forecourse sail. By the time we had finished, the gale was upon us. Captain Calico Jack were a seaman and an old sea dog, to be sure. He ran under the storm jib and deeply reefed mainsail. Since we were too far out to run for cover, we headed out to open water for sea room.

As the storm grew more violent, Captain Jack hollered out to Willie, "Heave-to!"

"Aye, aye, Captain! Heave-to, lads! Away!"

We ran towards the bow and started to trim the jib aback, trim the mainsail in hard, and lash the helm. The jib began to push the bow down, turning off the wind and the mainsail fills, moving the boat forward. The ship began to make headway as the lashed helm turned the ship toward the wind again, causing the mainsail to catch the force of the wind, slowing the vessel's forward progress.

The storm were a beast. Many a man thought we were all to be lost. But I kept me eye on old Calico Jack, who stood for six hours stoically by the helmsman on the quarter-deck barking orders, and nary a once did I see him flinch. I knew then that he be a man of the sea.

By the time the sunset, the sky had cleared, and thar be a bright red sunset, and we all knew the worst be over, because red sky at night, sailor's delight; red sky in the morning, sailor take warning.

We sailors are full of superstitions, like never set sail on a Friday. Never hath bananas on a ship; thar be no whistling. Some say whistling is challenging the wind, bringing about a storm. Thar are to be no women on board, women make the seas angry, and one should always step onboard a ship with your right foot.

At eight bells, the cook, Roger Woods, called everyone to chow. Since weathering such a storm, the Captain ordered that we all be given an extra ration of oranges before they went bad. We ravenously ate our hearty servings of beans, pulses, and hardtack, saving the oranges as a treat. After dinner, we all sat around drinking rum and singing sea shanties.

Oh, blow the man down, bullies, blow the man down!
To me, way-aye, blow the man down.
Oh, Blow the man down, bullies, blow him right down!
Give me some time to blow the man down!

So, I tailed her my flipper and took her in tow,
And yardarm to yardarm away we did go.
Oh, Blow the man down, bullies, blow him right down!
Give me some time to blow the man down!

But as we were going, she said unto me,
"Thar's a spanking full-rigger just ready for sea."
Oh, Blow the man down, bullies, blow him right down!
Give me some time to blow the man down!

And as soon as that packet was out on the sea,
'Twas devilish hard treatment of every degree.
Oh, Blow the man down, bullies, blow him right down!
Give me some time to blow the man down!

So, I give you fair warning before we belay;
Don't never take heed of what pretty girls say.
Oh, Blow the man down, bullies, blow him right down!
Give me some time to blow the man down!

Oh, blow the man down, bullies, blow the man down!
To me, way-aye, blow the man down.
Oh, Blow the man down, bullies, blow him right down!
Give me some time to blow the man down!

We sang, danced, and drank until the wee hours of the morning. I woke up three sheets to the wind, having slept in the bottom of the longboat. My ribs and back ached from having spent the night sleeping on the burden boards and frame gusset plates. Whilst me head be a thumping as if I had been a dancing the hempen jig.

Most days were routine, keeping the ship tidy. We'd wash the deck planks so they wouldn't dry out, crack, or get moldy; other days, we'd mend the sails from any rips or tears. When all the work be done, we would practice our swordsmanship. Being that I were a whaler, I would observe the most adroit and skilled fencer. That be the second mate, Mr. Twigg, better known as Black Dog Billy Twigg. Black Dog had once been the Captain of the infamous *Devils Harlot*. She went down in a ferocious sea battle with no less than six of Her Majesty's warships. A then twenty-one-year-old pirate, Captain Black Dog Billy Twigg, was able to scupper two of the British man-o'-warships and incapacitate another before having to surrender. He and the remanding surviving nineteen crew members were cast into irons and thrown into the brig of the *H.M.S. Poseidon* to be taken back to England to be tried and then hung by the neck until dead.

But it weren't to be, thanks to a young American conscripted sailor, Jack Finch, whose hate for the British grew daily for their brutal mistreatment of the American conscripted seamen that they impressed to supplement their fleet.

Late one evening Jack Finch and six other conscripted sailors made their way down to the brig, overpowered the guards, and freed the pirate prisoners. Once freed, Black Dog and his crew, along with their emancipators, were able to capture the Captain and officers and commandeer the *H.M.S. Poseidon* for their own.

The pirate crew and their newly acquired ship were able to slip away and escape the other British man-o'-warships in the dead of night. Once they were safely away, they stuck the Royal Red Ensign and hoisted the Jolly Roger. Captain Black Dog Billy Twigg and his band of pirates managed to confiscate a 120-gun first-rate ship of the line. Being that its bad luck to rename a ship, the crew just removed the letters *H.M.S.* From that day forth, she be known as *The Poseidon.*

As for the British Captain and officers, Captain Black Dog Billy Twigg sent word to Port Royal that they be available for ransom. If'n they be interested in parley, they needed to send a signal by flying the Jolly Roger above the Union Jack in the town center. If they did not comply within two weeks, the Captain and officers would be killed.

The Jamaican governor, William Montagu, 5th Duke of Manchester, scoffed at a bold and brazen demand by a band of cutthroats and scallywags.

He was known to hath said, "By God, sir, the only thing that will hang in the town center other than the Union Jack will be these bold scoundrels."

Three weeks later, a longboat was spotted floating off Port Royal. When the boat was salvaged, thar lay five dead officers from the *H.M.S. Poseidon.* They found one man alive, the youngest officer, seventeen-year-old Master Henry Barnes. He was brought before Governor Montagu for questioning.

"What say ye young Barnes?" Governor Montagu asked.

"It were awful, me Lord. When they had not heard the news of a parley, they hung all the officers, 'cept me." The lad said as he began to weep.

"How is it that they spared ye?" Montagu asked.

"The Captain says to me, 'No need to fear me, boy. I always leave one man to tell the tale.' They then put the officers' bodies in the longboat along with me and cast us adrift." Master Barnes recounted.

"And what became of Captain Sewall?"

"As we were out to sea, I could see them making the good Captain walk the plank. He be bound from hand to foot. As he be falling to his death, he shouted out God save the Queen."

Governor Montagu pounded his fist on his desk and bellowed, "I want those men's heads stuck on a pike in the town center. Is that understood, Admiral Rowley?"

Admiral Sir Charles Rowley, 1st Baronet, was recently appointed Commander-in-Chief, Jamaica Station, having secured victories in the War of the Sixth Coalition and capturing the seaports of Flume and Trieste.

"I'll hath them before ye within the month, sir," Rowley promised. A promise he was unable to keep.

For nearly six months, Admiral Sir Charles Rowley chased Captain Black Dog Billy Twigg and his rowdy band of buccaneers throughout the waters of the Caribbean. All the whilst, Black Dog attacked and plundered over a dozen British merchant vessels, thereby amassing riches worth several hundred thousands of pounds of ill-gotten booty, making every member of the crew rich.

Many a man decided to take their treasure and go ashore and leave pirating behind. Some stayed in the islands of the Caribbean, a few went to America, and the rest buried their treasure and continued a life of pirating.

Jack Finch, the sailor who saved Captain Black Dog Billy Twigg, took his share and bought his own ship, the *Flying Dragon,* and took the moniker Captain Calico Jack.

Captain Black Dog Billy Twigg and the *Poseidon*

were eventually caught by surprise by the U.S.S. Constitution off the coast of South Carolina whilst they were in the process of raiding an American merchant vessel. Black Dog and a small company of the crew were able to escape as night fell. They managed to lower the longboat and make it to shore, landing on Pawleys Island. From thar, they made their way to Georgetown, where they commandeered a fishing schooner and sailed down to the island of Nassau. It was thar that Black Dog Billy and his crew signed on with Calico Jack and the *Flying Dragon.*

I spent as much time as Mr. Twigg would give me learning the art of swordsmanship. I learned the essential offensive moves of posture and footwork. Black Dog taught me the basic moves of the lunge, the feint, thrusting attack, the disengage, remise, the flick, and the beat attack. And the equally critical defensive moves. The riposte, the parry, and the circle parry.

After weeks of practice, Mr. Twigg bowed and says, "Young lad, I thinks ye be ready for fightin' and scuttlin'."

This pirate's life be nothing like whalers. A whaler's life be hard and back-breaking. Course, I haven't truly lived the pirate's life yet. But that would soon change.

"Mister Willie! Chart a new course." Calico Jack hollered.

"Aye, aye, Captain. Where be we heading?"

"Tortuga." Captain Jack replied.

Willie turned to the helmsman and repeated, "Helmsman, chart a new course to Tortuga."

"Why Tortuga?" Willie inquired.

"We lost a bit of sail during the storm that we need to replenish, and we could freshen up the stores," Jack answered.

"Aye, aye, sir."

We sailed all that day with a steady breeze and in fair winds. It was Francis Bonnet standing watch in the crow's nest who alerted the crew, "Ship ho!" as he pointed off to the starboard side.

"What see ye?" Mr. Twigg, the second mate, yelled.

"A merchant ship carrying the Royal Red Ensign and flying *Foxtrot*, sir," Bonnet called out.

"Are ye sure?" Mr. Twigg hollered.

"Aye. It be the *Foxtrot*." Bonnet yelled.

I knew that flying the *Foxtrot* ensign meant the ship was disabled. She be a sitting duck for the likes of us. A white banner with a ruby red diamond sitting in the center be a pirate's dream.

"All hands hoay!" Captain Calico Jack shouted.

The entire crew gathered on the quarter deck as summoned. Calico Jack stood dressed in all of his splendiferous glory, holding a cutlass and a dirk.

"Well, me buckos, are ye up for a wee bit of scuttlin'?"

A unanimous thunderous roar erupted. Everyone ran to get their swords and weapons. Since me and the other new men had no weapons of our own, One-Eyed Willie issued us each a naval boarding cutlass and a Colt 1851 Navy Revolver.

"Hoist the Jolly Roger. Fire the chase gun and run a

shot across her bow." Captain Jack ordered.

"Ready the grappling hooks!" One-Eyed Willie commanded.

As we were bringing the *Flying Dragon* near, we could see and hear some of the men on the British merchant ship, the *H.M.S. Abercromby* panicked and screamed in fear. The ship tried to make a run for it, but they be carrying too much cargo. We caught up to them easily.

Captain Calico Jack stood on the ship's side with his cutlass in the air as the grappling hooks flew over and brought the *Dragon* side by side with the *Abercromby Revenge*.

Jack shouted, "If they be wanting a fight, show them no quarter! Yyaarrrrgggghhhhh!" as he swung over to the deck of the *Abercromby Revenge* by a halyard.

As the two ships collided, the men of the *Flying Dragon* jumped onto *Abercromby Revenge's* main deck. We were met with the majority of their crew wanting to engage in battle. Others ran to seek shelter and safety, fearing for their lives.

My first deadly encounter was with a ship's officer, who I thought must hath had some training in the Royal Marines by his demeanor. He came at me with ferociousness and malice. I knew that this was to be the true test of me metal.

Our swords clashed with such vigor that white sparks flew, the likes I had never witnessed. I became suddenly aware that I be surrounded by bladed weapons, swords, daggers, and boarding axes. As the battle raged on, I found that I would hath the advantage at some point, and then me adversary would gain the momentum. We fought back and forth in a frenzy. I realized that I was driving him further toward defeat with each stroke of my sword. I soon forced him to his knees, and as he raised his sword to block another assault. I rained me cutlass down hard, slashing his right hand off at the wrist. As I readied myself to run him through, a blade pierces his body from behind; the bloody point of the sword is staring me in the face. I see that it be Black Dog Billy's sword. He smiled at me as he used his boot to disengage his rapier from the officer's dead body with a sturdy kick to the dead man's back, forcing him to fall face down upon the deck.

"Damn fine swordsmanship, young lad!" Black Dog Billy said with a toothy grin.

"You killed him." Says I.

"Aye, the Captain required to show no quarter. This one here would hath shown none to thee. Now, come on, lad, the fight is yet to be won."

The men of the *H.M.S. Abercromby* put up a valent but futile defense. The battle was over in less than an hour's time. After the hostilities were over, those who put up resistance along with the Captain and officers were placed in chains and those who did not were offered the opportunity to join the brethren of pirates. If they did, they were welcomed. The ones that chose not to were promised safe passage to a favorable port.

Captain Calico Jack and the rest of the crew voted on whether to scuttle the merchant ship or convert her into another pirate vessel. The vote was unanimous—the *H.M.S. Abercromby* would become the *Abercromby Revenge* and fly the Jolly Roger under the newly elected Captain Black Dog Billy Twigg.

Having two ships in our small armada would give us

a much-needed advantage in our ability to overtake and capture merchant ships, as well as provide a more vigorous defense against British, French, and American man-o'-warships. It were up to each man to sail whichever Captain he wanted to follow. Me, I chose to crew for Captain Black Dog Billy Twigg.

We headed to Cockburn Town on the tiny island in the Turks and Caicos Islands to convert and refit the *Abercromby Revenge* with 32 guns. She now be a proper pirate vessel. Once that were accomplished, we made way to Tortuga to sell our treasure and split our spoils equally among the crew.

On the way to Tortuga, we buried the four men who perished during the taking of *H.M.S. Abercromby* at sea. Charles Mosby, the ship's sailmaker, sewed each sailor into a shroud making sure that the last suture would pass through the nose of the deceased. The reason being that if the man be not dead, he would not stand for this painful Parthian stitch. It were a simple ceremony; Captain Jack wished each man God speed and a fare thee well.

On our way to Tortuga, we spied a small, deserted island west of Castle Island, where we marooned the Captain, officers, and the mutinous crew of the *H.M.S. Abercromby*. We left enough water for three days, no food, and a single pistol with one shot.

I tell you, true pirating were a feeling that I've only had when I were whaling. Coming face to face with Moby Dick and the possibility of meeting me death, I found it thrilling to see fifty of me hearties fighting hand to hand. I must admit that thar be no place for the faint of heart. It be a cruel and bloody adventure, but God forgive me; I never felt so alive.

Before going to Tortuga, we stopped in Port-de-Paix on the northern coast of Haiti. The port sits just eight miles from Tortuga Island, but the difference between the two were night and day. Tortuga were a pirate haunt, with nothing more than dozens of taverns and whore houses. A place where pirates go to squander their ill-gotten booty. Port-de-Prix were a commercial center with banks, shops, and a black market, and that's where we be heading to turn our plunder into coin of the realm.

When we're in a British or French port, we will strike the Jolly Roger and will fly the Stars and Bars of the United States so as not to discommode the local authorities unless they are at war with each other.

Since Port-de-Prix is under French rule and our contraband is only English goods, we expect no complications from the regional jurisdiction except the usual bribes.

Whilst Captains Calico Jack and Black Dog Billy went into town to negotiate the terms for the sale of our spoils; we were waiting to get underway to unload the cargo to the dozens of longboats waiting alongside our ships once we received the signal. The signal came as a pistol shot into the air by Captain Jack as they were returning to the ship.

Each man received his fair share for all the goods as stated in the Code of the Pirate Brethren, which had been drawn up when Calico Jack and the original band of sailors turned to pirating. It were the code that provided rules for discipline, division of goods, and compensation for the injured. Whenever a new man came aboard to join the Company, he had to swear to obey the code, and he then had to put his name or mark on the articles. Each pirate Captain and crew would draft their own code.

Here be Calico Jack's Code of the Pirate Brethren:

I. Every Man Shall obey civil Command; the Captain shall hath one full share and a half of all prizes; the First Mate, Carpenter, Boatswain, and Gunner shall one Share and quarter.

II. If any Man shall offer to run away or keep any Secret from the Company, he shall be marooned with one Bottle of Powder, one Bottle of Water, one small Arm, and Shot.

III. If any Man shall steal any Thing from any member of the Company, or game, to the Value of a Piece of Eight, he shall be marooned or put to Death Punishment as the Captain and Company shall think fit.

IV. If any time we shall meet another Marooner that Man shall sign his Articles without the Consent of our Company, shall suffer such Punishment as the Captain and Company shall think fit.

V. That Man that shall strike another whilst these Articles are in force shall receive Moses' Law (40 Stripes lacking one) on the bare Back.

VI. That Man that shall snap his Arms, smoke Tobacco in the Hold, without a Cap to his Pipe, or carry a Candle lighted without a Lanthorn, shall suffer the same Punishment as in the former Article.

VII. That Man shall not keep his Arms clean, fit for

an Engagement, or neglect his Business, shall be cut off from his Share, and suffer such other Punishment as the Captain and the Company shall think fit.

VIII. If any Man shall lose a Joint in time of an Engagement shall hath 400 Pieces of Eight; if a Limb, 800.

IX. If at any time you meet with a prudent Woman, that Man that offers to meddle with her, without her Consent, shall suffer present Death.

X. Any Man has the right to Parlay.

XI. Killing a surrendered enemy is not allowed.

XI. Any captives who choose not to join the Company shall be ransomed or marooned.

XIII. Any Man who falls behind is left behind.

Every man of the Company received 600 Pieces of Eight. It were an extraordinary sum, to be sure. I did not feel agreeable to take such a sum ashore to Tortuga. Having seen much skullduggery and chicanery. I, therefore, decided to leave 500 Pieces of Eight behind in me bunk feeling secure that it be safe. I be wrong.

When I returned on board after a night of carousing and merriment, I found all me goods to be stolen. I ran up to Captain's quarters and announced me self, "Captain Twigg, it is I, Ishmael, I hath been a victim of banditry most foul. Some ne'er-do-well villain has stolen 500 Pieces of Eight. It were stored in a fanciful black leather pouch. I hereby invoke the pirate's code."

"Aye. It shall be done." Black Dog said.

Black Dog called upon his first mate Mister Gibbs to assemble the crew on the master deck.

"Avast! All hands-on deck!" He bellowed.

The call was repeated throughout the ship until all hands had convened on the master deck facing the Captain standing by the helmsman's wheel.

"Men, I fear that we hath a thief amongst us." Captain Twigg announced.

Thar were a multitude of mumbles, shaking of heads, and shock that ran through the assembled.

"We aboard the *Abercromby Revenge* will not stand for such aggression. If'n any of ye knows who this scoundrel be and does not come forth, he too shall face the wrath of Calico Jack's Code of the Pirate Brethren. What say ye?" Black Dog Billy asked.

Silence cloaked the Company for what seemed to be an eternity. Finally, Roger Woods, our cook, shouts out, "It were Jack Van Røan!"

"That be a lie! I did no such thing!" Van Røan protests.

Van Røan was set upon by no less than six able-bodied men and brought before Captain Twigg. Black Dog Billy slowly strolls toward the accused and turns out his pockets, removing all of Van Røan's trappings that he possessed on his body.

"Let's see what ye hath here." The Captain said as he began to hold up each item that he would find.

"One W&S Butcher large folding knife. One briar pipe and a tobacco pouch. A pair of dice made from ivory. Ah! What be this?" The Captain queried as he held a black leather pouch full of coins aloft.

"I found that, I swear." Van Røan persisted.

"Cook Woods, come forth."

The ship's cook, Roger Woods, made his way through the throngs of sailors to where the Captain be standing.

"How is it that ye hath knowledge of Mister Van Røan having possession of such an article?"

"I were in the King's Head tavern last night, and I got to hearing young Mister Van Røan bragging to several lads whilst playing a spirited game of five-card cribbage how he had absconded with some poor fool's purse that be filled to the rim with pieces of silver." Woods recounted.

"What say ye, Mister Van Røan?" The Captain asked.

"Nay, that be a falsehood. Cook Woods ne'er warmed to me, sir. That is why he bears false witness again me. I swear I found the purse, and I admit that it were wrong not to turn it in. But I ne'er stole the purse." Van Røan pleaded, looking amongst the Company for a sympathetic face.

He found none.

"I swear that I be many a thing, a rascal, a scoundrel, but ne'er a thief." Van Røan beseeched.

Captain Twigg called upon me, "Ishmael come forth."

I made me way through the Company and up to where the Captain stood.

"Aye, Captain." Says I.

"Ishmael, since ye be the wounded party. What say ye, guilty or innocent?"

"I know not this man, Van Røan, Nor do I know if he be telling the truth or lie. He did hath a passion of me purse, so he should hath punishment, but I cannot say to what degree."

The Captain looked at me and then turned his gaze over the Company, then asked, "Be thar any man who can bear witness for or again this man? Any of ye that were at said card game?"

Nary, a soul spoke. The Captain pointed to Van Røan and gestured for him to come forth. As he made his way through the human gauntlet, thar be scores of men that spat upon him, struck him, and called him many scandalous names.

"Mister Van Røan, I find you guilty of having in thyne possession an article that does not belong to ye. I hereby sentence ye to a flogging of ten lashes with the cat o' nine tails and banishment from the *Abercromby Revenge*. Sentence to be carried out forthwith. Mister Cotton, carry out the punishment."

"Aye, aye, Captain." Mr. Cotton, the Boatswain mate, replied.

As Cotton were leaving the main deck to retrieve his cat o' nine tails, he barked orders to the Company, "Lash him to the foremast and bear his back!"

Van Røan was quickly removed from the quarter deck and taken towards the bow of the ship, stripped of his shirt and bound to the foremast with his back exposed. The entire Company gathered around to view the proceedings.

The Company were all facing Van Røan's back, whereas the Captain and I were positioned to view his face. Mr. Cotton stood ready with his whip in hand, awaiting the Captain's command.

"Proceed," Twigg said with a nod.

When the flogging began, Van Røan's face contorted in pain and grimace, but as the number of lashes increased, he began to cry out in pain until, as the last blow was delivered, he screamed and passed out. The Company seemed to relish Van Røan's agony, cheering and laughing with each strike of the whip.

Once the punishment had been administered, Van Røan was left tied to the mast unaided for several hours. After he had regained consciousness, a bucket of seawater was thrown upon his raw and scared back as an additional punishment. He stayed strapped to the mast all night, given no food nor water. Nary, a soul, approached him until morning when he was escorted off the ship, taken to Tortuga Island, and left standing on the beach a marked man as we sailed away.

The *Abercromby Revenge* and *Flying Dragon* set off for the ten-day sail to the pirate-friendly Island of Nassau. Back on Tortuga, where we had heard some scuttlebutt that thar were to be a flotilla of twenty to thirty British merchant ships heading towards the Carolinas.

As we sailed into the waters where we expected to see the armada of merchant ships, we spied two other vessels flying their version of the Jolly Roger. Ours were a black flag with two crossed bones sitting under a human skull. As for the two other ships, one displayed a black flag with a red human skeleton holding a cutlass o'er his head. That be the flag of the *Black Hawk*, captained by Edward Foxx, a brutal and savage pirate known for always the burning of captured ships and torturing prisoners.

The other ship, the *Laughing Ghost,* were that of Captain Christopher Roberts. His ensign were blood-red that pictured a white skull with two crossed sabers and an hourglass, telling all that your time be up and thar be no quarter given to those who don't surrender.

Onboard the *Flying Dragon*, it were a sight to behold it was four of the most notorious pirate Captains ever to sail the seven seas plotting, scheming, and strategizing the upcoming attack on the fleet of merchant ships heading to the Carolinas. It were decided that the best battle plan would be that of a unified attack. To hunt as a wolf pack might by singling out the least vulnerable ships first, attacking them without mercy, showing the others that it be futile to resist.

Captains Roberts, Foxx, Twigg, and Calico Jack each signed their mark to said agreement. They each had a copy signed by the others, and each swore an oath to honor the accord by invoking the pirate's code.

As the Captains were preparing to head back to their ships. One-Eyed Willie posed a question, "What be the plan if'n thar be British Frigates or Man O Wars?"

"Aye. Good thinking, Willie." Calico Jack said.

That got the Captains to thinking. They sat back down; each took a bowl of tobacco in their pipes and began cogitating. It were Captain Foxx who suggested, "Thar be strength in numbers. I say we employ the wolf pack attack to the Jack Tars; we concentrate on one vessel at a time."

"Aye, attack from all sides. Strike and run. He hit them hard and moved on to the next." Black Dog remarked.

"Then, it be agreed. Thank ye, One-Eyed Willie." Captain Roberts said with gratitude.

As the Captains were leaving the *Flying Dragon*, Captain Calico Jack wished them all good luck, "Fare thee well, me Buckos. Be seeing ye on the other side."

"Avast, ships ahoy! Off the starboard side!" Me good mate Smitty shouted down from the crow's nest.

"How many?" Mister Turner, Captain Twigg's first mate, asked.

"As far as me eye can see!"

"Can ye see any warships?"

"Aye. I can see at least three frigates!"

Mister Turner rushed down to the captain's quarters to alert him of the flotilla.

"Captain! Flotilla off the starboard side. The barrelman spies dozens of ships and at least three warships."

Black Dog Billy orders the first mate to signal an alert to other pirate ships.

"Aye, aye, Captain." Mister Turner replies.

Turner stands at the bow of the *Abercromby Revenge* and fires his pistol into the air whilst I wave a black flag to signal that thar be warships amongst the flotilla.

The prearranged plan was that the *Black Hawk* would attack from the starboard side, the *Laughing*

Ghost from the port side, the *Abercromby Revenge* head-on, and the *Flying Dragon* would attack the most vulnerable, the stern.

The first ship we attacked were the *H.M.S. Colossus*, an 80-gun second-rate Vanguard-class ship of the line built for the Royal Navy in the 1840s. She were a swift frigate but no match for the nimble and maneuverable ships we sailed.

The *Black Hawk* and the *Laughing Ghost* would stay just outside the range of the frigate's cannons, taunting them and keeping them busy. At the same time, the *Abercromby Revenge* and the *Flying Dragon* would pass back and forth in front of and in back of the vessel, firing their broadside guns, creating damage to the bow and stern of the ship. The *Abercromby Revenge* and *Flying Dragon* intentionally aimed at firing their cannons below the waterline. In doing so, the *Flying Dragon* crippled the *H.M.S. Colossus*'s rudder, impeding her ability to steer properly. The *Abercromby Revenge* blew several holes in the ship's bow, causing her to take on water.

We made quick work of her knocking the frigate out of commission in minutes. Our sole purpose in attacking Her Majesty's guardianships were not to do a long-drawn-out gun battle with them or to sink them, just to inflict enough damage and hardship to slow them down so we could attack, board, and plunder the merchant ships of their prize possessions.

After the crippling of the *H.M.S. Colossus*, we encircled the *H.M.S. Goliath*, another 80-gun two-deck second rate ship of the line built for the Royal Navy in the 1840s. We commenced the same tactics, which were proving to be effective when the barrelman on the

Laughing Ghost spotted the *H.M.S. Queen* advancing towards the skirmish at high speed.

The *H.M.S. Queen* was a triple-decker 110-gun first-rate ship of the line of the Royal Navy, launched in 1839 at Portsmouth. She was the last purely sailing-built battleship to be ordered. In order to hold the *Queen* off, Black Dog Billy broke away from the altercation and tried to draw her away, acting as a decoy.

Because the *Queen* had the battle advantage firing at long range when fighting broadside, Captain Twigg sailed straight at her as if we were going to collide with her head-on. Twigg took the wheel from the helmsman as he shouted, "Mister Turner, ready the guns!"

"Aye, aye, Captain. Company, ready the guns!" Turner screamed.

"Mr. Turner, shorten sails on my order!"

"Aye, aye, Captain. You men go aloft and stand by on my order to shorten sails!"

I were one of the sailors that tended the sails, so up we scrambled up the rigg'g. I were assigned to the main topgallant sail up near the crow's nest. I had me self quite a view of what were to happen next.

Just as the two ships were about to collide, Captain Twigg veered slightly to the starboard side, causing the two ships to scrape our port sides against one another. Seconds before Black Dog Billy shouted to Mister Turner, "Shorten sails!"

"Aye, aye, Captain, Shorten sails!"

At that moment, every mainsail on each of the three masts dropped. Next, we heard Captain Twigg hollered, "Fire in the Hole!"

Mister Turner bellowed, "Fire in the Hole!"

Fire in the Hole were the warning given to the crew before a cannon is fired. The gun crews on the port side were at the ready; guns were loaded with powder and shot. At each cannon were a man holding a botafuego that held a burning rope that would be placed on the cannon's priming hole setting off the cannon.

As the *Abercromby Revenge* were significantly shorter in stature than that of the *Queen*, thus when the *Queen* fired its cannons, they fired over our heads and did minimal damage to just our fore topgallant mast, and the maintop gallant staysail. Since we had dropped all our mainsails, that be the only damage to the ship we sustained. But as the fore topgallant mast exploded and splintered from the cannonball hitting the mast, shards of the wooden mast hit poor Smitty's left hand, removing three of his fingers and severing his hand at the wrist.

As I be stationed up on the main topgallant mast, I were near the crow's nest when the fore topgallant mast fractured and soon after heard the screams from Smitty's injuries. Edward Low and me self-went to the aid of our wounded comrade. I tied me neckerchief around his hand, and me and Edward helped Smitty down the rigg'g to the main deck where Doctor Cotton, the ship's doctor, were waiting.

"Smitty, me lad, I'm afeared that I must remove that hand. For I cannot save it, it be too damaged." Doctor Cotton said.

"Are ye sure, Doc? I can live with two fingers!"

"Smitty, try an move them two fingers."

As hard as he tried, he could not. Smitty started to sob as Doctor Cotton took out his saw. He turned to me and handed me a broad axe.

"Ishmael, go stoke this axe in yonder hearth until it be glowing red hot."

"Aye, aye, Doc." Says I, as I ran to the hearth, placed the ax on the coals, and began to use the bellows to fan the flames.

"Mister Low, if'n you'd be so kind as to hold Smitty's down onto the taffrail. Do not let him move it!" Doctor Cotton ordered.

"Aye, aye, Doc." Low replied as he held on tight to Smitty's arm, pressing it down onto the railing with all his might.

Doctor Cotton poured some rum onto the saw blade, and then with three quick moves back and forth, Smitty's hand fell overboard. I arrived with the white-hot broad axe, and handed it to the Doc, who placed the blade of the axe against Smitty's stump to cauterize it.

"*AAAAIIIEEEEEEEEE!*" Smitty screamed, then he passed out.

The smell of burning flesh turned my stomach, causing me to spew onto the deck.

"Away with ye! If'n ye must retch, do it over the taffrail into the sea. " Doctor Cotton shouted angrily.

"Begging ye pardon." Says I apologetically.

"Here, you and Mister Low take Smitty down to his bunk. I'll be down shortly.

We did as we were told.

After the *Queen* fired all of her cannons, then it were our turn, Captain Twigg gave the order, "Fire!"

"Fire!" Mister Turner barked.

Because the *Abercromby Revenge* sat lower next to the *Queen* and as we aimed our guns to fire below the waterline, when we fired our twelve guns on the port side, the *Queen* sustained heavy damage in the storage holds where the freshwater, foodstuffs, and spare sails and rigging are stowed.

We sailed past the wounded battleship we saw that she were listing on her port side. We saw the crew frantically dropping their sails and sending men over the side to try and repair the damage done. As Captain Black Dog Billy would say later, "Being bigger tweren't always better."

As Edward Low and I returned to our posts, I noticed that we were sailing past the ailing *Queen*; the *Abercromby Revenge* proceeded to make a wide circle around the *Queen* so as to be far away from her guns. Even as they fired, their shots fell short, and the *Abercromby Revenge* made our way back to rejoin the fight against the *H.M.S. Goliath*. Seeing all the damage that we inflected onto the *Queen*, we began to holler cheers and jeers; a few of the men dropped their pants and exposed their arses to the British Tars.

Before we were able to rejoin the fray against the *Goliath*, we could see that the *Black Hawk*, the *Laughing Ghost*, and the *Fly Dragon* had disposed of the *Goliath's* ability to be a further threat. Now, all that were left to do was to chase down the merchant ships and then plunder their loot and booty. The four Captains had agreed that each ship would be on its own to attack any ship once the military escorts were dispensed of. Thar were plenty of ships to choose from.

Once the escorts were out of commission, the flotilla broke apart all the ships spread out since the strength in numbers no longer applied; it were each ship for themselves.

The pickings were lush. Of the twenty-two ships of the flotilla, we managed to attack and plunder five trading vessels. Most were carrying commercial items, silk cloth, tea, spices, and weapons such as swords, guns, and ammunition. We managed to obtain several chests of coin of the realm and one large box of assorted jewels, rings, and gold pocket watches.

With our cargo hold full, we set sail back towards Tortuga Island to sell our ill-gotten booty and meet up with our sister ship, the *Flying Dragon*. On our journey, we came across a slave ship, the *White Tiger*. A United States merchant vessel that not only carried slaves but cargo as well. Since the international slave trade was banned in 1807, the *White Tiger* were operating illegally, making her fair game. They couldn't object to the U.S. authorities because they themselves were breaking international law.

Captain Twigg gathered the Company to put it to a vote.

"Mateys, though our belly be full, what say ye? Shall we bring down the *White Tiger*?"

A thunderous roar of "Ayes" erupted, nary a man objected.

Captain Black Dog Billy hollered, "Mister Turner, man the cannons!"

"Aye, aye, Captain. Company, man the cannons!" Turner yelled.

As the *Abercromby Revenge* drew nearer to the

White Tiger, we could see their men frantically trying to outmaneuver us. They would hath too if it weren't for the shot we fired over their bow.

"Avast! Heave to, or we *will* lay siege to ye!" Black Dog roared.

Captain Grosjean of the *White Tiger* knew he couldn't outrun our cannons, so he ordered his crew to heave to so we could board her. We pulled up broadside and boarded the vessel with weapons drawn, and at the ready, in case they foolishly tried anything.

"What be ye carrying?" Twigg asked.

"We carry no loot, just general goods. Nothing that would temp ye." Grosjean answered.

"Wouldn't be carrying any human cargo, would ye? Cause that be illegal, me bucko."

Grosjean began to sweat, "Ah, Captain…"

"Twigg."

"Ah, Captain Twigg, we both be men of the world. Pirates in our own way. Look, sir, if God didn't want them to be slaves, he wouldn't hath made them black. Am I right?" Grosjean said with a sneer.

Twigg turned to Mister Turner, "Mister Turner, go and set those poor devils free."

Turner took six men, including me, down below where thar be eighty men, twenty-two women, and eleven children lying head to foot chained together with nary an inch between them. The stench were so bad that we all grew ill to our stomachs, as these poor wretches were forced to lie in their own waste.

We unchained them and had them go topside into the fresh air and sunshine, where they were given the means to bath.

Captain Twigg walked over to the crowd of men and

asked, "Be thar any of ye that speak English?"

No one came forth; they just looked quizzical. Then thar was a soft voice from the group of women, "English, speak little."

Twigg approached her and asked, "How is it ye speak English?"

"Missionaries." She said.

"What be ye name, miss?"

"Adila."

"And what be ye tribe?"

"Bantu."

Twigg turned to the crew and asked, "What say ye? What shall we do?"

Mister Turner spoke first, "Well, Captain, I don't think it possible to sail them back to Africa. And we can't send them to any southern port, as they would just be taken and sold off as slaves. Might I suggest we sail them to a northern port where their chances be better?"

"Aye, that be an idea. But who would captain the vessels? I do not trust these scurvy dogs to undertake such a task." Twigg said, pointing to Grosjean and his crew.

"Nor I." Turner agreed.

Twigg looked at our Company and inquired, "Any of ye hath a thought?"

"Aye, I hath a thought." Francis Bonnet, a former sailor of the *Rachel* said.

"And what might that be, me hearty?" Twigg inquired.

"I would be willing to captain this ship to a northern port if'n I had the help of some other like-minded mates." He said.

"And why would you be wanting to that, lad?"

"For the reward given for these slaving scoundrels, Captain," Bonnet replied.

"Aye, I like the cut of ye jib, me bucko," Twigg said with a hearty smile.

"I only need two or three mates," Bonnet said.

"Be thar any men wanting to take part in such a venture?" Twigg queried.

Three men stepped forward, Henry Roberts, Jack Morgan, and Bartholomew Davis, all former shipmates on the *Rachel*.

"Captain, hath mercy. I beseech thee, set us loose in a longboat. We will be willing to take our chances. For we shall all surely hang if taken north." Grosjean pleaded.

Black Dog Billy smiled and smirked, "My good Captain, we will all hath a date to dance with Jack Ketch. Take these sons of a biscuit eater down below and put them in the same chains as they had placed their human cargo before them."

We compelled Captain Grosjean and his crew down below at the point of our swords, threw them into the chains that the slaves had been in, and lay amongst the filth and excrement. As we made our way topside, we heard their screams and pleads for pity and forgiveness, but we had none to give.

Captain Twigg, along with Francis Bonnet, spoke to the Bantu woman, Adila, explaining what was going to happen. She seemed to grasp the idea and translated what was being said to the other members of her tribe. All appeared to be in agreement; thar seemed to be no hostilities against Francis Bonnet and the others. As we were making ready to continue onto Tortuga, it was unanimously decided that now Captain Francis Bonnet and the other members of his crew shall keep any spoils on board the *White Tiger* for themselves.

Before Twigg departed, he whispered to Bonnet, "Don't be letting me hear that ye hath turned slaver."

"You hath me word. I swear on the pirate's code, Captain."

"Well then. Fare thee well and fair winds."

Once we set sail again for Tortuga, I went down to see how Smitty was faring. I found him lying on his bunk passed out, moaning in his sleep. On me way topside I ran, into Doctor Cotton, "Hath ye any idea how long Smitty will be ailing?" I ask.

"Hard to say, lad. Ye might go asking Bo'sun's mate Dax Drury. He lost a hand two year ago, and he's doing fine."

"Thanks, Doc." Says I.

Dax Drury were what people think of when they picture what a pirate be looking like. He were tall, rugged-looking, with broad shoulders. He wore a blood-red bandana on his head, sported a gold earring in his left ear, and had many a tattoo on his person. One of a rope around his right wrist indicating he be a deckhand, two swallows on his chest, each one for every 5,000 nautical sea miles traveled, and a nautical star so he could always find his way home. Then thar were the hook where his left hand once was. He lost it in a sword fight with a British Lieutenant when the

British Frigate, the *H.M.S. Cumberland* did battle with the *Flying Dragon* off the coast of Cuba. It were a good day for the *Flying Dragon* as they won the day, but a bad day for Dax, who lost his left hand, and even a worse day for the British Lieutenant, who lost his life.

I found Bo'sun's mate Dax up near the bow of the ship, checking on the Jib Boom.

"Dax."

"Aye."

"Smitty, me mate just lost his hand to the Tars."

"I heard. How's the old salt doing?"

"He's still out cold. How long do ye think before he's shipshape?" I asked.

"Well, I were laid up for several weeks before I got my sea legs back. I tell ye what; I s'pose I could go down and see old Smitty for too long and hath a bit of a chat."

"Thank ye, I be much obliged," I said as I turned to make my way to the main deck as it were my turn in the barrel.

Mister Turner were standing at the base of the main mast, holding a spyglass that he handed to me.

"Up ye go lad, Keep ye a weather eye on the horizon, and don't let me catch ye taking a caulk."

"Aye, aye." Says I.

I proceeded to climb the ship's rigg'g past the main yard, the main top yard, and climbed into the crow's nest, which were near 100 feet above the main deck. Not fer the faint of heart, aside from the height, in rough seas, the sway could throw a man out and down into the briny deep.

But today, the seas were calm, and the wind were serving us to a desire. I were my first time in the barrel, the ship was gently rocking, and high up in the crow's nest, it were a swaying back and forth like a baby's cradle. I found myself fighting the urge to take a caulk. It were a severe offense to be caught sleeping when on watch, punishable by flogging with the cat o'nine tails. Having seen others go under the whip forced me to abandon any notion of closing me eyes. I were to stay on guard for at least four hours or until I were relieved.

As I scanned the horizons over and over for nearly three hours, thar be nothing. Then from our stern, I spied a ship.

"Sail, Ho!" I shouted down to the main deck.

"What see ye?" Mister Turner asked.

"Off our stern!" Says I pointing to the aft.

Mister Turner and Captain Twigg open their spyglasses and peered aft.

"Aye. I see it." Twigg announced.

Whilst I were looking hard, it appeared to me to be the *Flying Dragon* flying the Jolly Roger. So, I holler out, "She looks to be the *Flying Dragon.*"

"Aye, I thinks ye be right. I see she's flying the Jolly Roger. But let us not be slothful, Mister Turner prepare all cannons." Captain Twigg ordered.

"Aye, aye, Captain. All hands, man the guns and stand by!" Mister Turner hollered.

It be a wonderous sight from high above watching forty-odd men scamper about the deck below, readying the cannons for battle.

"Barrelman, keep a sharp eye out!" Twigg hollered.

I gave a wave of me hand and shouted, "Aye, aye, Captain!"

"Mister Turner, let all sails and sheets fly free, slack the boom vang, cast off the jib sheet, and ease the main sheet all the way." Captain Twigg's orders were intended to stop the *Abercromby Revenge* to let the *Flying Dragon* catch up.

"Aye, Captain." Turner acknowledged.

"Ye heard the Captain, let all sails and sheets fly free, slack the boom vang, cast off the jib sheet, and ease the main sheet all the way! But stand by to get underway!"

Once all the sails and sheets were freed the ship drastically lost speed and the *Flying Dragon* caught up quickly and came about broadside. I could see Captain Calico Jack and One-eyed Willie standing on the quarter-deck, with Willie standing at the helm.

"Ahoy, Captain Twigg. How'd ye fare? Our cargo hold be brimming. I hope ye did well." Calico Jack yelled.

"Avast, me hearties! I be glad to hear of ye good fortune. We too hath been blessed by Neptune's daughter. Our coffers be full, so now we be heading to Tortuga Island; care to join us?" Twigg asked.

"Aye, Captain Twigg. Let us proceed to venture on to cash in our good fortune." Captain Jack replied.

Whilst all the conviviality were continuing, I spied what looked to be a French man o'war sailing in our direction.

"Ship ahoy! She looks to be a large man o'war sailing a French ensign off the port bow!" I screamed.

Captain Twigg and Calico Jack, along with Mister Turner and One-eyed Willie, all ran toward the bow of the ships and looked out to the port side with spyglasses in hand.

"She looks to be a Hercule class," Twigg remarked.

Calico Jack agreed, "Aye, she be a 100-gun ship of

the line."

"What say ye. Shall we attack?" Twigg barked over the bow of the *Abercromby Revenge* to Captain Jack.

"Aye. I don't want her dogging us all the way to Tortuga." Calico Jack replied.

I spied the name of the vessel and shouted down, "She be the *le Tage*. Looks to be carrying a full complement of crew."

"A ship that size will carry over eight hundred men." Mister Turner stated.

"Do ye prefer bow or stern?" Twigg inquired.

"We'll take the stern," Jack said.

The plan would be similar to the attack plan for the British frigates. The *Abercromby Revenge* would sail towards the bow of the French man o'war, firing our cannons broadside at the front of the vessel as we sail past her. The *Flying Dragon* will do the same at the back of the *le Tage*. The bow and aft of any ship are the most vulnerable as all of a ship's armament is on either side.

Our cannons will be aimed high so as to inflict damage to the foremast by firing chain shots. Chain shots were two subcaliber iron balls joined by a chain. These projectiles could sweep across the deck of the ship wreaking havoc on anything in their path, including human limbs, or crippling any number of sailing structures such as masts and rigg'g having catastrophic effects of their ability to navigate. We also plan on firing many a hotshot. We be heating the cannonballs until they be red-hot, serving as an incendiary device; if we be lucky, some of our hot shots might penetrate the main deck and do damage to the gun room below or at least cause a fire on deck taking away men from their fighting positions.

Howsomever, the *Flying Dragon's* cannons will be regular round shots aimed low to try and hit the rudder, corroding the vessel's ability to maneuver as well as possibly blowing holes in the aft of the ship below the waterline causing flooding.

As we prepared for battle Captain Black Dog Billy Twigg shouted out his call to arms, "Cry, Havoc!"

Capitaine Jacques Lafitte, just twenty-six years of age, has been the captain of *le Tage* for less than six months. His rapid rise to the rank of captain was a result of the dire need for naval officers due to the war of the Second French Republic. The officer corps was drained through attrition of constant wars starting with the war of the First French Empire, the Bourbon Restoration, the July Monarchy, and now the Second French Republic.

"Capitaine, Capitaine! Deux bateaux pirates à tribord!" The lookout shouted down from the crow's nest. Lafitte gazed at the two vessels that were flying the black flags with skull and crossed bones. Horror and panic ran through the young officer, but he tried to steel himself so as not to show fear to the crew. He turned to his first officer, *Lieutenant de vaisseau* Hugo Blanchet and calmly said, *"Tous les hommes à leurs postes de combat."* The officer barked the order and the crew scrabbled to the battle stations.

"*Préparez-vous à tirer sur mes orders!*" Lafitte hollered.

As the *Abercromby Revenge* and the *Flying Dragon* swung apart from each other, it became clear to young Capitaine Lafitte that these two adversaries weren't going to play by the traditional rules of engagement of firing shots broadside to broadside. The *Abercromby Revenge* were approaching from the east and the *Flying Dragon* were approaching from the west. So, no matter which direction they turned it would be to the other pirate ship's advantage. The naval academy hadn't covered this sort of combat tacit in the young captain's classes. He was lost, he turned to Blanchet for help and asked, "*Que ferons-nous jamais?*"

Lieutenant de vaisseau Hugo Blanchet had been a ship-of-the-line officer for over eighteen years. He had been through dozens of sea battles and was wounded four times. He was the recipient of the *Ordre national de la Légion d'Honneur* and the *Ordre da la Croix de Juillet.*

Blanchet had never been asked his advice on military strategy before. He looked at the terrified kid in front of him and thought that the best plan would be to try and concentrate on the ship that would be attacking our most vulnerable position, the aft. They would need to sail towards the port side in hopes that they could at least protect their rudder. He said, "*Nous devons protéger l'arrière. Donc braquer à bàbord.*"

Lafitte gave a thankful smile and asked Blanchet to give the order to the helmsman to steer hard port side.

"*Timonier difficile à bâbord* !" Blanchet barked.

Sadly, for young *Capitaine* Jacques Lafitte and for most of the world's navies whose mindsets where all the same, build the biggest more powerful ships and they would win the day. They never figured on the run and gun, guerrilla warfare tactics that these smaller lively, dexterous, and swifter ships can wreak.

The gun crews of the *le Tage* stood ready to fire, unfortunately thar weren't anything to fire at. *Capitaine* Lafitte were no match for either Captain Black Dog Billy Twigg or Captain Calico Jack. It tweren't a fair match, *le Tage* got assaulted from stem to stern.

The *Abercromby Revenge* peppered the French man o'war's main deck with hot shots generated numerous fires that caused chaos and mayhem and the firing of the chain shots produced devastation to *le Tage's* sailing structure, severing the foremast at the base, causing it to collapse. Our attack not only brought about the destruction of the foremast, its three foremast sails, the flying jib, and jib sails but also damaged a third of the ship's rigg'g. Many a French sailor perished that afternoon; we lost none.

Whilst we were having our way with *le Tage*, Captain Calico Jack and the *Flying Dragon* were raining Hell down from above upon the Frogs. After damaging *le Tage's* rudder, Calico Jack ordered the gun crews to concentrate their fire at the navigation room, the captain's cabin, and officers' mess, all stacked on top of one another at the stern of the ship.

The barrage lasted over five hours before the *Abercromby Revenge* and the *Flying Dragon* sailed off leaving the crippled *le Tage* floundering helplessly, bobbing up and down in the water unable to sail or steer like a fishing float as we made off to Tortuga Island to cash in our booty for silver and gold.

As we approached Tortuga, we struck the Jolly Roger and hoisted the Stars and Bars, a neutral friendly country. Having just plundered a British flotilla of merchant ships and battling both British and French frigates, we didn't think the Jolly Roger would be a welcome sight.

"Drop anchor!" Shouted Mister Turner.

The thunderous clanking of the metal chain that held the 3000-pound anchor that measured over eleven feet tall, and seven feet arms made a fearsome plash as it hit the water. We sat off of the small port village of Trou Basseux, where smugglers and pirates go to do business. Whilst we unloaded our cache of booty onto several longboats that sat on our port and starboard sides, Captain Twigg went ashore to negotiate the terms of the financial transaction with an unscrupulous character named Bloody Bartholomew.

Jonathan Bartholomew received the moniker Bloody Bartholomew many years ago in London when he and his gang of gunrunner's hideout were surrounded by over two dozen armed constables. The building was an old warehouse on the banks of the River Thames, just south of Lambeth Bridge.

"Jonathan Bartholomew, this is Scotland Yard, the building is surrounded. I need for everyone to come out with your hands above your heads."

"Bloody Hell, it's the bobbies." Bartholomew squawked.

"Whadda we going to do, Gov?" One of his gang implored.

Bartholomew gave an icy stare to his gang of fifteen and remarked, "I don't know about ye blokes, but I'm not going back to Newgate again. I'd rather die than go back to prison."

He then began to load several handguns and said, "What say ye lads, are ye with me?"

Once everyone was armed to the teeth, Bartholomew cracked open the warehouse door and shouted, "If ye want me, come and get me!"

With that, he and his gang rushed out of the building guns a-blazing. The plan was to try and reach a skiff docked on the shore nearly sixty meters away. During the melee, hundreds of rounds were fired in every direction; in all the confusion, police wounded other police as well as many of Bartholomew's gang members. After the smoke had cleared, nine of Bartholomew's gang were either dead or wounded as well as six bobbies. It was reported as the bloodiest gun battle in London's history. As for Jonathan Bartholomew, he took a bullet in his left shoulder, yet he was able to make it to the skiff sailed downriver to Chelsea to the home of his aged mother, who tended his wounds, and eventually, he was able to make his way to the island of Tortuga. Thar is still a reward of eight hundred pounds for his capture, dead or alive.

Since Tortuga is a French colony, and since he has committed no crimes against the French, he is a free man. Bartholomew has established himself as a purveyor of various goods of unknown provenance. He buys items, no questions asked.

After several hours of intense negotiations, both

Captains Twigg and Calico Jack had struck an accord.

"So, gentlemen, we hath an accord?" Bartholomew asked.

"Aye, ye old bilge rat. And a proper one it be." Twigg stated.

"Aye, ye hath an agreeance." Calico Jack agreed.

They then each spit in the palms of their hand and proceeded to shake each other's hand as a symbol that the deal was set.

Once Black Dog Billy and Mister Turner returned, and the last of the cargo was unloaded, the celebration began.

"Break out the rum, and splice the mainbrace, Mister Turner."

"Aye, aye, Captain."

A couple of large casks of Jamaican rum was brought topside. As everyone began to revel in our good fortune, I decided to go and see how Smitty was doing. I hath not given him thought during our sea battles and pirating ways. On me way to see him, I spied Doctor Cotton.

"Doctor Cotton, Smitty?"

"Healthwise, he be fine, but he is full of melancholy and self-pity. Try and be of good cheer."

"Thank ye, Doc."

I took two tankards of rum down to where Smitty's bunk were.

"Ahoy, matey," I said as I held out the tankard to him.

"Nay."

"Nay! Don't make me drink alone. Here." I says as I handed him the pewter stoup.

After a couple of drinks, Smitty started to become

more jovial and buoyant. It were the first time in days that I had seen a smile beam across his face.

"How are ye faring?"

"Thar still be throbbing. It be strange, I would swear that I feel me fingers itch." He said as he held up the stump.

"What does the Doc say?"

"It be not strange. But in time, it will pass."

"Has Bo'sun's mate Dax been by?"

"Aye. He showed me much kindness. Of that, I be thankful. I guess that I be feeling sorry for me self."

"What saith Doctor Cotton?" I asked.

"He is reading a fitting for me hook within a fortnight."

"That be great. How 'bout ye come topside and join the festivities?"

"Nay. I not be feeling right just yet."

"Well, think 'bout coming ashore this evening. What ye needs is a strumpet to crack Jenny's teacup." I says with a grin.

"I don't know if I'm ready for quiffing?"

"Nay, that's exactly what ye needs. I'll come to get ye when the longboat is ready to leave. Once we get our share of the booty, we'll be flush and ready for rum and quim. Now, ye get some rest, ye old sea dog. Ye will need all ye strength."

Whilst anchored off Tortuga, I spied something that I had only heard about but had never laid eyes upon. A steam-powered warship. She was the *Napoléon*, the first purpose-built steam battleship in the world a 90-gun ship of the line. I could see that our days of pirating were closing fast.

Whilst on leave in Tortuga, I cozied up to one of her English-speaking sailors so as to inquire about the *Napoléon's* capabilities, strengths, and weaknesses. The man's name was Raphaël Archambeau; he were a gunner's mate ever since she were launched back around the time of the encounter with Moby Dick.

This voyage was the *Napoléon's* first shakedown cruise. They were out this way intentionally looking for pirates to engage in battle for some real-world experience.

"What ship be ye sailing on, mon ami?" Archambeau asked.

"The *Abercromby Revenge*. We be an American privateer escort for American merchant ships."

"Ah, très intelligent! And have vous had any encounters with pirates recently?"

"Nay. Not for a whilst, although I hear that thar be some in the seas off of Nassau Island."

"Merci." Archambeau said with a grin.

"Can I buy ye another rum?" Says I wanting him to loosen up to answering questions about the *Napoléon*.

"Oui, merci."

"Hey, barkeep, two more rums!" I shouted.

The barkeeper were an ex-pirate who went by the name Billy Bones. He looked to me to be an ancient mariner, his skin looked like an old, weathered canvas tarp from too many years out on the open sea, the lower half of his face be covered with a large gray scraggly beard with brown chewing tobacco stains, he wore an eye patch over his left eye and cobbled along on a wooden peg leg. Old Bolly Bones weren't lucky in battle, that be for sure, the poor sod. Although unlucky in combat, Billy did manage to squirrel away enough to buy the Drovers Inn; it tweren't much, but it were something.

"Here ye be," Billy said as he plopped two tankards of rum on the table.

I tossed him two silver pieces as I held up me flagon and said, "Cheers."

After Archambeau finished his tankard, I asked him, "So, Raphaël, what be the top speed of the *Napoléon*?"

Proudful, he answered, "Thirteen knots."

"Shiver me timbers!" I said shocked. The *Abercromby Revenge*, on a good day, could only do six knots.

"And she be truly yar, well balanced on the helm, quick, and handy." Archambeau boasted.

"How long will ye be staying in Tortuga?" I asked.

"Trois jours." He slurred as the fifth tankard of rum was finally taking its toll.

"Three days. Hmmm, well, me hearty, I must be shoving off. Au revoir, fair winds to thee." I says as up I got and hastened back to the *Abercromby Revenge*.

"Sink me! Thirteen knots!" Black Dog Billy Twigg gasped.

"Arrggghhh, do you believe he were speaking the truth, me bucko?" Calico Jack asked.

"Aye, I felt it were no trickery, Captain. He be telling genuineness." Says I.

"If'n that be true, we be in a terrible predicament. I fear our days of pirating be near an end." Twigg said forlornly.

"Aye, that be true. It seems that we be at the edge of the map." Calico Jack said.

The three of us sat in Captain Calico Jack's cabin, contemplating what the future be when Captain Twigg stood up, paced the room, and finally said, "I think we leave it to the crew to decide."

Thar we stood, the two companies from the *Abercromby Revenge* and the *Flying Dragon* standing on the main deck of the *Flying Dragon*, all ninety-four of us facing our two Captains standing on the quarter-deck.

"Lads, we be standing at the edge of the map, and I fear thar be monsters. And that monster be anchored over yonder." Twigg said pointing to the *Napoléon*.

"Thar be the future. We the past. She can do thirteen knots. Twice as fast as we can." Calico Jack revealed.

"The question now is, what do ye want to do? We could continue to loot and pillage, knowing that sooner than later, we be captured or killed. Or do we take our spoils and give up our thieving ways? What say ye?" Black Dog Billy asked.

We stood mumbling and questioning amongst ourselves for several minutes when One-Eyed Willie, Captain Calico Jack's first mate, raised his hand and shouted, "I be a buccaneer all me life. Thar be no going back fer me. I'd druther die a pirate than a farmer!"

The crews erupted with roars of elation and excitement. Once the noise quieted down, Captain

Twigg asked, "So say you all? For if'n thar be those who wish to end these days of pirating fear not, say yer piece now."

I feared mockery, and yet I raised me hand and spoke, "I for one see only folly in continuing such endeavor knowing that the deck be stacked against us. As many of ye know, I were a whaler before pirating lo these many months. I fear not death, nor do I wish death upon me foolishly. This new breed of steam-powered ships can outgun us, outmaneuver us, and outrun us. Nay, I fear to continue would be madness. I vote for changing course."

"And what course might that be?" Mister Turner inquired.

"I don't rightly know off hand. But thar might be opportunity out California way. I hear say that thar be gold in them thar hills." Says I.

"California! And how do ye figure to get thar?" Scoffed One-Eyed Willie.

"Going round the Cape." Black Dog Billy announced.

"Ye thinking of sailing round Cape Horn? What are ye, daft, man?" One-Eyed Willie sneered. And many of the company laughed and jeered.

"It be madness." Someone in the crowd shouted out.

Calico Jack stepped forward, raising his hands, calming the crowd down, and said, "If'n thar be a man who could sail the Horn, it be Black Dog Billy Twigg.

"If thar be those that want to try to go to California, step towards the port side. Them that wants to go on pirating head starboard." Captain Twigg barked.

As I counted, thar seemed to be an even split for each. Although thar were many from either company that would be crossing over from crewing for the *Abercromby Revenge* to be crewing for the *Flying Dragon* and vice versa. Thar seemed to be no hard feeling towards each man's decision. Yet thar be a great sadness that permeated throughout companies as we would be leaving many a mate behind. Me mate, Smitty chose to continue the pirate's life. But that be each man's lot. It were hard to say goodbye, but we lose many a soul to Davy Jones' locker during each voyage.

"Mister Turner snap to and set sail." Captain Twigg ordered.

"Aye, aye, Captain." Mister Turner said as he turned to the company and began shouting orders to get underway like a whirling dervish. He were running from stem to stern, shouting orders.

"Ye heard the Captain, snap to and set sail! Castaway all lines! Let go, the hawser! Weigh anchor! Brace the forearm and hoist those mainsails, lads."

Once both ships were out in deep water, the *Flying Dragon* hoisted the Jolly Roger. As we went our own ways, I saw Captain Calico Jack standing upright on the quarter-deck next to the helmsman. It were the last time that I saw either him or the *Flying Dragon* ever again.

Years later, I heard that the *Flying Dragon* was attacked by no less than three British frigates on the inner side of Ocracoke Island off the coast of North Carolina. The British frigates, *HMS Tribune* and *HMS*

Newcastle carried out a broadside attack, whilst the *HMS Furious*, a screw-driven powered frigate, stunted the *Flying Dragon*'s forward progress by boxing her in causing a collision.

Over two hundred British Marines from the three ships boarded the *Flying Dragon*, commencing in hand-to-hand combat that lasted over forty-five minutes over decks slick with blood from those killed or injured. Against a superior force, the pirates were pushed back toward the stern to make a desperate stand.

The tale I were told was that One-Eyed Jack and Captain Calico Jack were among the last to die. Willie was stabbed in the back by a Marine bayonet. During a sword battle with two British officers, Calico Jack's cutlass broke in half. It be said that he were offered surrender, but he stood defiant and said, "I rather die like a man than be hanged like a dog!" And with that, he charged the two officers, his broken sword raised in spite. They cleaved him to the brisket, nearly cutting him in half.

Of the forty-eight men on board the *Flying Dragon*, all but eight were killed in battle; one were me mate, Smitty, who was captured and taken back to England where were tried, convicted of murder, and six counts of piracy, and hanged. He had to be hanged twice. On the first attempt, the rope broke, and Smitty survived. Whilst they were stringing up a new rope, some in the crowd called for his release, claiming it were a sign from God. The Crown did not agree, and poor Smitty was hanged again, this time successfully. Like so many before him, Smitty was gibbeted over the River Thames as a warning to future would-be pirates. His body hung thar for three years. The *Flying Dragon* were set on fire and scuttled. She be no more.

We decided to fly the First Navy Jack flag, which consisted of thirteen red and white stripes with an uncoiled rattlesnake and the motto "Don't Tread on Me." And as a precaution, even though we feared it were bad luck, we changed the name of the *Abercromby Revenge* to that of the *Hornet's Nest*.

As we made our way south towards Cape Horn, we were constantly vigilant to avoid other ships. Once we crossed the equator, the days were tediously long. We spent the majority of our time during the days washing and scrubbing the decks, keeping the brightwork shine, and just in case, we continue to practice our sword fighting and combat skills. At night, we drink grog and sing sea shanties.

It happened one night off the coast of Brazil when we were awakened by the screams of Tom Thumb, the young cabin boy of Calico Jack. When given the choice, Tom wanted not to continue the pirate's life, so Captain Jack allowed him to come aboard the *Abercromby Revenge.*

We found a seaman named Nathan Evers and Tom Thumb down below in one of the cargo holds. Evers had Tom Thumb forced over a wooden water casket on his stomach, naked from the waist down, whilst Evers were buggering and having his way with the poor lad.

Several of us grabbed Evers and subdued him,

eventually placing him in chains, and dragged him up to the Captain's quarters. Doctor Cotton came down to console the young lad, who were severely traumatized. It came to be that the young lad became withdrawn and even stopped talking.

Nathan Evers stood sobbing before Captain Twigg, trousers down around his ankles, his member fully exposed. Twigg were sitting behind his table, displayed with all sorts of maps and his logbook. He rose from the table and made his way to be nose to nose with the accused.

"What have ye to say? Twigg demanded.

"He made advances to me, Captain." Evers wept.

"He be nothing more than a child, you scurvy dog!"

"It tweren't me fault, Captain. I swear."

Twigg stepped back from Evers and looked down at his state of undress, and ordered, "Make yourself decent, man."

Evers slowly leaned down and righted himself. As he were about to stand up, he fell to his knees and cried out, "Have mercy, Captain. I beg ye."

"Stand up! Thar be one thing I cannot abide, a lily-livered scallywag. Come morn, ye shall be taken onto the main deck and where ye shall be keelhauled."

"Please, Captain, no!"

"Take this black-hearted villain down to the brig and out of my sight."

As he was being taken down below he was set upon many times, savagely beaten and spat upon by many members of the crew before finally being thrown into the brig where he awaited his death sentence.

"Tomorrow, ye be nothing more than shark bait, ye wretched rogue!" Mr. Turner said as he slammed and locked the brig's iron door.

"Noooooooo! Please, have mercy. I beg ye, Captain. Beat me, whip me, maroon me, anything but keelhauling."

"Mister Evers, ye have committed a most heinous crime against young Master Thumb, and I say let the punishment fit the crime. Therefore, Mister Evers, I'm disinclined to acquiesce to your request. Mr. Turner, proceed with the chastisement."

Of all my years at sea, I had never witnessed a keelhauling. Evers were suspended by chains that were attached to his hands and legs then anchored to a pulley on the starboard main yard, a rope is fastened to the opposite extremities of the main yard, and a weight of lead is hung upon his legs to sink him to a competent depth. The purpose of this apparatus is so he will be drawn close up to the yard-arm, and thence he be thrown into the sea, he then will be dragged under the ship's keel which be covered in barnacles, he is then hoisted up on the port side of the vessel.

I stood amongst the company next to Smitty who whispered to me, "If he's lucky, he'll drown, before the barnacles shred him to ribbon."

"Barnacles?"

"Like a thousand knives across your back. And, of course, the blood attracts sharks."

Nathan Evers stood shaking chained on the starboard railing, Mister Turner placed a black canvas bag over his head as to somewhat prevent severe damage to Evers' head.

Captain Twigg looked at Mister Turner and said, "Proceed."

Turner then pushed Evers overboard feet first, so when he was pulled up on the port side, he would be hanging head down to help expel water from his lungs. Evers hit the water hard, probably knocking the wind out of him. Once he had gone under, Mister Turner gave the order for the men on the port side to begin hauling Evers under the ship.

"Haul fast or slow, Captain?" Mister Turner asked.

"Let us not belay this, Mister Turner."

"Ye heard the Captain, heave to men."

The fifteen men assigned to the ropes began to pull quickly, but it tweren't easy going as the ship was under sail. It seemed an eternity. Once Evers was retrieved from the water, his face was bleeding and torn, his clothes hanging in sherds, and his hands were dripping blood.

"Again!" Captain Twigg ordered.

Once again, Evers was dropped into the sea, and the men now ran to the other side to begin hauling him starboard. They hauled him up and swung him over on to the main deck. He lay there not moving, the bag that were placed over his head torn open; his eyes were open and filled with blood. His body was as shredded as mincemeat. After Doctor Cotton had examined Mister Evers, he pronounced that he sustained four broken ribs, a fractured skull, and his left leg had been broken.

"Will he live?" Mister Turner asked.

"If'n he don't get infected, he might live." Cotton replied.

"Take him below and put him in his bunk." Turner barked.

Six men, including me self, carried his limp, lifeless body down and deposited him onto his bunk, Doctor Cotton following close behind. As we were heading topside, we heard moans and gurgling sounds emanating from Evers, such sounds as I had never heard produced from any human.

By the time we arrived on deck, there were no sign that thar had been any keelhauling, all the pulleys and ropes had been stowed, and the men were back at work. As I were climbing up the main mast rigg'g to take me turn in the barrel, I saw little Tom Thumb huddled in a corner of the quarter-deck hiding behind the helmsman just staring out to sea.

It were nine days later when it were discovered that Tom Thumb were nowhere to be seen. We searched the ship top to bottom, stem to stern, but alas no Tom Thumb. He apparently went overboard. It were at that point that Captain Twigg feared for Nathan Evers' life. He called for all hands to gather on the main deck.

"As ye all know, Master Tom Thumb has been lost at sea. And this is why I am ordering all hands do no harm to Mister Evers or ye shall receive the same punishment that he received. I have decided to cast off Mister Evers at the nearest port, which by my calculations shall be tomorrow at the port of Cayenne, the capital of French Guiana. That is all."

"Company dismissed." Shouted Mr. Turner.

Evers was bedridden, still recovering from the

injuries that he had sustained from the keelhauling. It were hard sleeping as Evers moaned constantly even when Doctor Cotton administered morphine. Many a man cursed Evers wishing him ill will and even spat upon him. The Doctor tended to his wounds as best he could but one injury that were little he could do to help heal. During the keelhauling, the barnacles on the ship's keel shredded a huge portion of his lower face, it ripped away the flesh around his mouth exposing his teeth and jawbone. In some respects, I felt bad for the poor wretch. I know that he needed to be punished, but after seeing what keelhauling can do to a man shook me to the core. I would have been in favor of caning or even the use of the cat o' nine tails, but this were too much castigation.

The next afternoon, we dropped anchor off the port of Cayenne. Evers was escorted off the *Hornet's Nest* to boos, jeers, and death threats. He was then rowed ashore on the longboat, Doctor Cotton accompanied him to the *Cathédrale Saint-Sauver*.

"Speak French?"

Evers shook his head no.

"Are ye a Catholic?" The Doctor asked.

Evers mumbled, "Nay."

"It would be better that they think ye are. I will speak to them and tell them that ye are a Catholic in hopes that they will take ye in."

Cathédrale Saint-Sauver stood in the town square towering over the city. The church has a light brown exterior thar be seven towering arcs in the front with a central bell tower. Inside thar be tall white pillars that form arches all the way down to the alter.

Doctor Cotton and Nathan Evers were greeted by a

young nun as they entered the narthex of the church.

"*Parles-tu anglaise*?" The Doctor asked.

The nun shook her head no. She held up her hand in a gesture for them to wait.

"*Un moment.*" She said as she hurried away.

Minutes later an older nun approached.

"I speak some little English. May I help you?" With a thick French accent, she queried.

"I am Doctor Cotton, and this poor lad is in need of spiritual and medical assistance that I cannot administer."

"*Que lest son nom*?" She asked.

"His name is Nathan Evers." Cotton answered.

"*Est-il catholique*?"

"Oui, sister, he is a Catholic."

"What has happened?" She asked caressing Evers' face.

"He was injured onboard ship during a *tempête*."

Evers looked quizzical at Cotton, who whispered, "During a storm."

The aged nun gave Evers a reassuring smile and gestured for the Doctor and Evers to follow her.

"*Suivez-moi.*" She said as she led them down through the nave, turning left into the North Transept, out the massive wooden door, and out into an outdoor colonnade to a small infirmary. Inside were a dozen beds, all but one was occupied. Thar were women and men, some European and a couple of indigenous natives being tended by the order of nuns. Evers changed into a white hospital gown and was seated on the edge of a bed before being attended to by a superfluity of nuns that surrounded him. Doctor Cotton waited long enough to see that Evers was being adequately taken care of. He then headed back to the longboat and the *Hornet's Nest.*

As he boarded the ship, I asked him what he thought Evers's chances were.

"I fear it will not end well for Mister Evers." Doctor Cotton said.

"Why are his wounds so bad?"

"Nay, lad. It be my assumption that he will recover from his injuries but will take his life soon thereafter."

"Why?"

"I believe that he will find living in society with such a facial deformity will be too much for him to bear. Nay, Ishmael, by this time next year, Nathan Evers will be dead by his own hand." Doctor Cotton surmised.

He proved to be right.

It were but three days later that we found that we were in need of freshwater; our current supplies had turned brackish. We sent six crew members, including me self and Mister Turner, with several empty barrels to be filled with fresh water from the river Amazon. It were tedious work rowing upstream against the currents. We did not know it at the time, but we were in Munduruku territory. Munduruku means "red ants," based on the historical Munduruku tactic of attacking en masse.

We had been rowing several hours upstream to

make sure that the water be pure when we were suddenly surrounded by a dozen or so native canoes occupied by warriors armed with spears and bows and arrows.

Mister Turner spoke in a low voice, "Steady men. Let's not do anything hasty. But be at the ready to use ye guns if'n it comes to that."

They forced us to the riverbank where their village was. They lived in thatched huts that sat upon wooden stilts high above the ground to keep them dry when the river flooded, and I imagined to keep themselves safe from the jungle's nocturnal predators. Thar must have been eight or nine huts with women and children sitting around campfires roasting some sort of meat.

As we entered the camp we saw six shrunken heads of white men, the heads looked to be that of Catholic priests with their pectoral crosses draped over their heads, much to our disgust.

The chief noticed that we were all staring at the shrunken heads, he pointed to the heads, made the sign of the cross, and spat on the ground growling, "*Pûera karaíba!*"

None of us had any idea what he said, but the meaning came through in his actions and his tone. They tweren't at all ready for the white man's religion.

Mister Turner kept his hand on his pistol as he tried to communicate with the savages.

"Do ye speak English?" He asked.

Thar be no response.

"*Est-ce que tu parles français?*" He asked.

Nothing just strange looks from the chief.

"*Você fala português?*"

The chief nodded.

"*O que é que você quer de nós?*" Turner asked.

I whispered, "What did you ask?"

"What do they want of us."

The chief pointed to the rifles that we be carrying, and said, "*Queremos bastões de fogo.*"

Turner softly said, "He wants rifles."

Between the six of us, we had three Leichte Percussions-Gewehr single-shot rifles, three Jennings repeating rifles, and each man had a sidearm. Thar be no way in hell that we were going to give these savages repeating rifles, nor any of our pistols.

Mister Turner nodded, held up three fingers, and said, "*Três.*"

The chief shook his head and demanded, "*Mais!*"

Turner held up his hands to try and appease him and said, "*E vamos dar para balas.*"

The chief gave thought before answering with a nod and saying, "*Multar.*"

"Lads hand them over the three Leichte Percussions-Gewehr rifles and the ammunition. And then let us depart post haste." Turner said.

We laid the three rifles on the ground along with approximately forty rounds of ammunition as we then began to head back to the longboat.

"*Esperar!*" The chief barked.

We all froze, steeling ourselves for battle, the chief called to one of the warriors in their native language of Tupi, to go and retrieve two of the shrunken heads and present them to Mister Turner in exchange for the rifles.

Mister Turner took them, bowed, and thanked the chief saying, "*Obrigada.*" As we kept backing away not daring to turn our backs on them, our hands nonchalantly resting on our pistols.

With the barrels full of water and our lives intact, we rowed like Hell to return to the *Hornet's Nest*.

Once back onboard the wildly exaggerated stories flowed like the rum that we received. Mister Turner was voted an extra share of the ship's loot for his bravery, cool-headedness, and sheer guile.

When asked what he were going to do with those two shrunken heads, Turner smiled and replied, "Keep 'em of course. Hadn't ye ever heard that two heads are better than one?"

The voyage down to the Cape was uneventful, the weather were pleasant. We be lucky it being January to try and traverse the Cape when the temperatures are on average sixty degrees. Had we tried to negotiate sailing the Cape during the summer months, being below the equator, we would encounter terrible storms and the possibility of icebergs. As it were, the seas were rough and a tough slog.

We started in Ushuaia in Argentina, we then sailed down the Beagle Channel and turned south around Isla Navarino to Isla Herschel where we say for the best conditions to attempt to round the Horn. We waited for two days before we made the voyage. During the six days, it took us to pass through the Cape, all hands were on deck for most of the crossing tending the sails. The winds served us to our desire, and now hauled the *Hornet's Nest* west into the Pacific Ocean. Nary a one of the company had ever sailed on the Pacific. What we noticed first were the difference in the color between the Atlantic, which is emerald green, and the Pacific which is cobalt blue.

We sailed the length of Chile, keeping the land in sight at all times off the starboard side. Until we came upon the port city of Iquique as we were very much in want of everyday necessities, stores like food and water, and some things we men considered just as or more necessary, women. We stayed in the port of Iquique for three days, until one day a Spanish man o' war dropped anchor off the port. The Captain and several of the officers of the Spanish warship *Nuestra Señora de Begoña* requested permission to come aboard. They came aboard all neatly dressed in their naval uniforms. They were visibly surprised to see how casually dressed the crew and especially the officers of the *Hornet's Nest* were. Captain Black Dog Billy Twigg and Doctor Cotton greeted them as they asked permission to come aboard.

"Permiso para subir a bordo. Yo soy el Capitán Gutiérrez." The Captain said with a sharp salute.

Black Dog returned the salute and nodded to Doctor Cotton to translate.

"Bienvenido a bordo. Este es el Capitán Twigg." Cotton replied with a sweeping gesture to come on board.

Twigg whispered to Cotton, ask them what they want.

"¿Qué podemos hacer por usted, Capitán?"

Captain Gutiérrez smiled and said in broken English, "What be your business is in *estas aquas*?"

Taken aback Twigg answered, "We stopped for

supplies. Our destination is that of San Francisco."

"Argentina?"

"Nay, America. We just sailed the Cape Horn. We be going north."

"And are *ustedes piratas*?" Gutiérrez asked with a sneer.

"Pirates? Nay, we be not pirates. Merchant seamen."

"Ah, merchant seamen, why do you carry *muchos cañones* as a merchant ship."

"It's a dangerous world, Capitán," Twigg replied with a snarky grin.

"*Sí, sí*. How much longer will you be in Iquique?"

"We sail tonight."

"That is good." Captain Gutiérrez said as he looked at the sky. "It is a *buen día* to sail. Be sure you do. *Ve con Dios*."

Gutiérrez gave a short bow, turned, and led his men off of the *Hornet's Nest* and back on board the *Nuestra Señora de Begoña*.

Twigg asked Mister Turner is everyone back on board.

"All but Mister Scott. He were arrested for fighting and stabbing a whore." Turner answered.

"Well, I be in no truculent mood, Mister Turner. I hereby invoke the pirate's code. Fall behind, stay behind. Prepare to set sail, Mister Turner."

"Aye, aye, Captain." Turner acknowledged.

"We be off, lads. Castaway all lines fore-and-aft! Let go, clear the hawsers! Weigh anchor! Brace the forearm and hoist those mainsails. Ishmael, get ye up in the barrel and keep a keen eye on that Spanish frigate. I don't trust them scallywags." Turner bellowed.

"Aye, aye." Says I, as I scrambled up the rigg'n. Once settled in, I pulled out the spyglass and watched as the crew on the frigate looked to be going about their normal duties. Thar weren't any casting off of lines and the sails were all stowed. The Captain and his officers were standing on the quarter-deck observing our getting underway.

Soon the anchor were hoisted, sails were full, and we be off. I heard Captain Twigg with Mister Turner talk about trying to make it to San Francisco without stopping anymore. We had enough stores and water to make the journey, it would just mean several weeks or months of boredom and tedium. Little did we know that we would soon be in for the fight of our lives.

"Ship ho! Off the port bow" Shouted John Whizkey, the barrel man.

"What see ye?" Mister Turner hollered up.

Whizkey strained to peer through the spyglass, and called out, "It be a frigate. Flying the French flag."

Captain Twigg hurriedly appeared out from his cabin carrying his spyglass.

He scanned the horizon until he spied the vessel and with the monocular still up to his eye he said, "A French man o' war here in the Pacific, and it appears to be steam-powered. What say ye to that, Mister Turner?" Twigg asked.

"I fear roguery, Captain."

"As do I, Mister Turner. Call the men to arms."

"Aye, aye, Captain."

Mister Turner shouted out, "Hands aloft to lose the gallants! Haul on the mainbrace! Make ready the guns! And run out the sweeps."

The men of the gun crew be scrambling and a scurrying making ready the cannons, whilst the of the rest men scrambled up in the rigg'g to set the sails for battle.

The French frigate sailed head-on towards our ship the barrel man, John Whizkey shouted down, "Captain, she stuck down the French flag and has raised the Jolly Roger. Thar be pirates."

"Mister Turner, strike the stars and stripes and raise our Jolly Rogers. Prepare to fire on my command!"

"Aye, aye Captain. All guns armed and ready."

Captain Twigg and the men of the *Hornet's Nest* didn't know it, but they were going up against the most feared pirate in all of the Pacific, Hipólito Baudelaire, a French-born Peruvian sailor, privateer, who fought for Peru, Chile, and Ecuador before becoming a pirate.

He and his men were notorious for raiding Spanish ports all up and down Central America as well plundering the Mission at San Juan Capistrano in Southern California. He sailed as far west as Manila and Hawaii, blocking their ports and holding them for ransom.

His ship, a French frigate, named *le Fléau,* (the Scourge) was a 32-gun Concorde-class frigate carrying 12-pounder long guns as her main armament. She posed to be a most mortiferous adversary. Twigg could see that they were outgunned and overpowered, being that the *le Fléau* were steam-driven. He believed that their only hope was to try and outmaneuver them.

"Heave down and bring a spring upon 'er, Mister Turner," Twigg ordered.

"Aye, aye, Captain," Turner said as he barked the order to the helmsman.

As the *le Fléau* began to catch the *Hornet's Nest*, Captain Twigg took the helm and commenced to initiate evasive action by turning the ship around, so we be heading south. Now the *le Fléau* were on our stern and coming fast. Our sails were beginning to luff, as the wind tweren't pushing us forward for *le Fléau,* being so much larger than us were blocking the wind.

"Captain, she be closing down on us. Soon she will rake us!" Mister Turner shouted.

Captain Twigg saw that thar be no outrunning nor outmaneuvering the *le Fléau*, so he decided to try something he had never tried. But despite times call for despite thinking.

"Lower the starboard anchor!" Twigg yelled.

Turner stood frozen watching the *le Fléau* get closer.

"Do it now, I say!" Twigg demanded.

Turner all of a sudden came to life and hollered, "Lower the starboard anchor!"

"After we're finished club-haulin', Mister Turner prepare the men to open fire on my command!" Twigg announced.

Once the starboard anchor were dropped, which slowed the *Hornet's Nest's* forward movement and caused us to spin around 180 degrees face to face with our pursuer.

Thrown completely off guard, Captain Hipólito Baudelaire unexpectedly had to adjust his course to the port side giving the *Hornet's Nest* the advantage. When the *Hornet's Nest* swung around to be parallel with Baudelaire's ship Twigg ordered, "Fire!"

"Fire!" Screamed Mister Turner.

All 12 of our cannons fired as one hitting the *le Fléau* broadside causing considerable damage to their guns and creating mayhem. The *Hornet's Nest* continued to swing on our anchor bringing us aft of the *le Fléau*. Where thar be no cannons to attack us and whilst we be coming around to attack their port side we had time to reload.

"Cannons seven through twelve prepare to fire on me command!" Twigg charged.

"Cannons seven through twelve prepare to fire!" Turner shouted.

When the *Hornet's Nest* were approaching the port side, the *le Fléau's* cannons were aimed straight ahead, whilst ours were coming at them on a three-quarter angle from behind their ship. When we fired, we destroyed half of their port side armament.

Captain Twigg bellowed, "All hands, grapnels, at the ready!"

Mister Turner grabbed hold of a hawser with his left hand, and yelled, "Give no quarter." Placed a dagger in his mouth, whilst holding his cutlass in his right hand, then swung onto the deck of the *le Fléau* knocking down a group of sailors all the whilst hacking them to pieces.

With that, we threw the grappling hooks over to the railings of the *le Fléau* and tugged to bring the two ships together. Then with swords and pistols in hand, each crew began to board the other's ship.

For a long time, I was unable to board the *le Fléau*, for I was defending the *Hornet's Nest* along with

Captain Twigg and a couple of dozen others of our company. The smoke from the gunfire and the blazing fire from the *le Fléau* created by our cannon attack filled the air so thick it were hard to distinguish friend from foe. It were such brutal fighting as swords clashed, fists flew, and guns fired, the likes that I had never seen before. Thar be bodies and limbs of dead and wounded buccaneers lying about everywhere. The decks ran cold with blood.

The battle raged on for over an hour, ebbing back and forth like the tides of the ocean. The one thing that turned the hostility to our favor were that being a pirate on the Pacific Ocean, Captain Hipólito Baudelaire and his crew tweren't privy to the latest advancement in weaponry of the repeating rifles and pistols. Months ago, we be lucky to have had plundered an arms shipment from England on its way to America carrying several hundred repeating rifles and pistols along with thousands of rounds of ammunition.

Finally, we pushed what were left of Baudelaire's men back onto the poop deck leaving them nowhere to go. It were either surrender or fight to the death. Among them were Captain Hipólito Baudelaire who were felled with three shots in him and ten dismal cuts in several parts of his body, he appeared to be dying. It were he that offered surrender saying, "We fight no more. Take what ye will and leave us be."

Captain Twigg victorious, raised his sword to Baudelaire lying before him and asked, "Where be the booty?"

"In me cabin." Baudelaire acquiesced.

Mister Turner and several men ran below to Baudelaire's cabin and found four large chests filled with jewels and gold which they took and carried over to the *Hornet's Nest*. There be cheers and jubilation upon our victory. But the conquest did not come without much loss. We lost over half of our company, and many were wounded. I, me self were wounded thrice, with two cuts one on me chest, one on me back, and a trivial gunshot wound in me left shoulder.

As Captain Twigg were leaving Baudelaire and his men, Captain Baudelaire asked in a failing voice, "Damn you villain, who are you?"

"Black Dog Billy Twigg, Captain of the *Hornet's Nest*."

Baudelaire gave a gestured salute then succumbed to his wounds and died.

After we set sail, leaving the *le Fléau* badly damaged, her decks smoldering from the fires, and listing to the starboard side, we spent the next hours throwing the dead overboard and scrubbing the decks to be free of blood and guts, whilst Doc Cotton worked on all of the wounded.

Thar tweren't a soul that didn't receive some wound, be it minor or life-threatening. I considered me self amongst the lucky, with only negligible injuries and no limbs lost.

Our company were down to half strength. We had just enough hands to crew the *Hornet's Nest* without any disturbance. Captain Twigg estimated six weeks until we reach San Francisco harbor. We needed to stop one more time for stores and freshwater. While sailing north along the Mexican coast we were looking for a port to take shelter and finally found the port of Mazatlán.

Before we docked, we had hoisted the colors of the American flag. There were over a dozen ships that had dropped anchor, carrying fortune hunters from the East Coast, most were aspiring miners making their way to San Francisco to seek fame and fortune. The others were scallywags who were traveling to gold camps to take advantage of and or rob the miners of their hard-earned gold, mostly through commercial enterprise. Thar be many a whore looking to get rich as well working in the multitude of houses of ill repute.

Back in 1846-1848, Mazatlán had been occupied by the Americans during the Mexican–American War, so many of the locals were able to speak English. It were agreed upon by the company that we stay in port for three days for a little rest, which meant drinking and whoring. We felt that we deserved it after our deadly encounter with the *le Fléau*.

Mazatlán had not only a small local police force but a small garrison of federales that kept the peace. All of us were aware that if any of us were to be seized and held for any time longer than the three days when the *Hornet's Nest* is to set sail we would be subject to the pirate's code, fall behind & stay behind. If that were to happen, you would lose out on a huge share of the booty that we have accumulated over the year and a half that I have been with Captain Twigg, especially what we had taken as spoils from our encounter with the *le Fléau*.

We tended to look out for one another, but as in life

nothing rarely goes as planned. With only hours before we were to set sail onward to California, one of our gunners, Thomas Fogg had gotten into an altercation with a Madam of one of the more popular brothels over the price of services rendered. Madam Emilla, who stood a mere four foot five inches demanded immediate payment or she would call the Federales.

"Ju pay!" She shouted.

"Go fuck ye self, bitch! She tweren't be wasting me jeez on her!" Fogg barked.

Madam Emilla got nose to nose with the six-foot completely naked Thomas Fogg and before he knew what had happened, Emilla had both of his testicles in her left hand and her right hand was underneath holding a very sharp paring knife.

"Ju pay now?" Emilla whispered softly.

Fogg looked down, gulped, nodded, and said, "I pay now."

The whore brought him his trousers, he reached into the pocket and took out two silver doubloons and handed them to the half-naked girl. She showed them to Madam Emilla who brought the knife tightly up to the skin and shook her head saying, "*Más*."

Fogg nervously reached back into the pocket and pulled out two more doubloons and dropped them into the girl's palm.

"*Más*." The old woman said pushing the knife blade harder up against him, and she began to squeeze Fogg's ballocks until his face grimaced. Once again he quickly retrieved two doubloons and gave them to the girl.

The old madam released his cullions and gave him a slap on his arse, smiled, and said, "*Gracias, chico*."

Fogg couldn't get dressed fast enough. He ran out of

there half-naked, forgetting his boots as he sprinted out the door and down the street towards the docks towards the last trip of the longboat back to the ship before we set sail for San Francisco.

I was in the barrel on lookout when I spied something I hadn't seen in over two years, whales. Hundreds of Gray Whales as far as the eye could see migrating north hugging the California coastline, and nary a whaling ship to be seen. I saw several dozen merchant ships traveling north and south, so many we didn't bother calling them out since we were longer pirating. Captain Twigg told the helmsman to follow the merchant ships traveling north toward San Francisco.

When we entered San Francisco Bay thar must have been thirty ships anchored out in the harbor. We nestled the *Hornet's Nest* in amongst six British merchant ships off what were called Embarcadero where the piers and docks were. Thar be busy unloading cargo from the ships out in the harbor all day and night.

That next morning Captain Twigg and Mister Turner went ashore to see about cashing in our booty into U.S coin of the realm. They were gone most of the day. When they returned to the *Hornet's Nest*, they had several gentlemen accompanying them to appraise our cache of loot. They all seemed excitedly impressed with our treasure and soon thar were a bidding war going on amongst themselves. In the end, each of the 48 surviving crew members of the original 92 received Ten thousand dollars each.

As Captain Twigg and Mister Turner were giving us our payout, I posed a question.

"Excuse me Captain," Says I.

"Aye, lad, what is it?"

"Well, sir, what is to become of the *Hornet's Nest*?" I asked.

"That be a good question." He said as he stood so all the company would hear.

"The question, what is to become of the *Hornet's Nest*. I know that some of ye have taken it upon yourselves that ye shall be giving up the seafaring life for other opportunities and to that I say, fare thee well. However, Mister Turner and a couple others of the company have decided to turn our talents to becoming sailors of the merchant trade. If'n any of ye wish to continue to sail together, ye are more than welcome. Like always we shall be sailing under the pirate's code and all who sail shall have an equal share. What say ye?" Twigg announced.

Thar be over thirty of the company who still had seawater running through their veins. But for me, I had wanderlust in me soul. I needed a new adventure. So, I said me goodbyes to me hearties, Mister Turner and Captain Black Dog Billy Twigg.

"Captain, it were an honor to sail with ye." Said I as I was making me way to the gangplank.

"Well, lad, ye shall always have a berth on the *Hornet's Nest* if'n ye ever want to go to sea again," Twigg said as he shook me hand. I threw me duffel bag over me shoulder and walked into the busy crowded docks of San Francisco harbor. The further I walked away from the docks I was greeted by many a whore, wanting me to go upstairs for a "ride." Thar were those who said they'd satisfy me right in the alley. Then thar were hustlers, shell men, con artists, and flimflammers belying good times and easy ways to make money.

THE GOLD RUSH

It felt like I were a fish out of water, which I guess I was. I hadn't decided what I were going to do yet with me life. As I were strolling down Market Street, I spied a bank down on Sansome Street. It were called Wells Fargo Bank, it looked to be a sturdy building built of all brick with metal bars on all of the windows and standing on the outside thar be two armed guards holding shotguns. When I went in thar be two more. I walked up to the bank teller and said I wanted to put me ten thousand dollars into their bank. Well, the place got so quiet ye could have heard a mouse walk across the floor.

The teller, looked pale and sweaty before stuttering, "One, one, one moment, sir." Then he ran off into this caged-looking area where he nervously whispered to a rather rotund fella and pointed at me.

They both returned, and the large man asked, "Good day, sir. I'm the bank's president, Mister Higgins, may I help you, sir?"

"Yes, as I was telling this man, I want to put me ten thousand dollars into ye bank. Is that going to be a problem?" I asked.

"No. No, of course not. Do you have the check?" Higgins said trying not to look excited. I was sure that he must have dealt with large sums of money, after all, thar is a gold rush going on.

"Check?" I answered as I reached into me duffel bag, pulled out a fistful of dollars, and piled them on the counter. Everyone in the bank gave a collective gasp, even Higgins.

"Why don't we conclude our business at my desk, Mister?"

"Ishmael," I replied

"Mister Ishmael," Higgins said with a grin from ear to ear.

"No. Just Ishmael." Says I.

"Fine. Ishmael. Please just follow me to my desk. Oh, and please bring the money."

I followed him into the caged area, to his desk. It were a large grand wooded desk made all of oak, He sat in an overstuffed leather chair, and on the wall behind him were a photograph of a rather disgusted-looking man.

"Is that your father?" I asked pointing to the picture.

Higgins turned around in his chair, looked at the photograph, smiled, and said, "Hardly. That's President Millard Fillmore."

"President of the bank?"

"No. President of the United States."

"Ah. Last I heard Polk were President."

"Have you been away, Ishmael?"

"I were a whaler. Ye don't keep up with such things out to sea."

"I must say, I had no idea that whaling could so profitable."

"I were out to sea for nearly four years. But I be through with such things."

"You're leaving whaling?" Higgins asked.

"Aye, I've given up the sea. I want to try me hand at something new."

"Well, I must say that's quite commendable. Any ideas?"

"I have given thought to prospecting."

"Prospecting. That is a hard life. Have you any experience?"

"Nay." Says I.

"I'll be honest with you, Ishmael. I have seen men who spent their entire lives saving and end up destitute, broken, become drunkards, lose their wives and when they can't see any way out they put a bullet in their head. Sure, there are those few who strike it rich. But for everyone that makes it big, there are hundreds that go bust.

Now, might I suggest that you consider investing your money in stocks and bonds rather than gambling it away on prospecting."

"Stocks and bonds? What be that?" I asked.

"Well, with a share of stock you own a fraction of a company. It entitles you to a portion of the company's assets and profits equal to how many shares of stock that you own. I would imagine it would compare to whalers. You receive a portion of the profits from the final sale of whale oil. Do you not?" Higgins asked.

"Indeed, sir."

"So, this is similar to that."

"But I have to work to get that money."

"With stocks, it's your money that does the work. A company needs money to expand, to grow. So, when you buy a share of stock they are using your money, and to thank you they reward you with a share of their profits quarterly. The more stock you purchase the bigger the reward." Higgins explained.

"That sounds good, but can I lose money, too?"

"Well, Ishmael it would be like if you went out whaling and didn't get any whales, you wouldn't get a share since they lost money, right?"

"Right."

"Now there are hundreds of stocks to choose from, Some are riskier than others and there are plenty of stocks that are very safe and secure. Of course, the risker ones have the greater potential of making more returns for your money and the greater risk of losing it, too."

"How do I know which is which?"

"I have a friend who could help advise you for a small fee. If you're interested."

"Couldn't hurt to talk to him."

"Great. Now you just sit tight, and I'll have someone go and fetch Mister Charles Sutton."

Charles Sutton was a short portly fellow with a face full of whiskers. He seemed a jolly sort with a large toothy grin. When he shook my hand it was like grabbing a large beefy piece of raw meat.

"Howdy, I'm Charles Sutton. I understand that you're interested in investing in the stock market."

"Maybe. I want to know more before I hand over me money."

"Why sure, young fella. What do ya what to know?"

"So, I give you my money and you invest it into different companies. And I then am a part-owner in those companies, is that right?"

"That is correct."

"And who chooses what companies you put my money into?"

"Well, most people let me decide. They tell me what sort of risk their willing to take and I then invest in the kind of companies that represent that type of risk. Now, some companies are riskier than others. For example, railroads are a pretty stable investment because they're well established, whereas newer companies without a history might have a higher risk. Understand?"

"I think so."

"So, Ishmael, are you a risk-taker? Or do you play it safe?"

"Just one question," I asked.

"What's that?" Sutton inquired with a slight smirk on his chubby face.

"Are you a risk-taker?"

"What do you mean?"

"I mean if'n you think you can take advantage of me and steal my money then you'd be a risk-taker."

"I can assure you that I am an honest man. I do not steal from my clients. I make money when you make money."

"I can attest to Mister Sutton's honesty and integrity," Higgins said.

I looked at them both, then reached inside my coat pocket and handed Sutton four thousand greenbacks.

"Here ya are. Just so you know, I am a risk-taker."

Sutton took the money and proceeded to write me a receipt. As he handed the slip of paper to me he said, "Rest assured that I will treat your money as if it were my own."

"Good to hear, cause if'n you don't, I will kill ya." Said I, as I walked out of the bank. Outside, I asked one of the bank guards where 62 Sacramento Street be.

He thought for a moment and then answered, "Ya,

just go down Sansome Street for five blocks and turn left. I think number sixty-two is just a couple blocks down on your right."

"Thank ye."

Well, that bank guard were spot on. Number sixty-two was right where he said it would be. I walked into the dry goods store, and they had everything that I would need to go off prospecting. The store was packed with men from all over with the same idea that I had. I stood there in the middle of the chaos just staring. It tweren't long when a portly man with chin whiskers approached me and said, "Welcome to Levi Strauss, how may I be of service?"

"Well, sir, I'll be going off prospecting and I will need some supplies. Can you help me?"

"Certainly, my good man. What is it you desire?"

"I have here a list," I said as I handed it to him.

He perused it for a few moments, "Mmmm Hmmm. Right this way, sir."

He called over a young assistant, "Jacob, this gentlemen requires prospector's tools. A pole pick, a drifting pick, a long handle shovel, a couple of drills, a heavy hammer, some blasting powder, dynamite, a pan, horn spoon, an iron spoon, and some fuses."

"Yes, sir." The young man said as he ran off to gather me goods.

"Will, ya be needing some clothing as well?" The old gent asked.

"That I will and some foodstuffs as well."

"Very good, I will set you up with some hardtack, coffee, beans, and assorted other rations."

"Much obliged."

I went and bought a couple of pairs of pants, two

shirts, a pair of work boots, a belt, a canvas jacket, and a large felt hat.

"Can ye hold me goods until I get me a horse and mule?" I asked.

"That will not be a problem. I can recommend an excellent, livery stable and reputable gunsmith as well if you haven't acquired those items as of yet. Tell 'em Levi sent ya over."

"That be mighty neighborly of ye matey." Says I.

'Where will you be staying while you're here in San Francisco if I might ask? If you haven't made arrangements yet, might I suggest the Hotel Charlotte? In the meantime, we will hold your purchases here at the store."

"Much obliged."

"Now, here is your bill, sir. That will be one hundred and thirty-seven dollars for the tools and clothing."

I thought that it might be costly but being in the midst of a gold rush and all, it seemed kinda reasonable. I paid the nice man his due, then ventured over to the livery stable to purchase a horse and pack mule.

I entered the stable and was met by a man who tweren't nice like the fella over at the dry goods store. He had his hair all slicked back, parted in the middle, sported a pencil-thin mustache. Reminded me of a weasel and was fidgety like one, too.

"What can I do you fer, friend." He said.

"The man over at the dry good store recommended you. I'd like to buy a horse and pack mule."

"Who?" He asks.

"Levi, at the dry good store."

"Ah, Levi. He's good people." He answers by being more friendly now that I mentioned Mister Strauss.

"I only have a couple left. Come on over here and take a look at the stock. I have two Quarter horses, two Mustangs, and an Appaloosa. How good a horseman are ya?"

"Fair. My pa had a farm back east and I use to do some riding. But it were mostly used for farm work." I explained.

"Mmmm Hmmm. Well, friend. I recommend the Appaloosa. She's easy-going, has a good, kind heart, a willingness to work hard, and is forgiving of your riding errors."

"How much?"

"Do ya have a saddle and pack for the mule?" He asked.

"Nay."

He looks me over, smiles, and says, "For a friend of Levi, I'll let you have everything for three hundred and fifty."

I examine the Appaloosa, mule, saddle, and pack. "Deal," I said as I pay the man three-fifty.

"What's her name?" I ask.

"*Chapawee*. It's Sioux. It means spirited. And the mule ain't got a proper name. But knowing mules you'll be calling it plenty of different names." He said laughing.

"Okay, If'n I pick them up tomorrow?"

"Sure thing. Come on into my office and I'll get you your bill of sale."

"How much for the Colt .45?" I inquired.

"The Peacemaker is twenty dollars. Box of cartridges is fifty cents each."

"I'll take the Colt and six boxes of cartridges. How much for the seven-shot Sharps Repeating Rifle?"

"Seventy-five for the Sharps."

"I'll take one of those and six boxes of those cartridges as well. And I'll need a holster, rifle scabbard, and saddlebags."

"That'll be one hundred and four dollars for the weapons and six for the holster, scabbard, and saddlebags for a total of one twenty."

I paid the man as I was trying on holsters. I settled on a right-hand smooth leather made of saddle-grade leather. It came with a leather hammer loop and leg tie to keep the gun secure.

I strapped on the gun belt, shoved the Sharps rifle into the scabbard, stuffed the twelve boxes of cartridges into the saddlebags, tossed it over me shoulder, and made me way to the Hotel Charlotte.

"And a good day to you, sir. May I help you?" The man behind the reservation desk asked.

"I'd like a room," I answered.

"Yes, sir. Our rooms start at two dollars and fifty cents a night."

"Two fifty, I only want to stay in the room, not buy it."

"Some go for as much as seven dollars a night."

"I'll take the room for two-fifty."

"Very good, sir. And for how many nights?"

"Just the one."

"All right, that will be two dollars and fifty cents. And I'll need you to sign the register." The man said as he held out an ink pen.

I took the pen from the man and sign me name. Then gave him a five-dollar gold coin.

"Excellent. Here's your key to room 624. Would you like some help with your luggage?"

"No thank ya. I be good."

"Well, the elevators are down the hall on your left."

"The what?"

"Elevator."

"And what is an elevator?"

The counterman had seen this many times before and so not as to try and explain the concept, he called the bellboy over.

"William, would you please escort this gentleman and show him the elevator."

"Yes, sir, Mister Collins. Sir, would you please follow me." The young fella was all decked out in a right spiffy uniform.

The lad led me to this tiny room where an old man wearing the same style uniform as William wore was standing inside by some contraption with a handle on it.

I waited on the outside looking at the young man urging me to enter the small room where the old man stood.

"Is this my room?" I asked.

"No, sir. This is an elevator. It will take you up to the sixth floor where your room is. There is nothing to be worried about, is there John?"

"No, sir. I think you'll find it quite enjoyable." John said smiling.

I slowly eased into the tiny chamber. Once I was in, John pulled a gate closed, grabbed hold of the handle, pulled towards him, and said, "Here we go."

There was a jolt beneath me feet that took me by surprise.

"Not to fear," John said with a grin.

As I peered out through the gate I saw the tiny room rising, past several floors of the hotel, until we reached the sixth floor.

"Here we are," John said as he slid open the gate.

"Well, shiver me timbers," I said.

"Beats climbing six flights of stairs, now doesn't it, young fella?" The old man replies.

"Aye, that it does."

"Now, when you're ready to come down, just press the button next to the gate."

"Thanks, fer the ride," I said as I went off looking for room 624.

On my first night in San Francisco, I thought I'd go and treat me self to an expensive meal. I asked the man at the front desk where I should go. He recommended that I eat at the Cliff House.

When he did, he mentioned that they might have a problem with my clothing. He said that they are a high-class restaurant and that people dress up real fancy to eat there. He weren't fooling. As I walked passed the window I saw that the men were all duded up, wearing fancy clothes with jackets, vests, and ties. And the women were all decked out in their finest dresses made of silks and satins.

I walked into the restaurant and was met by a big fella dressed in a black suit. He held up his hand to signal me to stop.

"Is there a problem, matey?" I asked.

"You can't come in here dressed like that. You need a jacket and tie."

"But I don't own a jacket and tie," I explained.

"Beat it!" He said as he poked me hard in me chest with his beefy finger.

I calmly said, "You do that again, matey and you're going to lose that finger."

"Beat it, matey! Before I throw ya out on the street." He said poking me even harder.

I grabbed his finger and twisted it back until there was a loud crack from his finger breaking, bringing the large man down to his knees in tears.

"You bastard. You broke my finger!" He screamed.

A couple of other men came rushing out of the restaurant.

"What going on here?"

"This bastard broke my finger!" The man moaned.

"What is the meaning of this?" The older of the two men asked.

"This man laid hands on me. Nobody lays hands on me." I exclaimed.

"I'm sorry, sir, but you cannot come into the restaurant without a coat and tie. That's the policy."

Looking down at the big man holding his hand in pain I said, "Give me your coat and tie, matey."

He sprung up from the ground and shouted, "You can go to Hell!" He started to poke me in the chest with his other hand but thought better of it.

I reached into me pocket and pulled out a ten-dollar

gold piece and tossed it to him.

"Your coat and tie."

Embarrassed, he sheepishly took off his jacket and tie and handed them to me. The man was quite a bit bigger than me, the jacket was big enough for another person to fit inside with me. I tied the tie around me neck and said to the older man, "Table for one."

The man looked me up and down, shook his head, shrugged, and said, "If you'll follow me."

I followed him through the entire restaurant past all the people having dinner. I heard some people snickering, while others were laughing. I was eventually seated at a small table in the back of the restaurant next to the kitchen.

That night I had the best T-bone steak dinner that money could buy. It cost me almost eighty cents, but it was worth every penny.

The next morning, I went back to the livery stable to pick up my horse and pack mule before heading over to the Levi Strauss dry good store to pick up what I had bought the day before. Mister Strauss greeted me as I entered his establishment.

"Ah, good day to you, sir." He said with a smile.

"Good morning, Mister Strauss."

He looked past me out into the street and spotted the Appaloosa and mule.

"Fine-looking horse and mule. I hope my friend did well by you."

"Aye, he did."

"Good. Good. Well, I suppose you're here for your goods. I'll just have Jacob bring everything out to you, so you can be on your way."

"Thank ye," I said.

Shortly, the lad Jacob began to bring out all of my supplies and gear. It took me near on an hour to pack and stow everything onto the mule, which I named Daisy. Once loaded, I said goodbye and thanks to Mister Strauss and began to make me way south. Mister Strauss was kind enough to give me a map of California to get me started. I will be glad to leave the city. San Francisco is too crammed fer me.

I traveled on the westernmost trail along the Pacific Ocean out of the city to avoid having to traverse San Bruno Mountain. I figured I'd be climbing plenty of mountains be for too long. Rode on the outskirts of San Mateo and began making me way eastward. As it were getting dark, I could see lots of lights off in the distance of a large city, San Jose. I didn't stop, no need to, the only reason to stop in a town is to spend money. I'm looking on making money and besides, as a man once said, "Thar's gold in them thar hills."

That first night I pitched camp at the foot of the Diablo Mountains at the edge of Coyote Lake. I had no tent, so after hobbling *Chapawee* and Daisy so as not to wander off. I just threw my bedroll on the ground, built a small campfire, ate a tin of beans with some hardtack, and used the saddle to rest my head, I just laid there staring up at the stars. I was fast asleep in minutes.

When I woke up thar be a thick fog surrounding me, so dense that I couldn't make out where *Chapawee* or Daisy be In fact, I couldn't even see my hand in front of my face. I thought it best that instead of me wandering all around and either getting lost or hurt, I'd just sit tight, make a pot of coffee and wait. It were several hours before the fog began to lift. I hadn't seen fog this bad since I were whaling off of New Bedford.

Finally, I was able to continue. Once I left the surrounding populated areas of the town of San Jose, I saw nary a soul for nearly eight days. Although I did pass an occasional sodbuster family every ten or twelve miles. As I approach, they scurry like frightened kittens back to their cabins to fetch their weapons. They all seemed to be fearful of strangers, scared of their own shadows, and who could blame them. Many have suffered attacks from bands of marauders, bandits, and Indian raiding parties. Stuck out in the middle of nowhere with no sheriff or constable for hundreds of miles for protection and most that I have seen have women folk and six or eight children trying to eke out a living dirt farming. I slowly clip-clop on by, wave, and always give a tip of my hat, so as to let them know I will be of no threat.

According to the map Mister Strauss gave me, I reckon I was just on the outskirts of *Los Banos,* located down in the San Joaquin Valley. It were there I decided to turn my travels north to where all of the major goldfields were located. As I traveled north I did come across the aftermath of what looked to be a US Army raid on a small Indian village. It were a terrible sight.

All the horses had been shot and there be only women, children, and old men lying dead. Many were hacked to pieces from the calvary's swords. Thar be women still holding their babies in their arms, both shot. In all me days of pirating, I had never seen such carnage, especially against the unarmed. Many of the women had been mutilated, their breasts had been cut off and they had been scalped.

Just outside of the camp, a scraggly half-starved camp dog began to follow me. He was so skinny and pitiful, I took out my pistol and cocked the hammer back and was about to put him out of his misery when he looked up at me with those big soulful brown eyes and gave a soft whimper. I reached back into the saddlebag that held some beef jerky and tossed him a piece. He gobbled it up and began to wag his tail, so I tossed him another, and another, and another. I soon realized that I had me a dog. I decided to call him Queequeg after the friend who saved my life all those many years ago.

Leaving the Indian camp behind, a feeling of disgust and hatred washed over me. I were in a foul mood for weeks and could not bear to be around people. I avoided all towns and those I spied as I traveled northward.

Weeks later I stumbled upon a small pristine valley with a narrow stream meandering through the middle that eventually flowed into Lake Tulloch many miles downstream. It appeared to me to be untouched.

I pitched camp just inside the tree line atop the ridge so as not to be easily spotted. The site gave me a bird's eye view of the whole valley. Once settled, I heated up and ate a can of beans, fed *Chapawee* and Daisy, shared some hardtack with Queequeg, and as the sun was setting, took a stroll down into the valley just to get familiar with my surroundings. I figured I'd get started prospecting in the morning after a good night's sleep.

While on my three-month journey to this valley, I would spend hours on end reading articles about prospecting and mining fer gold. Thar was this Scottish fella, John David Borthwick, who wrote about his three years of prospecting and this here New York newspaper writer who spent six months working in the gold mines just to name a few. I found them to be very informative as well as entertaining. Neither one of them fellas claimed to strike it rich, but they did come out ahead unlike so many hundreds of others who went belly up. I guess now, it's my time to see how I fair.

On the first day, I took my pan and walked down to the stream followed closely by Queequeg and while I waded into the stream up to my knees, Queequeg laid down on the bank and fell fast asleep. I stuck the pan in the sandy bottom and shook it vigorously several times. Back and forth and side to side. Then I gently began to swirl the pan in a circular motion, picking out the large rocks and pebbles. I did this for several hours when I spied a small golden fleck hidden amongst the wet sand. It sat there twinkling like a far-off star out on the ocean.

I picked it out of the pan and placed it in a leather

pull string pouch and I started again working that little stream until the sun began to set. By the day's end, I had a good size pinch of gold in that pouch of mine and a very sore back from bending over all day. Queequeg and I hiked back up to camp and where I built a small fire. To celebrate my good fortune, I made a pan of biscuits and opened a can of corn cause I was getting tired of eating them beans. After I filled up on them beans, sleep snuck up on me fast, I didn't hear anything until Queequeg started sniffing around looking for something to eat the next morning. I slowly rose, feeling all stiff and a bit achy, fix a pot of coffee, ate some hardtack, took *Chapawee* and Daisy for a short walk around the pasture followed closely by an overly enthusiastic Queequeg, who ran circles around us barking and leaping as we made our way back to the campsite.

I grabbed my pan, pickaxe, and shovel and walked down to the stream to try my hand at panning for gold. I spent the entire morning panning finding the odd flecks of gold until I worked my way to the mouth of the stream several hundred yards from where I started. It was there I began to find small nuggets. Around noon, my pouch was a quarter full. I decided to try testing the area off to the hilly side of the stream. I began to dig down into the earth randomly until I found a small nugget a couple of feet down. I then took some string and made a grid of the area so I could map out where I was finding gold. There was a pattern, it was almost as if the gold had been formed into an underground constellation. There must've been over twenty holes dug on that hill, most of 'em dug by me, but there were some dug by Queequeg.

The farther I moved away from the stream and up the hill the larger the gold nuggets were becoming. I was digging in a hole about four feet down into the ground when I spied a rock about the size of a small chicken, it appeared to have specks of gold. I peered all around to make sure I was alone. I kept digging, that's when I saw a large gold vein running horizontally all along the wall of the hole. Queequeg was running about sniffing all around the crater, the sun was such that his shadow kept darting down into the hole where I was carefully digging out the rock. I don't remember exactly when I noticed that Queequeg's shadow turned into the shape of a man. I froze. What was I to do? I could pretend not to notice and hope it would buy me some time, or I could pull my gun and try and get off a shot. I did neither, the last thing I remember before blacking out was hearing the cocking of the man's pistol, then…

KAPOW

The shot hit me on the left side of me back. It felt like someone walloped me with a sledgehammer, knocking the wind out of me and sending a black cloud floating over me. I laid there for a long time, I thought I was dead.

The villain that shot me jumped down into the hole and began to kick me in my side, wanting to know if'n I was dead. Then he rolled me over onto my side, which was the wrong thing to do. As he rolled me over, I felt my hand slide over the gun holster, and with my eyes still closed I drew my Colt and fired off six shots in the direction I thought he be.

The sound of my gun blasting away inside of the hole was deafening. I waited for the scoundrel to return fire and finish me off. But there was nothing, just silence. When I finally opened my eyes I saw that he lay dead. Of the six shots fired five missed him completely and my first shot hit its target and blew a large portion of his head clean off.

I laid there for a long time thinking I was going to die. After a while, I sat up and saw that the bullet had just passed clean through my side and didn't hit any major organs. I slowly made my way out of what I thought was my grave, carefully looking to see if there be any other vandals lurking about. As there were none that I could see, I crawled down the hill and fell into the stream, where I lay for some time. The cool water washed over me as I faded in and out of consciousness until nightfall. I then slowly worked my way back to camp. That's when I saw what that rascal had done to poor old Queequeg.

He had struck him on the head with his pistol, giving him a large gash on the side of his head. He whimpered sorely when he saw me. I knelt beside him and tried to ease his pain, he seemed to take comfort in that. I then searched through my gear to find anything medicinal. The best I could tell is that the bullet didn't hit any organs, just busted up a couple of ribs. I bound myself up real tight and then tended to Queequeg.

"Queequeg, old friend, we are a right poorly sight to behold," I said as he cocked his head while I spoke, seeming to understand me.

That night neither one of us got much sleep. I had me a fitful sleep as I was half excepting some other varmints to come charging into camp guns a-blazing. But there was no one outside of my imagination.

The next morning, I could barely move, so I spent most of the day just propped up against my saddle holding my Winchester while I drifted in and out of sleep with Queequeg lying by my side. The fella that tried to kill me, his horse wandered into camp and settled in right next to Daisy and *Chapawee*. Late in the afternoon, I was feeling well enough to wander over to where the man I kilt lay dead. Thar were dozens of buzzards swarming overhead preparing to descend and make a meal of the poor sot. I eased my way down into the hole where he lay. His head was all bloated and covered with flies and maggots. It were a terrible sight, I covered his face with dirt, to keep the flies away. I went through his pockets, took his gun and holster, finished digging out the rock of gold, and placed his saddle next to the body. Afterward, I left no marker to indicate that this was a gravesite, soon the valley would reclaim it all back to what it was before I ever came. I did leave a small hand pick lying ten paces north of the burrow, so I would find it when I returned.

I found it ironic that the blackguard that started out trying to steal my gold, ended up with only a small piece of lead.

I spent the next three weeks being on the mend, I

didn't spend any time prospecting. I did break down the rock of gold into smaller, more manageable size nuggets that I put in my saddlebags. I guessed that the amount of gold that I had in my bags might be worth close to three thousand dollars.

I decided that unless I wanted to make myself out to be a target, I would rid myself of all my prospecting gear. I placed it all into the grave of my assailant that I had yet to fill, which I did, and I left the head of a pickaxe to mark the spot. Not as a grave marker but as the location of what I hope would soon be a mine.

I let his horse go free, as I had no need nor desire to have to take care of another animal, *Chapawee*, Daisy, and Queequeg were quite enough. The three of us worked our way west over towards Stockton so I could lay my claim to my goldfield. We passed many a dirt farm through the Central Valley. Coming down from the hills it started flat and arid until we got closer to Stockton. The farms had irrigation from the San Joaquin River so the closer we got to the city, the greener the farms.

It took us two days to arrive in Stockton. I must say I was surprised at the advanced development of this western city. The city sat on the banks of the San Joaquin River, which had a thriving shipping commerce that provided services to all of the Central Valley. The Western Pacific Railroad had a station in Stockton as did Western Union Telegraph. It were quite the metropolis.

I entered the town on Centre Street and made my way to the city center at the corner of El Dorado and Weber Streets. I stopped in front of Jones & Hewlett Groceries, Provisions & Hardware, Purveyors of

Agricultural and Mining tools. I noticed a small Wells Fargo Bank sign tacked up on the outside of the store's entrance.

I tied off *Chapawee* and Daisy to the hitching post out front, grabbed my saddlebags, and me and Queequeg sauntered in. The interior was enormous, that had to be hundreds of items, everything from tools to women's finery.

I just stood gawking when a voice from behind me said, "Good afternoon. How might I be of assistance to you?"

I turned around and saw a short nondescript doughy middle-aged man wearing spectacles, a green eyeshade, and sleeve garters standing behind me.

"I have gold," I replied.

"Very good, sir. If you would be so kind as to follow me."

Me and Queequeg followed the man towards the back of the store, into an area that had two bank tellers and two armed guards standing on the outside. Inside the teller's cage, there was a door to a private office. Inside the office, on one side of the room stood an enormous safe, in the middle was a wooden desk, and off to the other side was a wooden counter with a large weighing scale with weights.

The man closed the door to the office, moved behind the counter, and smiled, "I'm Mister Darcey, branch manager of Wells Fargo Bank here in Stockton and you are?"

"Ishmael," I said.

"Well, Ishmael, won't you please have a seat."

"Thank ya," I replied as I sat down on a rather uncomfortable wooden chair.

Darcey sat across the counter from me behind the scales.

"The going rate for gold today is twenty dollars and eighty cents an ounce. Now, how much gold would you like to barter?"

I lifted my saddlebags and placed them onto the counter, untied the strap, and emptied the gold nuggets along with the small bag of gold flecks and dust that I had collected. The cluster of golden stones came tumbling out onto the counter, almost covering the entire surface and engulfing the weighing scale.

Mister Darcey's eyes got as large as saucers. He smiled and said, "My, my, my, looks like you've hit the motherload. I would suggest that you stake your claim over at the land office after we conclude our transaction before someone else does and jumps your claim."

"Aye, and where might I find the land office."

"Just three streets west of us on the corner of Lindsay and Hunter Streets."

"I were thinking of not filing a claim, just moving on."

"Oh, and why would that be? You could be a very rich man."

"Aye, or a dead man. I was bushwhacked and shot in the back while prospecting this."

"That's terrible. It is unfortunate that there are so many ruffians, rouges, and ne'er-do-wells about. Why just last week some scoundrel tried to come in here and rob this bank. His name was Bart Mackey, a real desperado. Suppose to have killed five men."

"What happened?" I asked.

"He was shot dead. They have him displayed outside of the Buckhorn Saloon over on Channel Street."

"That's awful."

"Yes, well, let's see what we have here," Darcey said as he began to weigh the gold nuggets.

Darcey's sausage-like fingers were quite nibble in adding up the weight of the nuggets and calculating the dollar value on this adding contraption machine. He would punch the buttons on the gadget, then pull down on a lever attached to its side that would print the total onto a roll of paper.

"Ishmael, I can offer you two thousand nine hundred dollars and eighty-seven cents for your gold."

"That sounds reasonable," I said.

"I can offer you cash or if you'd like you can open an account and deposit the money with us here at Wells Fargo Bank."

"Well, Mister Darcey, I already have a Wells Fargo account that I opened in San Francisco."

"Oh, you do?"

"Yes, sir. I think I'd like to deposit two thousand five hundred dollars into my account."

"Very good, sir. So, I shall give you four hundred dollars and eighty-seven cents in cash. Do you happen to know what your balance is on your account?"

"I'm sorry to say I do not?"

"Not a problem, sir. I'll just telegraph the San Francisco office and once I hear back we can conclude our business. Let me get you your four hundred dollars and eighty-seven cents." He said grinning.

IIe shouted out for a Mister Cobb, and one of the tellers came scurrying in.

"Yes, Mister Darcey?"

"Mister Cobb, please bring me four hundred dollars and eighty-seven cents if you would be so kind. Thank you."

"Yes, sir, right away." He said as he scampered away.

"Now, it will take a couple of hours to hear back from San Francisco. So, if you wouldn't mind, maybe you'd like to go and get something to eat, and then come back." Darcey announced.

"That'll be fine. I'll be back as soon as I find a place to stay and bed my horse and mule."

"I can recommend several nice hotels or if you prefer the names of some reputable boarding houses."

"I think I'd prefer a boarding house. They tend to be more homey."

"I think you might like the Driscoll House, run by the widow Driscoll. It's out west from the center of town on Elk Street. There's a livery stable not far and she allows well-behaved dogs. Just mention my name and she'll give you a special rate."

"Sounds perfect. We'll go and get settled and be back this afternoon. Much obliged, Mister Darcey. Thank ye."

Mister Cobb, the teller entered the office with my four hundred dollars and eighty-seven cents. I rose from the wooden chair and shook Mister Darcey's hand, collected my four hundred dollars and eighty-seven cents from Mister Cobb, and me and Queequeg headed for the street.

My first stop was to the land office to stake my claim. I had the map that I was given by the nice man, Levi Strauss back in San Francisco. I was able to make the exact location of the small valley where I found the gold.

"You're in luck, partner. There isn't any claim on

the piece of land. To lay a claim, I need to know how much land in that area you'll want to purchase." "I'll take a hundred acres."

We looked at the government's surveyors map and the claim's officer drew up a map and office deed for the hundred acres that I wanted. The total cost was three hundred dollars for the land and another fifty for the paperwork.

I was now the proud owner of what was to be known as The Devil Fish Mine.

"Good afternoon. Would you be the widow Driscoll?" I asked.

"That I would." The woman answered.

Sarah Driscoll was a woman in her late thirties who appeared to be several years older. It was a hard life, that of a pioneer woman, washing clothes by hand, cooking three meals a day, ironing, and cleaning a boarding house. Yet, she somehow managed to present herself with an air of beauty, grace, and femineity. Her hair was an auburn color; she had alabaster skin with emerald green eyes.

Her husband, the late Randolph Driscoll was gunned down as an innocent bystander during an attempted bank robbery six years ago. Randolph Driscoll was the owner of the Stockton Shipping & Freight company, one of the largest shipping companies in Stockton. Upon his death, he left the company and all of his worldly possessions to his wife Sarah.

Sarah Driscoll was a wealthy woman having sold her husband's shipping company for several thousand dollars, which was enough to pay off the mortgage of the house and all of her husband's debts. She could have lived comfortably without having to do another's days' work, but Sarah came from sterner stock. She couldn't foresee herself just lounging around doing nothing all day. No, she enjoyed meeting new people and keeping busy. So, she decided to open her home to strangers two years ago and hasn't regretted it a single day. She wore a woven flowered gingham day dress with a wide white collar of lace. Her hair, parted in the middle, was worn in a neat bun low on the neck. Over her left breast, she had a peach and white oval-shaped cameo cabochon with an engraved vintage-inspired lady gazing off in a distance.

"Mister Darcey over at the Wells Fargo Bank suggested that I talk to you about a room. My name is Ishmael."

"Well, I do have a room available. How long are you looking to stay in Stockton, Ishmael?"

"I'm not sure, but I'd say at least a week."

"I charge thirty dollars a week and that includes breakfast and dinner."

"I understand that you allow dogs. This here is Queequeg. He's a good boy and won't be no bother."

"For dogs, I charge a dollar a day and that includes leftovers and scrapes."

"That sounds fair, ma'am," I said.

"Excellent. Let me show you and Queequeg to your room."

The room was up on the second floor It was a corner room overlooking the backyard with a small orchard of pecan trees. There was a full-size brass bed covered with a patchwork quilt, a tall wooden chest of drawers, a washbowl, towels, and a pitcher of fresh water, along with a chamber pot. On the floor was a large area rag rug that Queequeg immediately plopped down and fell asleep on.

"This is perfect," I said as I gave her forty dollars.

"I'll go get your change."

"No need. I'm sure ole Queequeg will eat more than a dollar's worth a day. Right boy?"

Queequeg lay there sound asleep on the rag rug.

Sarah Driscoll looked down at the sleeping mutt and smiled, "Well, if you insist."

"I do. Now I'll just go down and get me gear."

Mrs. Driscoll and I went downstairs leaving Queequeg upstairs deep in slumber. As I was heading out the door, Mrs. Driscoll said, "Dinner will be served a six this evening."

"How many guests do you have?" I asked.

"Five, including you."

"I shall see you at six. Thank you again, Mrs. Driscoll."

"Good afternoon, Ishmael."

"Good day, Ishmael." Mister Darcey said very jovially shaking my hand enthusiastically like we had been long-lost friends. It seems that as long as one has money one is always welcome.

"It's good to see you again. I just received a telegram from the Wells Fargo Bank in San Francisco. They confirmed that you do indeed have an account with Wells Fargo and, I must say with a sizeable deposit. Now, with what you're depositing today your balance will be six thousand five hundred dollars." Darcey chirped proudly as if it were his money.

"Very good," I said nonchalantly. I was about to leave when I turned and said, "Oh, thank you for recommending the widow Driscoll's boarding house. She seems to be a very lovely lady."

"Yes. Yes, she is that. So, Ishmael what are your plans?" He asked.

"Well, I thought I'd gather some more supplies and see about hiring a couple of reliable hands to help me work the mine."

"So, you've been to the land office and placed a claim?"

"Aye, I laid a claim and purchased one hundred acres surrounding the mine. Do you happen to know where I might go to find experienced men, Mister Darcey?" I asked.

"Indeed, I do. In fact, my brother-in-law and a friend of his have much experience. If you'd like I could arrange that they come here to meet with you and discuss the possibility of employment tomorrow?" Darcey proposed.

"That would be most kind of you, Mister Darcey."

"Not at all. Shall we say tomorrow at 10 am?"

"Very good. Until tomorrow at 10 am." I said.

I rode back to the widow Driscoll's boarding house, where I found Queequeg sleeping on the front porch. He began to bark excitedly when he saw me and

Chapawee approaching. I dismounted and tied *Chapawee* off at the hitching post out front of the boarding house. Queequeg gave me such an exuberant greeting, it was almost like I'd been gone for days.

I went upstairs to wash up for dinner. I changed my shirt, combed my hair best I could, and took off my side holster and arm. When I came downstairs into the dining room, I found three men and a woman sitting at the dining room table. Two of the men appeared to me to be salesmen types by the way they were dressed. Both in their mid to late forties, duded up in suits with ties. The third man looked to be coupled with the woman. I surmised that they were husband and wife by the way they bickered at each other consistently.

Mrs. Driscoll entered the room from the kitchen carrying several bowls of food and a platter of fried chicken. As soon as she placed them down on the table people started grabbing at the food, I waited until the feeding frenzy had stopped before I attempted to reach for any of the dishes. Mrs. Driscoll looked at me with an embarrassing smile and said, "There's plenty more where that came from."

After a while, when things claimed down and everyone had seemed to be satisfied, Mrs. Driscoll said, "Everyone, this is our new guest Ishmael. He will be staying with us for a week."

I smiled and gave a quick nod in the direction of everyone and said, "How do."

"Ishmael, this is Mister Bracken, he's an anvil, forging, and wrought iron salesman. This gentleman is Doctor Schmidlap, he is a medicinal and herbal treatment salesman."

"You mean snake oil?" I queried.

"I sell a line of Clark Stanley's Snake Oil Liniments, but I also sell a variety of elixirs, such as Dalby's Carminative, Hadacol, Beecham's Pills, and Daffy's Elixir, my good man. All efficacies' products." The Doctor announced.

"What's in 'em?" I asked.

"Oh, all the finest ingredients. In the medicines, there are such compounds as cocaine, alcohol, and opium-based elixirs. In Clark Stanley's Snake Oil Liniments there are rattlesnake livers, mineral oil, tallow, chili peppers, and camphor."

"What's snake oil good for?"

"Clark Stanley's Snake Oil Liniments is good for a number of ailments, such as rheumatism, sciatica, lame back, toothaches, sprains, frostbite, bruises, sore throat, and bites of animals, insects, and reptiles. And it gives immediate relief or your money back." Schmidlap bragged.

"Hmmm," I smirked.

"How many bottles would you like?" He asked.

"How much?"

"Normally, it sells for one dollar, but for you two bits."

"Why not, I'll give it a go," I said as I fished out a quarter from my pants pocket.

"What's ailing you, Ishmael?" Doctor Schmidlap inquired.

"A recent bullet wound in me back. Don't sleep so good. It pains me at night." I said sheepishly.

"Well, my friend this will do the trick. Rub some of this on before you go to bed, and you'll sleep like a baby." Schmidlap said as we exchanged a bottle for a coin.

"Thank ye," I said.

After our sales transaction, Mrs. Driscoll continued with the introductions.

"Ishmael, these are the Kohls, Jeremy, and Sarah. Mister Kohl is a preacher with the First Baptist Church of Our Lady of the Waters."

"Preacher, ma'am," I said.

I was taken back by the fact that Preacher Kohl didn't bother saying grace before jumping in with both feet at dinner, but as this fella, Oscar Wilde said, "Religion is like a blind man looking in a black room for a black cat that isn't there and finding it."

Once dinner was over and the other guests had left I offered to give Mrs. Driscoll a hand cleaning up, but she refused.

"Would you care for a cup of coffee?" She asked.

"Aye, that would be most pleasant."

She cleared off the table, taking the dirty dishes into the kitchen, and brought out two cups of coffee on a tray.

"Here you are, Ishmael." She said as she offered me the cup.

"Thank ye, ma'am. Much obliged." I answered.

"So, Ishmael, where are you from? California?" She asked.

"Oh, no ma'am. I'm from back east, Massachusetts."

"My, you're a long way from home. What brings

you all the way out here?"

"I were a whaler for years, ma'am. But I had me fill, so I thought I'd try my hand at gold mining."

"You said that you had been shot. Was that a result of your gold mining?"

"Yeah, some villain tried to jump my claim. Shot me in the back while I was digging out a rock of gold. Lucky for me he wasn't a good shot. I played possum, laid on the ground till he thought I were dead, then I shot and kilt him dead."

"Goodness me, what are you going to do, now? You're not going back out there?"

"Yes, ma'am. I'm heading back to develop the mine. I going to get a couple of fellas and go back and dig for gold."

"But it's so dangerous."

"Well, now there will be three of us. So, it shouldn't be too bad. In fact, Mister Darcey down at the bank says his brother-in-law and his friend might be willing to come to work for me."

A look of concern passed her face, then she said, "I shouldn't say anything, but Ishmael, Mister Darcey's brother-in-law Billy Malone is a known deadbeat. Nobody in town will hire him. He's a malingerer, an idler. He's always looking to make an easy buck. And his friend Bobby Lang is no better. I'd say you be careful, if'n you do take these two with you."

"Why thank ye, Mrs. Driscoll. I truly appreciate your honesty."

She smiled, looked at her empty cup, and asked, "Would you care for some more?"

"Oh, no ma'am. It's been a long day. I think I'll just go to bed now."

"Well, good night, Ishmael."

"Good night, ma'am. Come on Queequeg, let's go. We got a big day tomorrow."

The next morning it was pouring rain. It was coming down in buckets. I had a hard time getting Queequeg to go out back and do his business and even a harder time trying to dry him off before coming back into the house.

When I finally got to the dinner table everyone had already finished their breakfast and left the house.

"Good morning, Mrs. Driscoll."

"Good morning, Ishmael. How did you sleep?"

"Ahhh, I slept like a baby."

"I'm glad. Would you care for something to eat this morning?"

"Yes, ma'am."

"How about a couple of eggs, some bacon, fresh biscuits, and coffee."

"Sounds wonderful."

"It shouldn't be too long. Mind if I join you?" She asked.

"I would love some company."

Moments later Mrs. Driscoll brought out two plates of eggs, sunny side up, with six slices of bacon, and three warm biscuits. After placing them down, she went back into the kitchen and got two cups and a pot of steaming hot coffee.

We sat, ate, and talked about nothing in particular. It was nice. She was easy to talk to and it had been ages since I had a pleasant conversation with a lady where I wasn't paying for her company.

We or I should say, I lost track of time until the grandfather clock in the parlor rang out that it was nine o'clock. I had to be at the Wells Fargo Bank to meet Mister Darcey's brother-in-law and friend.

"Would you excuse me, Mrs. Driscoll, I have to get ready to meet with Mister Darcey."

"Sarah, please."

"All right, Sarah. I must get ready."

"You go on, Ishmael. Have a good day."

"I will, and you as well. We'll see you later. And I'll keep in mind what you confided in me last night. Come on, Queequeg."

We went upstairs to my room, I changed my shirt, combed my hair, and strapped on my Colt. Went downstairs, saddled *Chapawee*, and the three of us trotted over to see Mister Darcey and meet his brother-in-law, Billy Malone, and his friend Bobby Lang.

Billy Malone was leaning against Darcey's wooden desk looking like a vagrant when I walked in. He looked to be in his late twenties, he was unkempt, unshaven, hair disheveled, his clothes were dirty, and he smelled like horse manure. Queequeg walked up to the dawdler, sniffed, stepped back, and growled. Darcey, looking embarrassed, tried to put on a brave face.

"Ishmael, I'd like you to meet my brother-in-law,

Billy Malone. Billy is currently working as a stable hand at Waldo Meyer's livery stable."

"How long have you been working there?

"Bout a year.' He mumbled.

"Have you ever worked digging a mine?" I asked.

"No. But me and Bobby have dug lots of ditches."

"Hmm." I mused.

"Ah, listen, Billy, why don't you go out into the store while I talk to Ishmael," Darcey said.

"Look, Mister Darcey, I don't think Billy is what I'm looking for. I need someone with mining experience, not a ditch digger."

"I understand. Billy and Bobby, both will probably not amount to much more than shoveling shit at Waldo Meyer's livery stable."

"I'm sorry," I said apologetically.

"Ishmael. Would you be interested in having a partner"

"A partner?"

"Yeah, someone to share the expenses of developing the mine. And of course, sharing in the profits."

"Who?"

"Me." Darcey proclaimed.

"You! You want to partner with me on a mine?"

"How about I buy half interest in the mine. I'll put up ten thousand dollars as capital to get the mine started. Once the mine starts producing, I will get my money back first and then we split everything after that fifty-fifty."

"And what if the mine goes bust? I don't know, I may have gotten everything that there is to get. Then what?" I asked.

"Then I'm out ten thousand dollars."

"And you're willing to take that chance?"

"I am."

"Okay, if you're willing to take a chance."

"Excellent. I'll have my attorney draw up a contract this afternoon."

"Okay. But I want it to read simple. I don't want a lot of mumbo jumbo."

"Understood. Oh, and I would feel more comfortable if I had Billy on-site to watch out for my interest."

"All right, but his pay comes out of your share. I'm not paying for a ditch digger."

"Agreed."

"What time should I come back?"

Darcey looked at his gold pocket watch, then at the clock on the wall, and said, "I think five o'clock."

"See you at five, partner."

Me and Queequeg left the bank and walked several blocks until I saw a tasteful sign on the front of a brick building.

"J. R. Lazarus, Attorney at Law"

I walked into what looked to be an empty office. There was a wooden banister separating the room into two sections. A waiting area where there were several overstuffed chairs and an office section. In the middle of the office was a large wooden desk flanked by two plush leather chairs. Surrounding the desk on three walls were bookshelves stuffed with hundreds of law books. The chair that sat behind the desk was turned to face the back wall bookshelf. From the back of the chair came a deep feminine voice.

"May I help you?" The faceless voice queried.

"Yes. I'd like to meet with Mister J.R. Lazarus." I said.

The chair slowly turned around, revealing a middle-aged woman with short, cropped hair, wearing a men's three-piece suit, and smoking a stogie. With the cheroot clutched in her teeth and smiling, she announced, "I am J.R. Lazarus."

"I. I. I." I stammered.

"Yeah, yeah. I know, you were expecting a man. If'n you'd feel more comfortable with a male lawyer, I can give you the names of some. They're not as good as me. But if you can't handle dealing with a woman, I'll understand."

"No, I'm sure you'll do fine."

"Good. Now, what can I do for you?" She asked, wanting to waste no time.

"I want to have a will made up."

"That's easy enough. Here, fill out this form and I can have it ready for you by tomorrow. That'll be three dollars, in advance." She said as she handed me a piece of paper and a pencil.

I answered the questions, gave her back the sheet of paper, gave her the three dollars, and said "See ya tomorrow."

I then rode six blocks down Levee Street to the offices of the Stockton Journal. I tied *Chapawee* to the hitching post out front and I and Queequeg entered the building.

"Hey! Get that mutt outta here. I don't abide dogs."

Snarled a tall skinny fella wearing a striped shirt with sleeve guards and a green eyeshade.

I ignored his demand and said, "I want to place an ad."

"I told you to get that dog out of here."

"No," I said defiantly.

"I'm not going to tell you again."

"Or what!?"

"Or I'll throw the both of you out."

"You want to take this out into the street?" I challenged.

He jumped over the counter, opened the door, and barked, "Let's go!"

"After you."

Once he was out the door, I slammed the door shut and proceeded to lock it. He stood outside banging on the door demanding to be let in. I went back to the counter and spoke to an elderly gentleman, "I want to place an ad."

"Yes, sir." The old man said pleasantly.

He handed me a blank piece of paper and a pencil. I wrote a want ad for men who had mining experience.

The man looked at the ad, smiled, and said, "That'll be two bits. The ad will be in tomorrow's edition. Thank you."

"Thank you," I replied.

"Oh, and you'd better watch out for Otto. He's probably waiting to jump you when you leave."

"Thanks again," I said as I unlocked the door and stepped out onto the sidewalk.

Sure enough, Otto was hiding in the doorway next door. As he started to advance towards me, I gave Queequeg the command, "Guard!"

Queequeg began to snarl and growl, stopping Otto in his tracks. He looked to be frozen in time, not moving an inch.

"Do you want to continue, or are we done here?" I asked.

A squeaky voice uttered, "We're done."

"Good. Come on Queequeg let's go."

At five o'clock me and Queequeg made our way through the Jones & Hewlett Groceries, Provisions & Hardware store to the back where the Wells Fargo bank was located. The tellers and the guards were gone since the bank was closed. There was a light in Mister Darcey's office, so I knocked on the teller's door.

"Mister Darcey, It's me, Ishmael." I bellowed.

Moments later, the office door opened, and Darcey emerged smiling.

"Ishmael, good to see you, and right on time. Come in."

When I entered his office there was his brother-in-law, Billy still looking like smelling worse than I saw him eight hours ago, and a man dressed in a suit and tie. I presumed that it was his attorney.

"Ishmael, this is my attorney, Mister Eric Webster. Mister Webster is here to witness the signing of our partnership agreement contract."

"Nice to meet you, Mister Webster. I'm Ishmael."

Webster held out his hand and said, "It's my

pleasure, Ishmael."

"And you remember Billy," Darcey said as a segue to get to the contract. He handed me a copy of the contract that read very simply, *"I Ishmael do hereby sell one-half partnership of the Devil Fish Mine to Mister Eugene Darcey. Who will be entitled to one-half of all profits and earnings that come out of said mine in perpetuity? The cost of one-half share in the Devil Fish Mine will be ten thousand dollars to be paid upon signing of this partnership agreement."*

"Any questions, Ishmael?"

"No. Where do I sign." I asked.

"You both sign each other's copies on these dotted lines. And the third copy, I will keep in my office for safekeeping." Webster replied

"Would you like my payment of ten thousand dollars to be paid here and now in cash, or would you like me to deposit the ten thousand dollars into your account and I will present you with a receipt of deposit, tomorrow?" Darcey asked.

"A receipt of deposit will be fine. Thank you." I said.

Mister Webster proceeded to finalize the documents by signing as being witnesses to our partnership. Handed me and Mister Darcey each a signed contract and kept one for himself.

"Gentlemen, that concludes the official business. Congratulations to you both. I hope that this proves to be a most profitable venture for you both." Webster said as he folded his copy and placed it into his coat pocket. He shook both Darcey's and my hand and was soon gone from the premises. That left me, Darcey, and The Devil Fish Mine alone in the Wells Fargo office.

"So, Ishmael, when do you think you'll be heading out to begin mining operations?" Darcey asked.

"Probably by the end of the week. I still need to find a couple of experienced hands. I'll keep you informed as to my progress. Come on, boy. Let's get." I said.

"Don't you want to go out and celebrate?" Darcey inquired.

"Naw, maybe some other time. I got some things I have to attend to. Good night, Mister Darcey."

I got back to Mrs. Driscoll's boarding house around six-thirty. Everyone had finished their dinner, the table was cleared, and I found Mrs. Driscoll sitting in the parlor knitting. I walked in after bedding down *Chapawee* for the night in the barn.

"Sorry, I'm late, Sarah. I hope I didn't put you out."

"Not at all, Ishmael. I have set a bowl of stew in the oven in case you hadn't eaten." She said with a warm smile.

"That's very kindly of you. A hot bowl of stew sounds wonderful."

"Come have a seat in the kitchen and I'll get it for you."

I followed her to the kitchen table and had a seat with Queequeg lying by my feet.

"Would you like a couple of biscuits as well?"

"Yes, please. Will you join me?" I asked."

"I've already eaten, but I will sit with you and have

a cup of tea. How did it go with Mister Darcey, today?"

"I sold half my gold mine to him for ten thousand dollars."

"Oh, my lord! That's wonderful." She exclaimed.

"My sense is not to trust him. He's paying his brother-in-law's salary to work the mine as I refused to support such a slacker. I placed an ad in the Stockton Journal to hire a couple of experienced men to help work the mine."

"That seems like sound advice."

"So, how was your day, Sarah?"

"Pretty much the same as every other day, I suppose. Make up the rooms, laundry, cooking, and cleaning. It's a hard life, but at least I get by." She said.

"Do you get lonely?" I asked.

"At times." She answered with a touch of an embarrassing smile as she gazed off into the distance as if she were somewhere else.

"I know that feeling as well." I confided.

"But your life seems so adventurous."

"Being surrounded by people doesn't necessarily mean you can't get lonely, it just means you're not alone."

She looked into my eyes, nodded, gave a slight beaming smile, and said, "I should get back to my knitting."

"Before you go, I just wanted to tell you that I had a will made up today and if there was something that was to happen to me while developing my Devil Fish Mine, I have you to inherit my half of the mine."

"Why me. Don't you have any family?"

"Sadly, no."

"But, why me. You only just met me."

"True. But you've been so kind to me. And besides, I would hate it see Darcey end up with it all. Hopefully, it will dissuade him and that dolt of a brother-in-law from trying to steal it from under me or try to bushwhack me if they know they won't benefit from my death."

"Ishmael, I'm flattered, but I can't accept this."

"Sarah, please, this will only happen if something happens to me. Please, you'd be doing me a big favor."

"Well, all right. I'll do it for you."

"Thank you."

"Promise me you'll be careful."

"I promise."

The next morning, I went to meet Mister Darcey to get my receipt and my copy of the partnership contract.

"Good morning, partner," Darcey said with a wolfish grin.

"Good morning."

"Here for your copies of our partnership?" He asked.

"Yep, and the deposit receipt," I added.

"Yes, of course, Here it is. Your balance is sixteen thousand five hundred dollars." He said as he handed me the statement.

"Thank you," I said.

"I saw in today's Stockton Journal that you're advertising for men."

"I am. I figure along with Billy, we'll need at least two more workers."

"And when do you think you'll be heading out?"

"I'm hoping by the end of next week."

"Ah, very good."

"I will of course keep you apprised."

"Excellent. Well, I must get back to work and I'm sure you have plenty to do to get ready as well. So, I'll say good day to you."

"Good day, Mister Darcey."

My next stop was to J.R. Lazarus, attorney at law to pick up my will. When I entered her office, there were several men seated in the waiting area, she peered up from reading a document on her desk and said, "Just have a seat, I'll be with you in a few moments."

I did as I was told and sat down in one of two vacant chairs. Queequeg laid down next to my chair. All the other men were sitting reading copies of the Stockton Journal. I asked one of the men who finished if I could take a look at his paper if he was through with it. He was very cordial and handed me his copy.

"I'll give it right back, I just want to check on an ad that I had placed."

"No need. I've read everything I wanted."

"Thank you."

I thumbed through the paper, all eight pages until I came to the want ad section. There it was, third from the bottom.

WANTED TWO MEN TO WORK A GOLD MINE Looking for two men to work digging mine. Experience a must! Will pay 25 Dollars a week, plus bonuses. See Ishmael at Mrs. Driscoll's boarding house located on Elk Street tomorrow between the hours of 10 am and 4 pm.

"Ishmael! I can see you now. Won't you please

come through?"

I stood and went back to her desk proudly carrying the newspaper with my ad showing. She gestured for me to sit at the chair positioned next to her desk.

"Now, I have drawn up your will. It's very simple as you can see." She said as she handed me a copy to read.

As I was looking at it, she read it aloud. When she was done, she asked, "Do you have any questions?"

"No Ma'am."

"Very good. Now, all you need to do is sign here at the bottom on both copies. One is for you and the other I will keep in my files."

As I finished signing my name she asked, "Is there anything else I can do for you?"

"No Ma'am. I believe that this will do nicely for now." I said as I rose. I shook her hand and left, Queequeg followed at my heels. We headed back to Mrs. Driscoll's boarding house to start interviewing potential mine workers.

Out of the fourteen men that came for the job, I picked two men that I thought were both experienced and whom I felt were trustworthy. The first fella I hired was Bob Grant, a grizzled old-timer who had worked in a half dozen gold and silver mines. He provided me with several names of people he had worked for. And I was able to contact three of the mining companies who confirmed his good standing and considered him to be an upright citizen.

The second fella was Jason Collins. Jason had solid mining experience as well. He wasn't as old as Bob, what he didn't have in the way of experience he made up with brawn. Once we agreed on their employment, I set a date of two days to head out to start digging the Devil Fish Mine. I gave Bob Grant two hundred dollars to start buying the supplies and gear that we would need. I stopped by the Wells Fargo bank to inform Mister Darcey of my plans and to have him tell his brother-in-law Billy Malone to be ready to travel in two days. He should meet up with me at the widow Driscoll's boarding house at sunrise. We leave at dawn with or without him.

After I had a hardy breakfast with Sarah Driscoll, I packed up my gear, saddled *Chapawee* and Daisy, gave my copy of my will to Sarah, and went outside to wait for Bob, Jason, and Billy Malone.

Sarah followed me out onto the porch, she brought with her a large gingham napkin folded over containing a fresh-baked iron skillet loaf of cornbread.

"Ishmael, I baked you a little something for your journey."

"Thank you, Sarah. That was mighty kind of you."

"Ishmael, you take care of yourself."

"I will."

"Will I ever see you again?" She asked, her eyes

tearing up.

"I'll be back."

"Promise." She asked.

She leaned close to me, closed her eyes, and I gave her a passionate kiss.

"I promise," I whispered.

Queequeg began to bark when he saw Bob Grant and Jason Collins arriving driving the buckboard full of gear and supplies. Their unsaddled horses were tied to the back of the buckboard. I took the cornbread-filled napkin, and gave Sarah another kiss, "I promise."

I then walked up to the two men seated on the buckboard, "You boys want some cornbread?"

"Sure," Bob said as I offered the loaf to them. I then tied Daisy's bridle to the back of the buckboard, mounted *Chapawee*, doffed my Stetson to Sarah, and headed down Elk Street towards El Dorado Street. We turned east making our way out of town.

"Ether one of ya seen Billy Malone this morning?" I asked.

"Not me," Bob answered with a mouth full of cornbread.

"I hadn't seen him either," Jason said.

We were about half a mile out of town when we heard a horse galloping at full speed towards us from behind.

"Hey, Ohhhhhhhhhhh!" The horseman hollered.

It was Billy Malone. He looked half drunk and smelled twice as bad as he looked. I stopped and rode back to him and said, "Look, Billy, we ain't got time for this bull shit. I don't care if Darcey is my partner and I don't care if he is paying you out of his own pocket, we don't need any slackers. So, if'n you aren't going to take this job seriously, you can just turn around and head on back to town. What's it going to be?"

"I want to go with you." He said.

I turned back towards the boys waiting in the buckboard and said, "Let's move out."

Our journey of two days was uneventful. We found the valley where the small stream meandered through the basin just as I remembered it. The grassland had quickly reclaimed the valley, it looked completely unspoiled. It was almost as if I had never been there, found the gold, or kilt that scoundrel.

The first thing we did was to clear an area so we could set up our campsite on the hilltop under a grove of cottonwoods. I chose that spot for its shade and more importantly for the cover and view. Having the high ground would come in handy if'n we got into a gunfight.

Once we had set up camp, we unloaded the wagon, secured the horses and pack animals, and looked for the hand pickax that I had left behind all those many months ago. Jason Collins found it.

"Hey, Ishmael. Over here, I think I found it!"

Sure, enough there it was. I counted off ten paces towards the stream and said, "Dig here."

The four of us began to dig and it didn't take very long to uncover the body, the saddle, and the rest of his belongings. In the months that the body had been buried, it had decomposed considerably, and the odor was putrefying. We had barely uncovered him when we were inundated with thousands of blowflies. It got so bad that we could barely see our hands in front of our faces. Finally, I reached down and grabbed the corpse by his shirt and dragged his body out of the hole and over a couple of hundred feet away, where I left him to the vultures and coyotes. As I was returning to the pit, I turned around to see the carcass appeared to be black, covered with flies. It wasn't but minutes when the vultures began their feast. By the next morning, every trace of the man was gone, the scavengers had erased any evidence that the reprobate ever existed.

The rest of the day we concentrated on digging the entrance of the mine. Using some of the timbers that we brought with us to build overhead crossbeams used to hold the back of the mine to prevent the dern thing collapsing down on our heads.

That night after dinner, we sat around the fire jawing about our pasts. I told about my whaling days, but nothing about my pirating. I repeated a story that I had heard, told to me one night while we were hunting after Moby Dick by Chief mate Starbuck upon the *Pequod*. I directed it to Billy.

"*Entre Chien et Loup.*" I said.

"What the Hell does that mean?" Billy Malone asked sarcastically.

"It's French. It means between the dog and wolf."

"Okay. But what the Hell does it mean?" Billy repeated.

"You know that time of day when the sun is starting to disappear over the horizon? When the bright light is such that it becomes difficult to make out what's coming at ya. Let's say that an animal is coming at ya and you're straining to see if it's a wolf or a dog, between a friend or a foe, between the known and the unknown.

Do you shoot or wait? If you shoot, you might kill a friend, and if you wait too long, you might be killed. You've only got seconds to act. What do you do?" I asked.

"That's easy. You shoot." Billy said without hesitation.

"And what if after you shoot, you find that you've killed your best friend or worse someone you love?" I asked.

"Well, it's their own damn fault. They should have shouted out to me." He snapped back.

I said nothing, I just looked at him, as did Bob and Jason. I knew from his answer that he was only out for himself.

"Well, what would you fellas do?" Billy asked defensively.

"I'd probably wait," I said.

"Bob? Jason?" Billy asked.

"I guess I'd hold off until I could make out who or what was coming at me," Bob answered.

"Yeah, I think I'd wait, too."

"Well, you'd all be dead," Billy said smugly.

"Maybe." I said as I stretched out on my blanket, rested my head on the saddle, covered my face with my Stetson, and fell fast asleep holding onto my Colt with Queequeg by my side."

Once we established the foundation of the mine, we began to work the mine. At first there appeared to be a small vein of gold that ran for several hundred yards slanting downwards deep underground. It seemed that every ten feet we would be forced to stop mining and work on the structure and stability of the shaft. It was soon apparent that we would be needing another couple of wagon loads of timber. The one wagon load of timber supports that we brought with us was about to run out.

I decided to stop the digging and have Billy Malone and Jason Collins accompany me back to Stockton to cash in the gold that we had collected thus far and return to camp with fresh supplies and timber. I would leave Bob Grant behind to safeguard the mine, I had found him to be a most honorable and trustworthy fellow. We would return within the week.

I dropped Billy and Jason off at Jones & Hewlett Groceries, Provisions & Hardware, Purveyors of Agricultural and Mining tools, while I went into the Wells Fargo Bank and cashed in the cache of gold.

"Ishmael! My boy, so glad to see you. How's everything?" Darcey asked greeting me like his long-lost son.

"It's going very well. We just came back to refresh our supplies and to get more timber."

"More timber? That must mean you're going further into the ground. So, the vein is running deep." Darcey uttered almost salivating.

"Yeah, Bob says it looks to be a possible bonanza."

"Bob?"

"Yeah, Bob Grant. He's back at the mine watching over her."

"Bob Grant? Do you trust him?" Darcey sounded in a bit of a panic.

"Yeah, I trust him. I trust him more than Billy." I shot back.

"How's Billy doing?"

"So far he's holding his own."

"Good. Good." Darcy replied with a relieved smile.

I plopped two large canvas bags filled with gold nuggets upon the weighing counter. Darcey weighed the gold. The total was worth twenty-seven thousand, sixty-nine hundred dollars. Darcey had opened a bank account in the name of Devil Fish Mine, Inc. with him and I both officers. Neither one could take any money out without the other co-signing the transaction.

When Billy and Jason completed the purchasing of supplies and timber. They also needed to obtain another wagon and a team of horses to transport the extra beams back to camp. I paid Jason his salary and a little extra for doing such a good job.

"Jason here's two hundred for the two months and another two hundred bonus. And there's more where that came from. I promise a hefty bonus once we get the mine in working order." I said as I handed him a wad of greenbacks.

Billy held out his hand towards me.

I said, "Your brother-in-law takes care of you."

Darcey looked disappointed that I paid Jason so much and more disappointed that I did it in front of Billy. I'm sure he was planning to stiff his brother-in-law.

"Fellas, let's plan on leaving at sunrise tomorrow morning. We'll meet at the livery stable and head out from there. See ya boys then. Bye Darcey."

"See ya partner," Darcey said.

I rode up to Sarah Driscoll's boarding house, tied *Chapawee* to the hitching post, and knocked on the screen door.

Sarah came to the door, she seemed to be preoccupied trying to open a jar of homemade pickles.

"Need some help with that, ma'am?" I asked.

"Ishmael!" She exclaimed.

"Sarah."

"What are you doing back? Is everything all right?"

"Everything is better than fine. We had to come back to gather more supplies."

"Come in." She said holding the screen door open.

I came in, leaned down, and kissed her. I was surprised when she kissed me back.

"How long can you stay?" She asked.

"I have to leave in the morning. Gotta get back. Is there a room available?" I inquired.

"Oh, Ishmael, all the rooms are taken."

"Well, I guess I'll head on into town and see about getting a room," I muttered.

"You know, now that I think about it I do have a room where you can stay. My room." She said slightly blushing.

The next morning over breakfast, the major topic of conversation was the impending war between the northern states and the thirteen southern Confederate states. It became a quite hot topic between a Mister Raymond J. Johnson from Memphis, Tennessee, and a Mister Charles Mann, who hailed from Chicago, Illinois. Mister Johnson came from a family that has slaves on their cotton plantation. He was pretty adamant that the negro was sub-human and that they were contented to work as slaves, even though on occasion they needed to be taught the discipline of the whip. His man-slave Abraham was sitting at the kitchen table having his breakfast. He wasn't allowed to have meals in the same room with his master.

"And you say they are contented, you using the whip?" Mann asked snidely.

"They crave discipline, sir! Otherwise, they are shiftless and lazy." Johnson shot back.

"I've never heard such rubbish. You, sir, are nothing more than a racist!"

"I take umbrage with that slanderous accusation! I demand satisfaction. I challenge you to a duel. Unless you are too much of a coward, sir!"

"You want to have a duel? With what swords?"

"No, sir. Dueling pistols. I shall meet to outback at sunrise. You will need a second; Abraham will act as mine.”

Mann, glanced over to me and asked, “Sir, would you be so kind as to act as my second?”

I looked at both of them and replied, “Why wait until the morning? Let's do it now.”

Mann stood up, pushed back his chair, and said, Fine with me. Johnson?”

“Very well. Abraham, go fetch my dueling pistols.”

“Yas, master.” The black man said as he ran up the stairs.

“I must tell you, sir, I am a crackerjack shot.” Johnson boasted.

Mann stared at Johnson and said, “We'll see.”

Seconds later, Abraham scrambled down the stairs carrying a polished wooden box. He handed the box to Johnson.

“Let us retire to the backyard, sir,” Johnson ordered.

“I suggest that you stay inside, Sarah. This is not for you.” I said.

The four of us went out into the backyard. Johnson opened the box revealing two identical dueling pistols. He held the box to Mann and said, “You may choose either one, they are identical, and both are loaded.”

Mann reached into the box, drew the one closet to him, examined it, and appeared content.

“Satisfied?” Johnson asked.

“This will do nicely.” Mann retorted.

Johnson took the other pistol and gave Abraham the box to hold.

“Now, we stand back-to-back. We turn and fire at the end of twenty paces, understood?” Johnson asked.

Mann, not looking at his opponent, was examining his pistol and just nodded.

"You, sir. If you would be so kind as to count off twenty paces?" Johnson asked of me.

"I will," I answered.

Johnson proceeded, "We shall each then turn and fire. Is that agreeable to you, sir?"

"Fine," Mann replied.

Both men stood back-to-back, holding their pistols at the ready. Johnson was about a foot shorter than Mann. And ten years older.

"Are you gentlemen ready?" I asked.

In unison, they said, "Ready."

I began to count, "One, two, three, four, five, six, seven, eight, nine, ten, eleven, twelve, thirteen, fourteen, fifteen, sixteen, seventeen, eighteen, nineteen, twenty."

Johnson turned a bit early and fired before Mann had completed his twentieth step.

POW

The shot grazed the top of Mann's back right shoulder, tearing a wad of fabric from his waistcoat and a small chunk of his shoulder.

Mann didn't flinch; he turned and aimed his pistol at a quivering Johnson. Johnson dropped his pistol and began to sob.

"Please, don't kill me," Johnson begged.

Mann lowered his pistol, looked at the shaking pusillanimous coward before him, scowled, and in a blink of an eye, raised his pistol and fired.

POW

Johnson lay dead, not three feet from Abraham.

Abraham Johnson had been an enslaved person for the Johnson family for twenty-two years, ever since he was six. He was born into slavery, and once he turned six, the slave broker sold him to the Johnson family, separating him from his mother and siblings. He was assigned to be a house boy. His duties were to maintain the house fires, hauling wood, emptying chamber pots, doing odd jobs for the master, and serving meals. He looked much older than a man of twenty-eight.

Abraham stood in shock, looking down at the body of the man who had at once controlled his every movement, thought, and decision.

"Abraham," I said.

He did not respond; he just stared at his fallen master.

"Abraham!" I said, raising my voice to get his attention.

"Yessa?" He mumbled.

"Are you all right?" I inquired.

"What's going to happen to me?" He asked.

"You're a free man." Mann proudly announced.

"Free?"

"Yes, free. You don't belong to anyone, Abraham. You can go anywhere and do anything that you want." Mann said.

"I don't know wheres I go or whats I do. I be a house slave, that's all I knows."

Sarah came out of the house, saw what had happened, looked at me, put her arms around Abraham, and said, "Listen, Abraham, I could use some help around here. Would you be interested?"

"Does that means that you own me?"

"No. It means that you would work for me. I would pay you wages. Abraham, you are no longer a slave. Do you understand?" She asked.

"Yessa ma'am."

"Now, let's go pack Mister Johnson's belonging so we can send them back to his family in Memphis." She said as she took him into the house.

"Mister Mann, that was a Hell of a shot. What is it you do?" I asked.

"I'm a Pinkerton agent. Have been for eleven years. In all that time, I've never been shot in the back. That man was a braggart and a bully. I detest slavers and the whole concept of slavery. If things go the way it looks that they are, I will be joining the Union Army to help put down these southern Confederates."

"Do you think it will come to a war?"

"I am afraid so. President Lincoln will not abide the tearing apart this nation. This aggression cannot stand. Now, sir, if you'll excuse me, I am in need of medical attention."

A few minutes after Mister Mann had left to see the doctor, Billy Malone and Jason Collins arrived, driving the two buckboards full of supplies up to the boarding house.

"I'll be right with you boys; I just need to get my gear."

I went into the house and found Sarah. She had packed Johnson's belongings and set them by the front door to be taken by the sheriff.

"That's a wonderful thing you're doing," I whispered.

"What?"

"Taken Abraham in."

"I really can use the help." She said with a smile.

"I know. I had a wonderful night last night." I said as I gave her a passionate kiss.

"When will you be back?"

"Probably in a month or so."
"Be safe."
"You too."
"Goodbye, my sweet."
"Goodbye," I said as I kissed her, and I was gone.

It's been several weeks since my travels to Stockton to make our gold deposit and supply run. When I returned, I discovered that on April 12th, 1861, Confederate troops fired on Fort Sumter in South Carolina. Thirty-six hours after the initial attack, Union forces surrendered. War has been declared.

I had a long talk with Sarah about my feelings toward the war. I told her that I felt that I needed to be involved as much as I could. I was torn between my love for her and my love of my country. I asked her to marry me, but she was hesitant. She was fearful of the possibility of becoming a widow again.

"Ishmael, I don't think I could live if I lost you." She said, weeping.

"Sarah, in life, there are no guarantees. Hell, I could die in the mine digging for gold; that would be a waste of my life, not dying for my country. I love you, Sarah. Marry me."

"Ishmael, I need time to think."

"Take all the time you need, my dear. I must talk to Mister Darcey. I will be back soon." I said.

I made my way to the Wells Fargo Bank to speak about my plans for the Devil Fish Mine.

"Ishmael, it's so good to see you, my boy."

"Eugene."

"Have you brought more nuggets from the mine?" Darcey asked with anticipation.

I said nothing. I sat down on the weighing table and hoisted two large canvas bags full of golden nuggets up next to me.

"Here you go," I said.

Darcey eagerly grabbed them and almost ripped them open.

"Ahhhh. Wonderful." He ogled.

"Eugene, can I ask you a question?"

"Ishmael, my boy, ask away."

"What is your position on slavery?"

"I am against it. Why?"

"I think I'd like to contribute to the Union cause. And I was hoping that you might feel the same."

"What are you proposing?" Darcey cautiously asked.

"I propose starting now that we contribute *25%* of our profits to the California Brigade to help put an end to the barbaric institution of slavery." I ventured.

He stood staring at me with a look of disbelief for several minutes before saying, "Ten percent."

I countered, "Twenty."

"Fifteen! Fifteen percent."

I could see that even a paltry fifteen percent was sticking in his craw.

"Agreed. Fifteen percent. It's for a good and noble cause, partner." I said as I reached my hand out. He took it, and we shook on fifteen percent of our profits.

He gave a slight harrumph as he went back to his desk. He sat down and looked up at me, and asked, "Is there anything else?"

"Aye, I will be signing on to the California Brigade to go and fight against the rebels."

"You're not serious; you're going to join the army to go fight in the war?"

"I am. Like I said, it is a good and noble cause." I proclaimed.

"You mad. You're going to get yourself killed!"

"Maybe. Anyway, I'll let you know about my plans. Good day partner."

My next stop was the office of J.R. Lazarus, my lawyer.

"Ishmael. Good day; what can I do for you?"

"I will be joining the California Brigade, and I want to have someone watch over my interests in the Devil Fish Mine and to be able to handle any affairs of mine while I'm away."

"Who did you have in mind?"

"You."

"Me? Very well. I'll draw up a power of attorney for you. When are you thinking of leaving?"

"Probably not for a couple of weeks."

"Well, I should have something for you to look over in a couple of days."

"Thank you," I said.

"Ishmael, you're doing a very noble thing." She said with a smile.

"See you in a couple of days."

"I Ishmael, take thee, Sarah, to be my wedded wife, to have and to hold from this day forward, for better, for worse, for richer, for poorer, in sickness and in health, to love and to cherish, till death us do part."

"By the power vested in me by the State of California, I now pronounce you husband and wife. You may kiss the bride." Preacher Thomas said.

Thar was just a handful of people at the wedding held in the boarding house. Most of them were friends of Sarah. The only people that attended that I knew were Mister Darcey, his wife Martha, and J.R. Lazarus. At the reception, I informed Darcey that J.R. Lazarus, my lawyer, was to have power of attorney over my day-to-day affairs and would be overseeing my share of the partnership. Darcey didn't seem too please when he heard that news.

Sarah and I spent our honeymoon week in San Francisco at the Cliff House just north of Ocean Beach, a fashionable resort for the wealthy. The modest one-story wood-frame structure was skillfully situated on top of the cliff overlooking Seal Rocks, providing breathtaking panoramic views of the Pacific Coastline. It felt good to be back by the sea. Oh, how I missed it. Someday, Sarah and I will have a place next to the sea, but until then, there are many things left to be done.

In April 1861, Oregon Senator Edward Baker was commissioned by Abraham Lincoln to raise a California brigade in Philadelphia. The first regiment

Baker organized, the 1st California, consisted of Philadelphians and was placed under the immediate charge of Colonel Isaac Wistar, who had been a ranger in California during the 1850s. By October, Baker's brigade had grown to its full size, consisting of the 1st, 2nd, 3rd, and 5th California Infantry.

That next week I joined the California Brigade and received the rank of First Lieutenant, assigned to the 5th California Infantry. Being that I was an officer, I was responsible for purchasing my uniform and weaponry. I already had my Colt, but I was required to have a sword as an officer. I purchased a regulation Union Staff & Field Officer's Sword. It was finely etched and ornamented with a hand-forged blade with leather handle grip and wired wrapped. I hadn't handled a saber since my pirating days. I felt at ease holding one again. My uniform was a double-breasted shell dark blue jacket with dome buttons. The trousers were navy blue with a gold stripe running down the sides. As for headgear, I wore the black wool Hardee hat adorned with a brass hat device and a sky-blue wool hat cord signifying infantry. The left side of the brim was pinned up, also signifying that I was an infantry officer. Sarah often remarked how fetching I looked in my uniform.

It was a grey foggy morning when I saddled *Chapawee,* gave my bride a long, slow kiss goodbye, and told her that I loved her and would return to her. She tied a yellow scarf that she wove for me about my neck.

"This shall keep you safe, my love." She whispered.

"I shall wear it always. Fare thee well, my darling." I said, smiling and with Queequeg by my side, I rode off.

THE WAR

I reported for duty with the 5th California Brigade three miles outside of Sacramento at Camp Union. I was assigned to Company E under the command of Captain S.P. Ford. We spend the next four months of military exercises and training preparing for a march east to join up with Major General George Mead's Army of the Potomac.

The journey took us three months to cross the country to join up with the Union forces; we finally arrived just outside of the small town of Gettysburg, Pennsylvania, on June 30th.

The California Brigade was placed under the command of Brigadier General Alexander Webb. At the time, the Union Army had suffered many losses; Gettysburg was to be a pivotal battle; a lot depended upon us to begin to turn the tide of the war.

We were bivouacked up on Cemetery Hill; as I looked out over the countryside, there were nothing but tents and soldiers, both Yankees and Rebels as far as the eye could see. There were over a hundred thousand Union soldiers, and the scuttlebutt was that the Rebs had close to seventy-five thousand.

Now, I had been in dozens of battles during my pirate days, and fierce they be, but this open field warfare was new to me. It seemed a fool hearty way to do battle, tens of thousands of men running across an open field straight into the enemy's waiting arms. It was sheer madness, men charging through cannon fire, traversing a constant barrage of Minié balls whizzing by their heads until, if they're lucky, lowering their bayonets and engaging in hand-to-hand combat. If victorious, they would revel in the glory of victory; if defeated and were not too severely wounded, captured, or dead, they would have to retreat over the same fields they came screaming and yelling just minutes earlier.

On the first day's fighting, 50,000 men went into battle, and 15,000 were killed, wounded, captured, or missing. General Lee's Confederate forces approached Gettysburg from the north and west. They had won the day, but not enough to claim victory. The fighting stopped just before sunset. A truce was called so that each army could go out into the field to collect their dead and wounded. All-day long during the battles, you could hear the cries and moans of the wounded lying in the fields dying.

Our orders were for Company E to hold Cemetery Hill. That first day we just had minor skirmishes throughout the day. There was no heavy assault made against our position, and we sustained no injuries.

Day two was intense; we had several attacks by the Johnny Rebs, and each time we were able to push them back. Later that day, Confederate Lt. General Richard S. Ewell began his attack at 4 p.m. For three hours, he chose to limit his demonstration to an artillery barrage from Benner's Hill, about a mile to the northeast of our position. Although our troops on Cemetery Hill received some damage from this fire, we returned counterbattery fire with a vengeance. And since Cemetery Hill is over 50 feet taller than Benner's Hill, it meant we had a decided advantage. Ewell's four batteries were forced to withdraw with heavy losses.

Then around 7 p.m., the Confederate's attack began with a Rebel yell as they charged up Cemetery Hill. This formed a gap that a regiment known as the

Louisiana Tigers exploited; they bounded over and breeched the stone wall. Other Rebel troops used other weak spots in the line, and soon some of the Confederates had reached the gun batteries at the top of the hill.

On the crest of the hill, the gunners of Captain Samuel Erdrich's New York battery and the men of the California Brigade engaged in hand-to-hand combat against the invaders. They came upon us with their bayonets, clubbed muskets, and even fists and rocks. Some of our boys fought with artillerists ramrods, wielding them like ball bats, bashing heads, and breaking bones. At one point in the thick of battle, a Rebel officer made a charge at me; my Colt pistol was empty. I had nothing but my saber. I was poised to strike when he raised his revolver; it was then that Queequeg bound upon the poor fellow, ripping his throat open. As a Rebel soldier ran towards Queequeg with bayonet raised, I jabbed him with my saber, killing him instantly.

I have to say that my days as a buccaneer came into good use. Thar were many a man that had never been in the throes of close-quarters combat. Those that froze or panicked paid the ultimate price, death.

It was a hard-fought battle; at one point, about seventy-five North Carolinians of the Sixth Regiment and twelve Louisianian Tiger brigades scaled the walls and planted the colors of the Sixth North Carolina and Ninth Louisiana on our guns. We soon retook those positions and drove the attackers back down the hill, keeping one of the keystones of the Union line.

On the third day, there were no infantry attacks on Cemetery Hill; the primary Confederate attacks were on Culp's Hill and the lower portion of Cemetery Ridge. We did repel a massive artillery assault, but we could still concentrate our cannons on the Confederate artillery barrage that preceded the failed Pickett's Charge. As a result of Pickett's fiasco, General Robert E. Lee was forced to retreat and ultimately abandon his attempt to reach Washington D.C. All toll 51,000 men died at the Battle of Gettysburg.

After all the smoked had cleared and the Southern troops retreated, we established a tented campsite atop Cemetery Hill to maintain a military presence, secure the battlefield from looters and curiosity seekers, and collect remaining military weapons. The men of Company E received multiple citations for holding the position and going beyond the call of duty.

Gettysburg was the first major defeat for the Southern Army. Thar had come news that the militias sympatric to the Southern Cause out west were planning on seizing the California gold fields to help finance the Confederate war effort. It was decided to send the California Brigade back west to defend the gold mines and put down the uprising.

Of the five hundred and forty men of the California Brigade that fought in the Battle of Gettysburg, four hundred and ninety-five rode west. Forty-five were left behind, buried on Cemetery Hill.

We headed west under the command of Colonel John K. Kellogg. Our orders were to travel post-haste.

Try, if possible not to have any encounters with the hostiles. We were to avoid any unnecessary skirmishes with the Indians. There had been several reports of Indian attacks on white settlers and Union troops crossing through the Oklahoma Indian Territories. We were heading into hostile territory, and not just because of the Indians; it was before the outbreak of war that the United States government relocated all soldiers in the Indian Territory to other vital areas, leaving the territory. The Confederates had alliances with the Cherokee, Chickasaw, Choctaw, Creek, and Seminole Nations. All of which we were going to have to travel through. Our expedition included four white regiments, two Indian regiments, and one artillery battalion.

Our first encounter with the enemy was at the Battle of Honey Springs. We attacked mid-afternoon. At the same time, heavy rain squalls began to fall, which caused much consternation and difficulties for the Confederate's ammunition. Their gunpowder was getting soaked, and they were hardly able to get much use of it.

It was my first battle in which I advanced on the opposing army on horseback, sword drawn at full gallop. My heart was in my throat, beating so hard that I could hear it beat outside my body. Thar were bullets flying all around me. That day, I not only led white men from the California Brigade into battle but many a negro troops as well as Indians from the 2nd Regiment of the Indian Home Guard. After the Graybacks retreated, it was then that I noticed that my steed, *Chapawee's* left ear, had been partly blown off by a rebel's bullet. I had the company Vet take a look; he applied some salve to his ear and bandaged it.

"It'll be good as new in a couple of days. Try and not let it get dirty." The Vet said.

"Thanks, Doc."

"That there's one fine specimen of horseflesh, Lieutenant."

"Thank you, sir. *Chapawee* and me, we go back a while."

"And is that mutt yours, too?" The Vet asked, pointing to Queequeg leaning against my leg.

"Yes, sir. This is Queequeg. I saved his life, and he's returned the favor many times." I replied.

"Queequeg. That's an unusual name. What does it mean?"

"He's named after a friend of mine who died saving my life many years ago."

"Well, I've got to attend to several other horses and mules. You take care, Lieutenant."

After the victory, Colonel John K. Kellogg stated that he had never seen such courageous fighting that was done by the Negro and Indian regiments. The question of whether or not negroes can fight was settled that day; they make as good or better soldiers in every respect than any troops I have ever had the honor to command.

Colonel Kellogg gave orders not to pursue the enemy because the horses and men were exhausted from the march and battle. We camped overnight at the battlefield; that night, Major Grayson's relief force arrived to help treat the wounded and bury the dead on both sides.

Years later, after the war, I heard that the Battle of Honey Springs was the largest ever fought in the Indian Territory and proved to be decisive in helping to win the war, as the victory opened the way for Union forces to capture Fort Smith and the Arkansas River Valley to the Mississippi River.

Over the months, I had sporadically received and sent letters to Sarah. Since the California Brigade had been moving from one front to another, it was hard to deliver the mail regularly. Occasionally Sarah would send a package of food items that she was sure that he wouldn't be able to obtain, such as tins of various fruits and vegetables, bars of soap, bread, jellybeans, and cheese.

One day after receiving a package from Sarah when the regiment was bivouacked a dozen miles north of Picacho Peak and about fifty miles north of Tucson, Arizona. The orders came down that we were to sit tight for a couple of days before confronting a small force of Confederate cavalrymen stationed in Tucson. Since I had the time, I figured that I would write my dear Sarah a letter while I could.

My Dearest Sarah,

This pleasant evening finds me well & willing to write to you. I was quite agreeably surprised last evening when I received the package that you so kindly sent to me. I am afraid you are sending things that you really need to use to benefit yourself. Now I am as thankful as anyone can be for any such thing & I can appreciate it now better than I ever could in any place that I have been. But after all, I do not want you to use me better than you do yourself.

How are things with Mister Darcey? Have there been any issues with the operation of the mine? Please ask him; next time you see him ask him to correspond with me and let me know how things are going.

We will be moving out in the next couple of days, heading down to Tucson to chase out a small garrison of Johnny Rebs that are trying to recruit men to try and take over the goldfields of California. It shouldn't be too much of an effort, but I promise I will be careful. I miss you and love you until next time my darling, all my love.

Your loving husband,

Two days after I sent that letter, we came across a party of Confederate pickets from Tucson. They were a small unit of Rebels placed on a defensive line forward of their main force to provide a timely warning against an enemy advance.

We were conducting a sweep of the Picacho Peak area, looking for Confederates reported to be nearby. Major Holmes, who was in command, was under orders not to engage them but to wait for the main column to come up.

However, Major Holmes took it upon himself to ignore the order and surprise the Rebels. We should have been able to capture them without firing a shot if he would have just waited for the main column.

Instead, Major Holmes led us into the thicket single file without dismounting. We were ambushed and returned fire. Three of the Confederates surrendered. Holmes secured one of the prisoners himself and had just remounted his horse when a bullet struck him in the head, killing him.

Fierce and confused fighting ensued among the mesquite and arroyos for over two hours, during the battle we sustained two Union fatalities and three wounded.

With Major Holmes dead, I became in command of the unit. I decided to break off fighting and retreat to the main unit since the advantage of a surprise attack had been compromised since Major Holmes's disobedience of orders had cost him his life and lost any chance of a surprise attack on Tucson.

We met up with the main column at Fort Barrett and advanced towards Tucson, when we arrived we learned that due to a lack of supplies, there weren't any Confederate reinforcements available, Captain Beauregard Jackson of the Texas 10th Calvary and his troops had to withdraw as soon as he learned of our advance. We entered unopposed.

We were welcomed by the local inhabitants. They were tired of the Rebel forces confiscating provisions due to their faulty supply chains. Before our presence, the Confederates were burning hay stored at all the stagecoach stations to delay our advance. They were, in fact, glad to be rid of the Rebels.

Once Tucson was considered secure, orders came

down from headquarters that we were to move out to the northern New Mexico Territory. There were reports that the Confederates were attempting to break the Northern force's hold on the West beginning with the Rocky Mountain railroads that supplied the Union troops.

Back in early 1862, the Confederacy established the Confederate Arizona Territory, which included the southern halves of both modern Arizona and New Mexico. The cash-strapped Confederacy's goal was to gain access to the gold and silver mines of California and the Colorado Territory to fill its treasury and take over and occupy the seaports in Southern California to evade the Union naval blockades.

The Rebels had moved into the southern New Mexico/Arizona territory and had captured the towns of Mesilla, Díaz Ana, and Tucson. The Rebs were 3,000 strong, under the command of General Henry H. Sibley, and were moving north against the Federal stronghold at Fort Craig on the Rio Grande, believing that if they could capture the fort that they would drive the Union out of the southwest.

We had arrived at Fort Craig with over 400 men, bolstering the fort's strength to just over thirteen hundred. I was surprised to find that there were some familiar faces from the 9th Cavalry and the 125th Infantry of the Buffalo Soldiers that I fought alongside at the Battle of Gettysburg. Aside from regular Union troops, there were hundreds of New Mexico volunteers under the command of Indian scout Lieutenant Colonel Christopher Houston Carson, better known as Kit Carson.

A couple of days after his arrival Lieutenant Colonel

Carson held a reception party for all the officers in the fort. He was an unassuming man. He stood about five feet five, weighed about one hundred forty pounds, squarely built, slightly bow-legged, and of iron temperament. When he spoke, his voice was as soft and gentle as a woman's. He seemed to let his actions speak louder than his words.

When I met him he was sitting alone at the improvised bar in the mess tent having a drink of whiskey. I approached him and introduced myself, Queequeg was by my side.

"Colonel Carson, it is a pleasure to meet you, sir."

"No need to be so formal, son. Just call me Kit. And you are?"

"Ishmael."

"Take a seat and have a drink with me, Ishmael."

As I sat down, he grabbed a glass off of the bar and poured me a large whiskey and topped off his glass as well.

"You from around these parts?" He asked.

"Oh, no sir. I'm originally from up north, New Bedford, Massachusetts. I was a whaler when I was younger."

"You don't say? What brought you all the way out here?"

"Gold," I said. I decided not to mention my pirating days.

"Gold." He laughed.

"Yup."

"Did ya find any?"

"Aye. I discovered a right healthy mine. Up near Stockton." Says I.

"Do tell! Whatcha doing out here in the middle of

this God-forsaken land?"

"Seems like as good a cause as any. Besides, Ima against slavery."

He looked at me like I was some kind of a fool, chuckled, and poured us each another large whiskey.

"Why you here?" I asked.

"They're paying me, son. You, you could be out tripping the light fantastic, living the good life. But instead, you're out here eating dust and risking your life for a *cause*. Well, don't that beat all."

He peered down at Queequeg and asked, "Is that your mutt?"

"Aye, this here's Queequeg. I saved him when I passed an Indian village that had been massacred."

"Them savages got what they deserved." Kit said with venom.

"They were just women and children. Mutilated and slaughtered like cattle."

"They are all savages, sir. I don't abide the killing of women and children, but the only good Indian is a dead Indian, is what I always say."

I stood up, finished my whiskey, saluted the Colonel, and said, "You sir are no better than the savages you profess to hate. We steal their land, and with murderous malice destroy their crops, kill their livestock and force march them to remoteness and desolate reservations that are unfit for any human to survive on. Thanks for the drink."

"Lieutenant! You will apologize at once or shall be placed under arrest!" Carson shouted.

"Colonel, you can go to hell before I apologize to you now or ever again!" I barked as I walked out of the mess tent.

I stormed back to my tent, fully expecting to be arrested and court-martialed. I sat on my cot and waited, but no one came. The next morning at morning mess, a sergeant stopped by my table and told me that I was to report to Lieutenant Colonel Carson's tent when I was finished.

As I entered Carson's tent I saw that he was in the process of shaving. I snapped to attention and waited. He spied me in his mirror. He gave a half-turn, and said, "At ease Lieutenant."

He then went about completing his morning ritual of shaving, grooming, and dressing in his uniform.

"Son, I like you. You got spunk. Although, I think you're a damn fool in your opinions about these savages. We are building a nation that will stretch from the Atlantic to the Pacific. The United States is destined to expand its dominion across the entire North American continent, and we aren't going to let those red devils get in our way, by God!" Carson exclaimed.

"Sir, if I may?"

"Go ahead."

"Don't you think it's ironic that we're standing here preparing to go into battle and perhaps die to give the Negro freedom? Someone who isn't even native to this land, who was brought over against their will, and yet we continue the extermination, slaughter, and massacre of the native people who have lived here for hundreds maybe thousands of years?" I asked.

Carson cast a cynical gaze at me and was about to say something when a sergeant came bursting into his tent and announced, "Sir, the Rebels are on the move. Sir!"

Carson grabbed his sword and gun belt off of his cot

and said as he rushed out, "Looks like we'll have to finish this discussion at a later date, Lieutenant. Let's go!"

I double-timed it back to my tent, and I too, grabbed my sword and gun belt, jumped on *Chapawee,* and ordered Queequeg to stay in my tent. He was none too pleased, as he barked and howled as I rode off into battle.

I joined my regiment of the California Brigade as we preparing to make our first attack against Confederate Major Powhatan Jordan of the 7th Texas Mounted Rifles.

We were signaled to announce if our regiments were ready to advance.

"First Regiment. Ready!"

"Second Regiment. Ready!"

"Third Regiment. Ready!"

"5th Infantry. Ready!"

"California Regiment. Ready!" I shouted.

Major Jordan drew his sword. Lieutenant Colonel Carson drew his saber. Then all of the Regiment officers, including myself drew our swords and waited for the attack order.

I faintly heard the order flowing down from regiment leader to regiment leader. When it came to me, I raised my sword over my head and screamed the order, *"Charge!"*

Unlike the Battle of Gettysburg, where I was dug in

and was defending a position, here we were charging over an open field towards an advancing enemy of almost equal force. We were 1300 strong, the Rebels fielded 1100 troops. I hacked through, what seemed to be hundreds of men from their first wave. I don't rightly recall how many men I sliced, slashed, gashed, gouged, and kerfed that day. I do know that with every pass I made I was able to cleave a path wide enough for my men to pass through onto the next wave of Graybacks.

The fighting dragged on throughout the day, seesawing back and forth the battleground. One moment it seemed that we were winning, the next Johnny Rebs was pushing us back to our lines. Finally, the Confederates gradually forced Lieutenant Colonel Carson and his men to retreat eastward. All seemed lost until a detachment of Union infantry and the California Brigade including my squad was able to sneak around their right flank and burn their supply train. When the Rebels realized that all their food, weapons, and ammunition had gone up in smoke they were forced to retreat.

Glorieta Pass has since been commonly referred to as the "Gettysburg of the West." It was here that our forces were finally able to turn back the Confederate invasion of the New Mexico Territory.

My Dearest Darling Ishmael,
It has been so long since I have heard from you, I wish and pray with all my heart that you are well and

safe. We get daily accounts about the war and of all the terrible numbers of deaths on both sides. Within the town of Stockton, there is a polarity between some of the citizens who are pro-slavery and those who are of a mind for anti-slavery. So far, there hasn't been any major civil discourse. Although at times emotions have run high at town meetings thanks to Sheriff Brookwood's even-handedness, peace has been maintained.

Things here at the boarding house have been busy. I have had the house full of guests almost since you've left. I have been getting monthly reports about the mine when Mister Darcey stops by at the beginning of every month. The excavation of gold from the mine has been extremely successful.

I was disheartened to hear of the death of his brother-in-law, Billy Malone. It seems that one evening at the mine Billy consumed too much alcohol whiskey and became belligerent and angry about his wages, drew his pistol, and fired. Wounding Jason Collins in the foot, resulting in the loss of two toes on his left foot. Bob Grant tried to restrain Billy, but when Billy took aim at him, Bob had no choice but to protect himself. In doing so he mortally wounded Billy Malone. Mister Darcey decided not to bring his body back for burial in the Darcey family plot, but instead had his remains buried not far from the Devil Fish Mine. A small headstone was placed at the gravesite and a simple service was held at the First Methodist Church, unfortunately, the turnout was poorly attended. I felt bad for the widow.

I pray that this conflict shall be over soon so I can have you come back safely to my waiting arms. I miss you terribly and worry so. I look forward to the day that you will return to me. Until then my love I pray that the good Lord will bring you safely back home to my waiting arms.

Your devoted wife
S

I received Sarah's letter while I was recuperating in the field hospital just outside of Santa Fe. My regiment was assigned to support Colonel John Chivington's 1st Colorado Calvary. We had gotten word that a Confederate force of just over 300 men was camped down at Apache Canyon. Our scouts discovered that they had a picket post of 50 men at the summit of the canyon.

Chivington ordered the regiment of the California Brigade that I was in charge of to attack the post. In the early hours of the morning before sunrise, my men and I sprung a sneak attack, capturing the entire picket post asleep. Meanwhile, Chivington's forces swung around and found their main army unprepared for battle, we were able to split their forces and force them into a retreat. The Colonel ordered a full-on frontal mounted attack against their artillery. The charge unnerved them and as a result, we were able to capture several of their cannons and surrender of dozens of Confederates, while scattering the rest, including their presiding officer, Colonel Pyron.

During the chaos, my men and I located the

Confederate supply wagons. We attacked, driving off and capturing the small attachment of guards. When Chivington and his men arrived, they proceeded to loot and burn the 80 wagons, spiked the cannons, and killed over 500 horses and mules. Which, at that the time, I had made a formal complaint against the unnecessary killing of the livestock. I had suggested that we should save the animals to be used for the Union. But Chivington wanted to show the Confederates that the Union were merciless and weren't willing to show any mercy. A view that many on both sides shared.

Chivington would gain infamy when he led a 700-man force in what would be called the Sand Creek Massacre. They killed over 230 peaceful Cheyenne and Arapahos, two-thirds were women, children, and infants. He and his troops took scalps and human body parts as trophies, including fetuses and the private parts of both men and women. Although there was an investigation into the massacre, no criminal charges were ever brought against either Chivington or any of his men.

Chivington is quoted as saying, "*Damn any man who sympathizes with Indians! ... I have come to kill Indians, and believe it is right and honorable to use any means under God's heaven to kill Indians. ... Kill and scalp all, big and little; nits make lice.*"

After our success at Apache Canyon, we were ambushed by a small group of steadfast Confederate calvary men who made a gallant charge against a much larger superior force. I drew my saber and ordered my regiment to attack. As we engaged the enemy a Confederate calvary man rammed his horse into *Chapawee*, knocking her down and me along with her.

As *Chapawee* fell my left foot got caught in the stirrup and as *Chapawee* landed I was trapped under momentarily. The weight and the force at which she fell had broken my tibia. As I lay there, the skirmish carried on all about me. At one point a Johnny Reb dismounted and had his sword at the ready, I had lost track of my saber during the fall but had the forethought to grab for my Colt and was able to get a shot off just as the scoundrel was going to attack a wounded man.

By the time Chivington and his men arrived the scuffle was over. It seemed that I was the only serious casualty of that incident. Since I couldn't ride *Chapawee*, who wasn't injured, I had to be transported to the field hospital by wagon with the men who sustained much more life-threatening injuries.

The journey to the hospital in Santa Fe took two days. During that time, we lost three men to their injuries. It was decided to bring them along with us and have them buried in Santa Fe instead out in the wild. When we arrived the field hospital staff was waiting for us. I was one of the first to be treated because they feared that if not treated immediately that my leg might become infected with gangrene and have to be amputated.

I was taken into an area of the hospital tent that they called surgery, placed upon a wooden table, and was told to take several deep breaths from a cloth cone with a sponge inside that was placed over my nose and mouth. I was later informed that the sponge had been soaked with chloroform. The last thing I remember before waking up in my cot was the doctor telling me to relax and try and breathe normally. Which I did and soon a cloud of blackness fell over me.

Hours later I woke up and with great trepidation, I slowly raised the blanket to see if they had indeed removed my leg. Thank God they didn't, I found my left leg was covered in a plaster cast.

Doctor Major Hanson and his orderly came into my tent that evening to see how I was doing and that's when I received Sarah's letter.

"So, how are you doing, Lieutenant?" Doctor Hanson asked.

"I have a raging headache and my leg is killing me, Doc."

"Here take these. They should help with the pain." He said as he handed me a glass of water and four pills.

"How's my leg?" I asked.

"You're lucky. Another day and we would have had to amputate."

"So, how soon before I will be up and around?"

"Hard to say. That was a nasty break you received. But for now, I need you to just lay back and rest. Let your body needs time to heal. Don't be foolish and try too soon or you'll only delay the healing, and you might do more damage and then we will have to amputate. Understand?"

"Loud and clear, Doc."

"Good. Now those pills should take effect in a couple of minutes. Get some rest and I'll check in on you tomorrow morning."

"Thanks, Doc."

The last thing I remember was him and the orderly walking away until he came around to check on me the next morning.

"Feeling better?" Hanson asked.

"Well, the headache is gone, the leg is throbbing, and I feel like I'm going to explode if I don't pee."

"Corporal Atwood, will you get the Lieutenant a bedpan. You did right not trying to get out of bed."

The corporal brought me a tin metal bedpan. It was oblong shaped with a short spout. The corporal assisted me by propping me up with extra pillows so I could achieve my mission. It felt so good, that I teared up.

"Lieutenant, after the corporal empties it, he will leave it by your bedside. And I suggest that you stay propped up, it will help in the healing."

"Thanks, Doc."

"Oh, I almost forgot. A Colonel Carson requested that he might be able to come by and see you. I said, yes. I hope that was all right?" The doctor asked.

"Colonel Carson wants to come by and see me? Did he say what it is in reference to?"

"I'm afraid he didn't."

"Did he say when?"

"Later today."

"Thank you."

"The nurses will be bringing breakfast shortly. I want you to eat everything. You need to build up your strength. That's an order."

"Aye, sir."

I spent the entire day watching the orderlies carrying the wounded in and carrying the dead out. It was after the lunch mess that Doctor Hanson came by to check on me. When he arrived, he frowned when he saw Queequeg laying at the foot of my bunk.

"I must say I don't approve of dogs in the ward."

"He's been by my side every day for over six years, Doc. He's no bother and he won't get in anybody's way. I promise."

"Well, all right. But if he disrupts the ward in any way, he'll have to leave."

"Fair enough."

"Now, how are you feeling, Lieutenant?"

"Much better, Doc."

"Excellent. Oh, I just got word that Colonel Carson will be stopping by within the hour."

"Thank you."

"Is there anything that I can get for you? The Chaplain, perhaps?"

"No, sir. I'm fine."

"Well, you let me know if there's anything that I can do."

"Thank you. You're very kind."

"Fine. I'll check in on you tomorrow."

As Doctor Hanson walked away he passed a familiar figure. A short squat bow-legged man headed towards me taking deliberate strides as if he was on a mission. He reached my bunk, looked me up and down, from stem to stern, smiled, and said laughing, "So, ya fell off your horse and broke your leg?"

"No. My horse fell on top of me and broke my leg. Doc says I was lucky, I coulda lost me leg."

He looked around at all the boys surrounding us with legs and arms missing, nodded, and muttered, "You were lucky, damn lucky, Lieutenant."

"What brings you by, sir?" I asked.

"Well, I have some good news and some not-so-good news," Carson announced.

"I'll take the bad news first. If you don't mind."

He looked somber, bowed his head, and whispered, "Unfortunately, it looks like you won't be shipping out with Colonel Chivington's 1st Colorado Calvary. I know how disappointed you must be."

I just looked at his sun-parched gravely face with his squinty eyes and feigned disappointment, "That is unfortunate, sir."

Laughing he said, "You're a lair, Lieutenant. You despised the man."

"Well, sir…" I stammered trying not to dig too big a hole for myself.

"I know you couldn't stand the man. Hell, you abhor me and my feeling towards the red savages. And God knows Chivington is ten times worse. Hell, If were up to him he'd love to slaughter every last Indian man, woman, and child. And yet the bastard recommended you for a field promotion for your leadership and unwavering courage in the face of the enemy. Congratulations, Captain." Carson said as he patted me on the shoulder and handed me my new Captain's shoulder boards.

I was stunned, speechless, I looked like I had been punched in the gut.

"I don't know what to say, sir," I said sheepishly.

"I've seen you in action, son. I would think that you deserve it, and although we don't agree on the issue and resolution of the Indians, you are a Hell of a soldier. Get well soon, Ishmael. We need you back in the fight."

"Thank you, sir."

"I talked to the Doc, and he says that you'll be out

of commission for at least four weeks, maybe longer. You just do what the Doc says. You'll have new orders waiting for you by the time you're released."

"Yes sir. Thank you for stopping by and personally telling me. It means a lot."

He shook my hand, and as he turned, he said, Fare thee well."

"And to you, sir. God speed."

My Darling,

I miss you terribly. I must tell you that I am writing this letter to you from a field hospital in Santa Fe, New Mexico. But I assure you that I am fine and have not been seriously injured. During a charge against the Greybacks, my horse Chapawee was knocked over and my foot was caught in the stirrups and the poor creature fell and landed atop my leg, breaking the tibia.

I was sent to the hospital in Santa Fe, where an excellent doctor fixed the break and soon I will be as good as new. So, there is no need to fear my darling. I am receiving exceptional care and soon will be up and around. Queequeg had been my bunk since I arrived, and I must say he has been a great comfort to me.

I did receive some good news today from Colonel Kit Carson. I have been awarded a field promotion to the rank of Captain. What is so ironic is that I was recommended for promotion by that zealot and xenophobe Colonel John Chivington. And another bit of good news is that I will not be assigned to him as he and his regiment have shipped out a week ago and by the time I will be released from the hospital I will finally be rid of him.

I was sorry to hear but not surprised about the death of Billy Malone. Please send my condolences to Mr. and Mrs. Darcey. It may sound callus my love but having been surrounded by so much death and misery on such a massive scale, although any man's death is still tragic, I can only hope that Billy that not suffer.

I miss you so and long to be in your arms again and feel your body close to mine. Stay safe my dear and I pray that this war will be over soon. I know that we will prevail for God is on our side.

Your loving husband,

I was released from the hospital six weeks after my surgery. Doctor Hanson came by to discharge me and to give me my new orders.

"Good day, Ishmael. How are you feeling today?"

"I'm feeling raring to go, Doc." I said with vigor.

"Good. Because I'm discharging you today. And here are your orders." Hanson said as he handed me an envelope with my name written on the outside.

"Thanks, Doc."

I tore open the envelope and read the orders for my next assignment. I was to be reassigned to the California Brigade. They were bivouacked about a mile outside of Santa Fe. I was to report to General Edward R. S. Canby and the regiment would march to Fort Craig, located along the El Camino Real de Tierra Adentro. Fort Craig was the largest fort in the Southwest, with over 2000 soldiers.

The scuttlebutt was that the fort was falling apart, there were leaky roofs, crumbling walls, chimneys, and it was overcrowded. However, despite all of its faults, the Confederates wanted no part in attacking. Due to the deception that was played upon them. On the forts, massive gravel bastons were "Quaker guns" (fake wooden cannons) with soldiers' caps alongside real cannons and real Union troops. The ruse worked, the Greybacks decided against a direct frontal attack on the too heavily fortified fort and retreated.

A couple of days later we did confront the Rebels at the Battle of Valverde. Both sides took heavy casualties, it had been the first time that I had to retreat from battle. I guess since the Confederates held the field of battle that they could lay claim to a victory. However, we still held Fort Craig.

Once again the Rebels left their rear flank unguarded, and we were able to attack and burn their supply wagons forcing them to march north towards Albuquerque without much-needed supplies.

We felt we had the Rebels on the run, they were retreating, and General Canby wanted them out of the New Mexico Territory for good. The word was that Sibley's Texas Mounted Volunteers were occupying Albuquerque as they were preparing to make their way back down to Texas.

Canby marched us up to Albuquerque from Fort Craig to ascertain the Rebel's strength. When we reached the edge of town he ordered the artillery to open fire, the barrage lasted for two days. On the third day, an old man who was a citizen of Albuquerque made his way to our camp and informed Canby that the Confederates wouldn't allow the civilians to seek shelter.

"The cowardly bastards! Using civilians as pawns. They are despicable and are anything other than gentlemen." Canby shared with the officer staff.

That night under the cover of darkness, Sibley and his Texas Volunteers snuck out of Albuquerque leaving behind his sick and wounded along with eight howitzer cannons that he had buried at the edge of town. With that, the Confederates had left the New Mexico Territory for good.

After making sure that the Confederates had left New Mexico Territory, we returned to Fort Craig. Once there the California Brigade received orders to return to California and continue to patrol the areas of the goldfields, mine included. They were telling us to go home and continue to do cursory and random scouting of the areas for any potential Confederate raids against the goldfields. We were going home at last.

LEE SURRENDERS: THE WAR IS OVER

The war is over! Lee and Grant met at Appomattox today and agreed to terms. Sad and tired, Lee signed a treaty that allowed the men on both sides to put down their guns. The years of bloodshed and tears are over for the North and the South, and the soldiers can return to their homes and families. Lee's men furled up the confederate flag for the last time. A horror that had lasted for more than four years has come to an end. At

4:00 P.M. Lee left Appomattox on his horse, "Traveler," and rejoined the remains of his once-mighty Army. He passed the blood-stained battlefields, sadly thinking of the friends he had lost during the war. The fighting was finished but the scars would never vanish.

A NEW BEGINNING

It was June 1864 when *Chapawee*, Queequeg, and I clip-clopped slowly down Hunter Street towards downtown Stockton. I was still wearing my dress blues uniform, several people that we passed gave us a wave and a few even cheered. There were a few southern sympathizers that booed or jeered. I did not let that bother me, for me the war was over, in the past. It was time for new beginnings.

As I passed through the center of town I spied Mr. Darcey walking with another man that I didn't recognize. As I approached, I hollered out, "Eugene."

He stopped and genuinely looked pleasantly surprised. He smiled as he asked, "Ishmael. Is that really you?"

"It is I. You're looking good." I said.

"Well, I must say you're looking a bit gaunt, old man. Are you all right?"

"War will do that to you," I answered as I dismounted.

I knew that I wasn't the man I was when I left. I had lost much weight and with my leg injury, I wasn't as strong as I once was. The war had even taken its toll on poor old *Chapawee* and Queequeg.

The gentleman he was walking with made his goodbyes and quickly left.

"I had heard that you had been wounded. Are you all right?" Darcey asked.

"Nothing too serious. I was more fortunate than most."

"Well, I see that you're now a captain. Are you planning on making the Army a career?"

"No. I've had enough of Army life. Oh, and I was sorry to hear about Billy."

"Yes, well, I always did have an uneasy feeling about poor old Billy."

"And how is Mrs. Darcey?" I inquired.

"She's well."

"I am glad to hear that. Well, Eugene, I must be going. I am anxious to see my misses. Good day to you. I will stop by in the next couple of days so that we can catch up on matters."

"I look forward to it. Good day."

I climbed up on *Chapawee* and we slowly meandered down Hunter Street till we reached Poplar Street, turned right, and rode six blocks to Elk Street, where I saw my darling Sarah standing out back hanging laundry on the washing line. I quietly rode up, hitched *Chapawee* to the hitching post, and Queequeg and I walked around to the back just as she turned around to go back into the house. That's when she saw me standing there, hat in hand.

"Ishmael! My love." She screamed as she ran to me arms outstretched.

We stood there embracing each other tight, kissing with long deep passionate affection. I then picked her up in my arms and carried her to our bedroom, where we engaged in amorous congress well into the evening.

As I had placed my captain's hat on the doorknob outside our bedroom the guests seemed to understand that we were not to be disturbed, that and the fact that Queequeg lay outside our bedroom door and would growl if anyone approached meant we were left undistracted. Afterward, we lay in each other's arms all night until the following morning when we made love again. And again.

When I finally arose I took a hot bath and put on the civilian clothes that I hadn't worn since before I joined the Army. I found that everything was too big and baggy. I looked at myself in the mirror and saw that I appeared to be a hobo. I decided to treat myself and travel into town and purchase a new set of clothes. Once I had done that, I would go and meet with J. R. Lazarus, my attorney, and then I would drop in on my partner Eugene Darcey and discuss the status and condition of the Devil Fish Mine are.

I saddled up old *Chapawee* and along with my trusty old friend Queequeg, we rode into town to Cowell & Howard Haberdashers located at 228 Main Street. I eased myself off *Chapawee*, tied her to the hitching post, and Queequeg and I opened the door and sauntered in.

"Good day, sir. How may I assist you?" A middle-aged fellow said as he approached me.

"Aye, as you can see, I'm in need of some new clothes. I just got back from the war, returning to civilian life only to find my old wardrobe doesn't fit me anymore."

"I must say you've come to the right place. What sort of things are you looking for, sir?"

"Well, I believe I will need a couple of suits, shirts, and some work clothes as well," I replied.

"Do you know your sizes, sir?" He asked.

"I'm afraid I don't"

"Very well, sir, may I take your measurements?"

When he was finished, he directed me to a rack of suits.

"Now, these are ready-made. Of course, we would

alter them as needed, or if you prefer we can most certainly make you a couple of suits that will be tailored made just for you.”

“I think I would prefer tailor-made.”

“Very good, sir.”

He then proceeded to show me different fabrics and styles. Having clothes made, which I had never done, turned out to be rather time-consuming. I did buy some premade clothes, so I wouldn’t walk around looking like a ragamuffin.

“If you could come back in three days, we will have something for you to try on for final alterations.”

“All right.”

“So, that will be two pure wool worsted dark navy-blue serge suits, four white dress cotton long-sleeve shirts, four pairs of work pants, and four work shirts. Now, let me see. The total will be fifty-four dollars.”

“Fifty-four dollars! My how the cost of things has gone up.” I said sounding shocked.

“I take it it’s been a while.”

“Four years in the war. I guess I just never had given it any thought. Oh, well. Here you are, my good man.” I said as I took sixty dollars from my pocket and handed it to the salesman.

“One moment, sir, let me get you your change.”

“No. That’s all right, keep the change. I appreciate all of your help.”

“Oh, that’s very generous of you, Mister?”

“Ishmael, just Ishmael.”

“Thank you again, Ishmael. We shall see you Thursday.”

“Good day to you,” I said.

“And a good day to you.”

"Come along Queequeg," I said as I opened the shop's door, and we took our leave.

I unhitched *Chapawee* and walked her the four blocks to J. R. Lazarus' office, my attorney.

I found her sitting at her desk busy working, not even looking up when she said, "Just have a seat, I'll be with you in a moment."

I sat down with Queequeg by my side. We were the only ones in the office. When she did look up it took her several seconds before it registered who I was. Then when she did recognize me. Her face lit up, she leaped up from behind her desk and hurried over to me and gave me a big hug.

"Ishmael, it is so good to see you. How are you?"

"I'm good."

"Let me take a look at you." She said as she backed up, giving me the once over from head to toe.

"Hmm. You've lost weight."

"Yeah, war will do that to you," I said.

"Are you all right?"

"Oh, yeah. I just have a minor injury. I broke my left leg when old *Chapawee*, my horse fell on top of me. But I'm all better now. Just a slight limp."

"Well, thank God you're safely home. How's Sarah?"

"She's fine. It is so good to be finally home."

"I can imagine. Was there something that I can do for you?"

"No. Not really. I just thought I'd stop by before heading over to meet with my partner Eugene Darcey. I was hoping that you might give me a head's up as to how the mine has been doing?"

"As far as I can ascertain he's been playing on the

up and up. Except for the death of his brother-in-law Billy Malone, there haven't been any irregularities."

"Well, that's a relief."

"If you find that anything is troubling you or suspicious, feel free to contact me and I'll see if there's anything I can do."

"Thank you, I will. It was good to see you again."

"And you, Ishmael. Please do give Sarah my best."

"I will. You have a good day."

"Bye."

"I'd like to see Mister Darcey," I said to one of the Wells Fargo bank tellers.

"Yes sir. And you are?"

"Tell him, Ishmael would like to see him. I believe he's expecting me."

"One moment, sir. I'll be right back." The young man said as he headed back to Darcey's office.

A few minutes later, Darcey's office door opened, and the young teller came out and approached me saying, "Mister Darcey will see you now."

I entered Darcey's office to find him sitting at his desk. He stood up, extended his hand, and gesturing said, "Ishmael, please have a seat."

I sat in an overstuffed leather wing chair opposite Darcey with Queequeg by my side.

"I think you're going to be rather pleased with the production and output of the Devil Fish Mine. I have developed a synopsis of the mine's profits as well as the totals for the expenditures. Over the four years that you have been away, we have seen a net profit of a quarter of a million dollars. Each. And I don't see any signs that there will be any slowdown. The vein seems to continue to go on forever." Darcey boasted as he handed me a copy of the prospectus.

I gave the document a cursory look over when I noticed a payout to Darcey in the amount of a thousand dollars a month for custodial administration fees.

"What's this?" I asked.

"Ah, that's my fee for overseeing the day-to-day operations of the mine."

"How long have you been collecting this fee?" I inquired.

"Ever since you left. Do you have a problem with that?" He answered with a tone.

"That's almost fifty thousand dollars."

"Well, now that you're back, how would you like to take over these duties?"

"Don't take offense. I'm thinking of putting my half share up for sale."

Darcey's ears perked up and he got a wolfish grin on his face.

"Really? You'd be willing to sell?"

"I'm thinking about it."

"For how much?"

"I'd like to go up to the mine and look things over. I'll let you know in the next two weeks."

"Very good." He said smiling.

"Do you think you'll want to buy it outright or get some investors?" I asked.

"That will depend."

"Of course."

I stood to leave when I remembered to ask, "Say, how would I contact Mister Charles Sutton? He's my stockbroker. I'm interested in finding out how my stock portfolio is doing over these past four years."

"Is Mister Sutton here in Stockton?"

"No. He's located in San Francisco."

"Well, if you not planning a trip to San Francisco, I would recommend sending him a telegraph. The telegraph office is located on the corner of Washington Street and Centre Street."

"Much obliged. We'll talk later, Eugene. Come on Queequeg."

On our way to the telegraph office, I marveled at the progress that Stockton had made since the last time I was here. Especially the downtown area. All the new businesses and shops. Stockton was becoming a vibrant city that had grown from the small town I first visited five years ago.

"Welcome to Western Union. May I help you, sir?"

"Yes, I'd like to send a telegraph to Mister Charles Sutton, San Francisco."

"All right. Go ahead." The operator said.

"PLANNING TO BE IN SAN FRANCISCO IN THE NEXT COUPLE OF WEEKS. STOP. WILL CONTACT YOU UPON ARRIVAL. STOP. NEED TO DISCUSS FINANCIAL MATTERS. STOP. ISHMAEL."

"That will be one dollar and twenty-five cents." The operator said, holding out his hand.

"How soon will it get there?" I asked.

"I'll send it out this afternoon. He should receive it tomorrow morning."

"Very good. Good day."

My next stop was back home to discuss my day with Sarah. She was waiting on the front porch, sitting on the front porch swing, gently rocking to and fro. She smiled big when she saw the three of us sauntering down the street. Old Queequeg loping out in front, tongue hanging out off to one side, he began to bark excitedly when he spotted Sarah. She got off the porch and was greeted by the old hound with dozens of sloppy kisses. By the time Queequeg was through welcoming Sarah, I had tied off *Chapawee* to the hitching post and was greeted with several kisses myself.

"So, how was your day?" She asked with a big grin on her face.

"It was good," I said as we walked by the front porch.

"Let's sit here on the swing and tell me all about it."

"Well, after stopping off at Cowell & Howard Haberdashers to get outfitted with some proper fitting clothes. I then went to see our attorney just to let her know that I was back. It was good to see her again. She said that everything that she's seen from Darcey seems to be on the up and up.

I then went to see Darcey have him give me a copy of the last four years of the Devil Fish Mine's earning statements, which I will drop off with J.R. tomorrow morning. I mentioned that I might be thinking of selling my mine shares and asked if you might be interested in buying me out."

"Really. You'd sell your half of the mine? Why?"

"Hmm, you see Sarah, ever since my whaling days, I've had this desire, this need for doing something new. Something with an air of danger. Since that day that I was rescued out at sea, everything I have done has been living life on the edge."

"Ishmael, don't you think it's time to settle down? Maybe start a family?" Sarah asked.

As I looked deep into her eyes, I could see the answer that she yearned for. And I said what I knew she wanted to hear. And yet I knew down in the roots of my soul, as hard as I would try, someday I would be gone. So, I lied and said, "My darling love, I will stay. My wandering days are over."

For the next couple of days, I spent all of my time doing the repairs around the house that four years of neglect by being off to war can accumulate. I stopped by Darcey and let him know that I would not be divesting myself of my half of the Devil Fish Gold Mine. He seemed genuinely disappointed. After about a week, I did travel up to the mine and inspected the mine. I was surprised to see that at least a dozen men worked the mine.

I went to meet with Bob Grant and Jason Collins to get a sense of their assessment of the mine is. As I approached them, at first, they didn't recognize me.

After all, it had been over four years.

"Can I help ya, Mister?" Bob said with his hand resting on the handle of his Colt revolver. Jason was standing a couple of feet behind with his weapon at the ready.

"Bob. Jason. It's me, Ishmael." I said, holding my hands away from my body so as not to be threatening.

It took a moment before it finally sunk in, then a big smile drew across both their faces.

"Ishmael! Well, I'll be damned." Grant exclaimed.

"My God! We didn't recognize you. You're so thin." Jason replied.

"How have you been?" Grant asked.

"I'm good. Still a little weary from the war. But, I must say you two haven't changed much. How have you both been?" I queried.

"Oh, Hell, we're doing great. The mine is showing no sign of drying out. In fact, we got men working round the clock. Mister Darcey leaves us alone ever since we had to shoot Billy Malone."

"Yeah, I heard about that. What the Hell happened, anyway?"

Jason looked at Grant and began, "It was well over two years ago; the three of us were sitting around the campfire drinking after a tough day. We had discovered another vein going off to the left, which meant that we would be going off into two different directions."

Bob Grant picked the story up, "Billy was drinking pretty hard and began complaining that he didn't think he was getting his fair share, especially now that the mine looked to be striking paydirt. I told him it tweren't up to us as to who gets what. But I said that since the mine looked to start producing more, you and Darcey would likely be prepared to give us a larger share in the profits."

"That's when he got surly and accused us of trying to cheat him. He said that we were all owners, and he wanted to be an owner too. He said that he deserved to be a part-owner as much as Bob and me because he did as much or more of the work. Which, of course, wasn't true. He did as little as possible. He'd be off, who knows where for hours at a time." Jason recalled.

"That's when he drew his Colt and threatened to kill us both if we didn't agree that he should become a partner," Bob said.

"Bob tried to talk some sense into him. The more Bob tried, the angrier Billy got until finally, Billy took a shot at Bob. Billy was too drunk to hit Bob, but we couldn't stand there and let Billy continue to take potshots at us. That's when Bob and I drew our firearms and kilted him dead." Jason sadly said.

"You boys did the right thing. Who knows, he might have shot you while you slept. So, what did Darcey say when you told him of the news?"

"Honestly, he was more interested in discovering a new vein than the death of his kinfolk."

"Hmm, that doesn't surprise me," I replied.

"Care to inspect the mine, Ishmael?" Bob offered.

"Sure."

As we approached the entrance, cool air smelling of dirt, kerosine, and human sweat wafted up from deep within the mine shaft. The further we descended, the warmer the temperature and the harder it was to breathe. The men working deep underground were all shirtless. If it weren't for the multitude of kerosine lamps, the world would be awash in blackness. The mine shaft was a good twelve feet high and nearly twenty feet wide. Giant wooden timbers held up the ceiling, and running down the middle of the ground was a small gauge iron rail that dozens of minecarts used to haul the dirt and gold from down in the mine to the surface ran all day and night.

We had gone down just to where the mine split off into two different directions when a large Polish miner named Miloš Brzezinski, one of the foremen, began herding a group of miners out of the mine shaft. "Everyone out! Fire in the hole!" Brzezinski screamed.

Everyone working in the mine scrambled up towards the light of the entrance. Just as we all scampered and made it out, there came a muffled rumble from down in the earth's bowels, followed by a belch of a thick black cloud of dirt and ebony raven dust billowing out of the mouth of the mine.

KA-BOOOOOM

It left a thick blanket of dreck, clay, and loam at least two inches thick over a quarter of a mile when it settled. We were also covered from head to toe in dirt and glebe. Twenty-eight men were standing in black faces looking like something out of Haverly's United Mastodon Minstrel Show.

"How often does that happen?" I asked Bob Grant.

"Oh, once or twice a day." He said nonchalantly.

"I'm going down to the creek and wash this muck off," I said as I walked *Chapawee* down into the valley.

I tied her off to a small pine tree. Luckily, I had brought a change of clothes that I had stuffed in my saddlebags. I stripped down to my nothingness and waded into the icy cold water, trying my best to get the black dirt and dust that had covered every inch of me off. I used the small gravel on the creek bottom to scour the grime off.

When I returned to the mining camp, they were carrying out the body of a miner who got crushed and killed while he and some others were trying to shore up the load-bearing timbers when there was a partial collapse of the ceiling.

"That's the second man this week," Grant muttered.

"How many men do you lose in a week?" I asked.

"Depends. On average, one or two. But for everyone who dies, there are four or five ready to take their place."

"How can that be?" I asked.

"It's because we pay top dollar. Men are willing to risk their lives for a decent wage. We pay more than the other mine owners, so we get the best workers." Grant replied.

"What happens to the men who die?"

"Well, we contact the paper and list their names; if'n no one comes to claim them in a couple of weeks, we just bury them over yonder," Grant said, pointing over to a makeshift boot hill.

There looked to be a half dozen gravesites with makeshift crosses stuck at the head of the graves.

"Are ya planning to stay the night? We have room in our tent if you'd like to stay." Jason asked.

"No, thanks. I think I'll start heading back to Stockton. I want to meet with Mister Darcey. You boys are doing a great job." I said as I shook each of their hands.

As I was riding off, I heard Brzezinski scream, "Fire in the hole!" And seconds later…*KA-BOOM.*

The look on Sutton's face was one of shock. He sprang to his feet when he saw me with Queequeg by my side. I was dressed in one of the new suits I had just purchased. I looked quite the city slicker with the exception of my holster and Colt strapped to my leg.

He began to stammer, searching for my name, "Ah. Ah. Ah."

"Ishmael," I said.

"Right. Ishmael. How are you? It's been what five years?"

"Six."

"Six years? My, my, how time goes by so fast. What can I do for you?" Sutton asked nervously.

"I came about my money."

"Of course. Please have a seat, and I'll get your file."

I took a seat across from Sutton's desk in a plush leather chair. As he was riffling through his file cabinet has asked, "So, how have you been?"

"I've been good."

"And what have you been up to lo these many years?"

"Well, I got married, and I've just returned from fighting in the war for the past four years, and before that, I founded a rather successful gold mine."

Sutton stopped looking in his filing cabinet, turned around, smiled, and asked, "Are you all right? I mean, were you wounded?"

"A couple of minor wounds, nothing serious."

"Thank God. And that's wonderful news about the mine." He said as he pulled my file out from the drawer. He carried it over to his desk. It appeared to be a relatively thick folder. He slowly opened it and read over the first couple of pages.

"I would have kept you abreast of your investments over these past six years, but I never received any address for you."

"Well, except for these last few months, I haven't had a steady address," I confessed.

"I understand. So, Ishmael, I am happy to report that your initial investment of four thousand dollars has grown to over one hundred and sixty-eight thousand dollars in the six years. With the majority of the profits coming from investments that I placed in the war market. War is good for business, sad to say. I hope you're pleased."

"Very. I must say that I was unsure what I would find, but Mister Sutton, I want to thank you. And apologize for doubting you six years ago." I admitted.

"That's quite all right," Sutton said with a smile.

"Well, we'll be off."

"What do you want to do with your earnings, Ishmael?"

"I will leave them with you, Mister Sutton. I believe that you will continue to treat them as your own as you have done these past six years. Good day." I said as Queequeg and I departed.

"And a good day to you, sir."

I met Sarah back at the Occidental Hotel on Montgomery Street between Bush and Sutter, close to Chinatown and Union Square.

The hotel was first-class, nothing that I had ever experienced before. The bedroom was spacious, the brass bed was soft and large, our own bathroom with hot and cold water; the dining room, or as Sarah called it, the *salle-a-manger,* was overly elaborate embellished with columns and a fella who played piano during meals.

One night after Sarah had retired for the evening, I decided to go down to the bar for a cigar and a drink. It was then that I met a most interesting gentleman. He was a funny-looking character. He wore an all-white three-piece suit, shaggy white hair, and a sizeable wooly mustache. I liked him right off. He introduced himself as Samuel Clemens, but later that evening, he suggested that I might know him as Mark Twain, the writer.

"And you are?" He asked.

"Ishmael."

"Ishmael, very Biblical. I am here in San Francisco promoting my book. Perhaps you may have read it, *The Innocents Abroad.*" He asked, holding up a hard-bound book.

"I can't say that I have. I bet ya that my Sarah has, however. She's quite the reader. She reads a couple of books a week."

He looked slightly disappointed and rejected before I said, "Might I purchase that one. I would appreciate it if you would sign it."

"Oh, that's very kind of you, Ishmael. Who shall I make it out to?"

"Sarah."

As he signed the book, he spoke what he inscribed, "To Sarah, Best Wishes. Mark Twain."

As I gave him four dollars, I said, "Thank you, Mister Twin. Sarah will be so thrilled."

"And what pray tell is your vocation?" He queried.

"Me? Well, I've been a whaler, a pirate, a prospector, and most recently, a Captain in the Union Army in the war."

"Hmmm, interesting. Ishmael, you seem to be a man of many talents. What do you do these days?"

"I am currently weighing my options."

"I take it then that you are a man of means?"

"I have been quite fortunate. The gold mine that I founded has proved to be quite profitable."

"How fortuitous for such a young man as yourself. Might I have heard of this mine?"

"I named it the Devil Fish Mine."

"What unusual name. How did you come to name it that?"

I proceeded to tell him of those fateful days on board the *Pequod*, of Captain Ahab, and the deadly encounter with Moby Dick. He listened with rapture to my tale of one man's obsession that ultimately begot the death of every soul on board that ship, nay one.

Samuel Clemens sat in silence for what seemed to be ages before speaking, "My God. Do people know of this story?”

“I would image just a handful might. I believe that most find it too fanciful and outrageous; they call me a liar to my face, as many have done. That is why I rarely speak of those days. They are quite painful.”

“I can fully understand that. Can I buy you another drink, Ishmael?” Clemens asked.

I looked at my pocket watch; it read twenty to two.

“No, thank you. That’s very kind of you, but it’s late, and Sarah and I will be off early tomorrow.”

“Well, Ishmael, I can’t tell how nice it was to meet you. I wish you all the best in your future endeavors.”

“I thank you again for the book, Mister Clemens. Er, Mister Twain, I mean. I’m sure Sarah will thoroughly enjoy it. And I will give it a read myself.”

“Goodnight, and goodbye,” Clemens said, hoisting his glass of whiskey in the air.

I reciprocated with a tip of my hat and a wink of the eye.

THE DEVIL FISH RANCH

Sarah and I decided to try our hand at cattle ranching on our return from San Francisco. I again called upon my whaling past to name and design our brand and called it The Devil Fish Ranch.

Later that month, we purchased a 30,000-acre ranch just thirteen miles east of Stockton. I bought two-thousand head of Hereford beef cattle, 65 bulls, and forty horses. Before the stock arrived, we hired ten ranch hands, two horse wranglers, a cook, and the ranch foreman. Buck Sawyer, the ranch foreman, oversaw the hiring of the ranch hands, horse wranglers, and the cook.

The first thing we did before the cattle arrived was to build the handling facility. We had half the ranch hands build the holding and sorting pens so we could start the branding of the stock. The other half were building the bunkhouse, barn, and the main folk house. While the buildings were being worked on at the ranch, Buck had hired several men to ride the ranch perimeter and install a cactus brand type barb-wire fence surrounding all 30,000-acres.

It took two weeks for the holding and sorting pens to be completed. When they were finished with the pens, those men jumped onto the finishing of the barn, bunk, Sarah's, and my folk house. Our house had a long wraparound porch, Queen Anne posts, and a railing. When you walked in, the front of the house served as a formal area, and there was a large kitchen and dining room with two bedrooms housed in the back. Unlike Sarah's boarding house, this house had no second floor. The siding was overlapping clapboard to help keep the wind and rain out. The house was painted white with black shutters and had a tin roof, making it noisy during rainstorms.

The barn was the traditional two-story structure, painted red. The bunkhouse was a single-story all-wood building with windows on all sides; it too was painted white with a tin roof. I had a spit-rail fence surrounding the entryway of the ranch with an eighteen-foot ranch gate with the Devil Fish Ranch spelled out on top with the devil fish brand hanging below the gate entrance. I left the decorating of the folk house completely to Sarah while I worked with Buck and the boys on the roping and branding of the herd.

The days were long, and the work was hard. Every three days, a couple of the boys and I would ride the ranch's perimeter to check the barb wire fencing. One day we came across several warriors from the *Sierra Miwok* tribe watching the herd from a hilltop. They had a couple of Indian ponies they were toting. I could see that they looked hungry.

Buck and two of our ranch hands, Josh Randall and Clint Cassidy, were with me.

The *Miwok* warriors were dressed in loincloths woven from grass with shirts made from deerskin. They were wearing one-piece moccasins with long tops that were wrapped around the calf. About their heads, they wore a crown-style headdress made of flicker quill that covered their forehead and was tied in the back. What I found most striking was they wore black and white horizontal striped face and body paint similar to the Mojave tribes that I saw in Arizona during the Civil War.

"Buck, I think I'd like to go and parley with them," I said.

"Parley?"

"Yeah, I'm thinking maybe we can trade them a couple of head of our cattle for a couple of those ponies."

"Why don't you just let me, and the boys run them outta here. Maybe shoot one or two of them."

"Shoot them? For what? They're not doing anything wrong."

"Yeah, but they might." He countered.

"So, you want to kill them for something they *might* do?"

He didn't reply; he just looked embarrassed.

"Look, why create hostilities when we can settle this peacefully. If we run them off, they'll just come back when we've left, steal several heads, and tear down the fencing. This way, they get something, and maybe next time, they'll come directly to me to trade. Come on." I said.

"You're crazy, boss." Buck barked.

I tied a white bandana onto the end of my Winchester rifle and slowly rode out towards the Indians with Buck and Josh, and Clint behind me, driving three head of cattle with us. Once the leader of the warriors saw that we looked non-threatening, he and his men rode towards us. Both groups stopped about fifty feet apart.

"You boys stay here," I ordered as I approached the group. The injun leader did the same.

I held up my right hand in a gesture of non-aggression and smiled. My counterpart held up his hand as well, but there was no smile.

"Trade?" I asked.

He looked at my men with the cattle and me. Then he looked back to his men. They had us outnumbered two to one. I could see that he wondered if this was some sort of treachery.

"Trade?" He replied.

"What can you trade me for the cattle?" I asked.

He turned to his men and said something to one of his men, who proceeded to bring a couple of Indian ponies to where the leader stood and handed him the reins.

"Trade." He said.

I smiled, nodded, and said, "Trade."

I turned and signaled to Buck for them to bring the cattle forward. As they drove the cattle towards us, I tapped myself on the chest and said, "Ishmael."

The Indian leader did the same, saying, "*Ča-ta-ta.*"

As the three head of cattle were brought forth, he reached out and handed me the reins to the Indian ponies. Once the cattle were turned over, his men began to drive them off to their village. As they were about to crest a hill, he turned to me and raised his hand as to say goodbye. I returned the gesture.

As I handed Buck the reins to the ponies, he snarked, "These ponies ain't worth one of them cows."

"I know. But I got a feeling that they won't be going stealing any cattle when they know that they can come trade hassle-free and get what they need." I replied.

"I'll say it again. Boss, you are crazy." Buck guffawed.

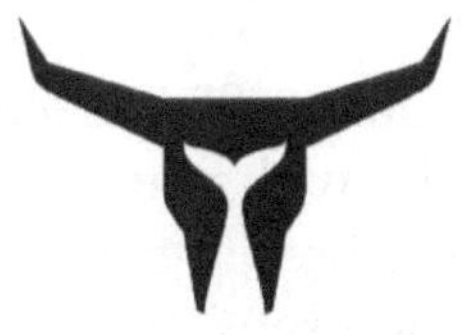

After the initial excitement of building and setting up the ranch, hiring the men, and settling the herd, life soon fell into a routine. Move the pack into different pastures, inspect the barb wire fencing around the perimeter, taking care of the bills, and do the general maintenance of the ranch.

It was getting close to when we were preparing to drive part of the herd to market when Sarah announced that she was expecting. What joyous news. I would never have thought that such a thing would be possible. Of all the extraordinary things that have happened in my life, this is the most amazing.

When Sarah was about six months into her pregnancy, we went into town to see Doctor Hamilton for a routine checkup. I sat in the waiting room with several other expecting couples who seemed considerably younger.

Eventually, Doctor Hamilton's nurse came out into the waiting room and said that the doctor would like to see me. I followed the nurse into the doctor's office, where I found Sarah in tears.

"Please, have a seat." The doctor said as I entered.

"What's wrong?" I asked, taking Sarah's hand.

Doctor Hamilton sat at his desk, hands crossed, and solemnly spoke, "Ishmael, due to Sarah's age, being that she's almost forty, there's a strong possibility that there may be complications at birth. That's not to say that there will be any. I am just alerting you that there could be problems."

"What kind of problems?" I asked.

"Well, I discussed it with your wife. It's not unusual for the possibility of a breech birth, where the baby is facing feet first or sideways, causing the labor to be much longer, which increases the danger.

There is such a thing as Child-bed Fever, which is a form of infection. And there is always the rare case of not being able to stop bleeding.

Now, I'm not saying that any of these *will* happen; I just thought it was my duty to inform you of these potential issues because of Sarah's age we have to be aware of and prepared for." Hamilton explained.

"Is there anything we can do?" I asked.

"Yes, Sarah should just try and take it as easy as much as possible. She should not do anything physically exhausting, and she should try and get as much bed rest as she can."

"I will make sure that she does," I said.

"Good."

"Is there anything else?"

"No. And for your next checkup, Sarah, I will come out to see you, so you won't have to make a trip to see me."

"Thank you, Doctor Hamilton," I said.

The ride home was quite emotional. Sarah was tearful most of the way home. I tried to comfort her best I could. I told her that I would go into town and see about hiring a maid and a cook to take the burden off of her. All she has to do is concentrate on getting plenty of rest and taking care of herself. Once we arrived home, I put her to bed, and she fell right to sleep.

The next day I rode back into town and hired a maid and a domestic cook to lift the burden off of my Sarah. With three months to go before she was scheduled to deliver, her mood was melancholy, although she was getting plenty of rest. All Doctor Hamilton could offer was to try and be as supportive as I could.

I telegraphed Jane Rogers, Sarah's spinster sister, in Sullivan, a small town outside of St. Louis, Missouri. Asked if at all possible to come and be with her sister. Sarah was the local schoolmarm and agreed to come to Stockton to stay with her sister. I insisted that I pay her fare for a first-class Pullman sleeper car on the Western Pacific Railroad. She would arrive in three days.

"Ishmael?" Asked a woman who looked nothing like Sarah, her younger sister.

Jane Rogers was tall and thin, with fire-red hair, alabaster skin like Sarah, and pale robin's egg blue eyes. She was dressed in a blue and white sailor striped cotton walking dress with a low square neckline. Her hair was dressed high in the back with complicated rolls that fell to her shoulders, adorned with blue ribbons. She wore a small navy-blue hat tilted forward to her forehead. I found her to look very fetching.

"Jane, it was so good of you to come," I said.

"How could I not? How is Sarah?" She queried.

"She is of low spirits."

"Well, have to see about that. Won't we?"

I took her two bags, put them in the back of the buckboard, helped her up onto the seat, snapped the reins, and we were off for the three-hour ride from Stockton to the Devil Fish Ranch. Along the way, we spotted several small herds of black-tailed deer, a coyote, and three grey foxes. Sarah commented that back in Missouri, she hadn't seen any such wildlife in many a year.

The weather was ideal; the conversation was stimulating, making the ride rather enjoyable. We were about three miles from the ranch when Jane spied a small band of Indians heading toward us.

"Oh my God. Indians!" She screamed.

I saw that they were the same band of Indians that I had encountered months ago when I traded cattle for ponies.

"Do not fear. I know these Indians. They do not mean us harm." I said, trying to reassure her.

"We are going to die! They will kill you and rape me!" She quivered.

"We are not."

As the band approached, I stopped the wagon, stood, held my hand up as a sign of friendship, and said, "*Yawa*."

"What did he say?" Jane asked nervously.

"It's hello in *Miwok*," I explained.

The leader of the warrior band was *Ča-ta-ta*, the person I had traded with months ago. He raised his hand, smiled, and greeted me, "*Yawa*."

As they slowly circled the wagon looking at what we had in the wagon and at Jane, I noticed that they had a string of six ponies that they were pulling.

"Trade," *Ča-ta-ta* said.

I nodded and said, "Trade."

I sat down on the buckboard seat, slapped the reins, and waved my hand to indicate for them to follow, which they did.

"What do they want to trade for?" Jane asked.

"Cattle. I let them trade ponies for cattle."

"Is that a fair trade?"

"Not really. But I feel that it's the Christian thing to do. After everything we've done and taken from these people."

Jane smiled and just nodded her approval. When we reached the ranch, Buck and a couple of the other hands rose out to meet us.

"Oh, I see you've brought along them prairie niggers. What do they want now?" Buck snickered.

"Buck, watch your language! There's a lady present, and even if there wasn't, I don't like that kind of talk. You got that!" I shot back.

"Yes, boss. Sorry, Ma'am." Buck muttered.

"You boys take those ponies and bring back six head of cattle."

"You heard the boss!" Buck snapped.

They took the ponies from the Miwok and drove six head of cattle back out to the Indians. Jane and I waited until the trade was completed.

Ča-ta-ta sidled up to me sitting in the wagon, held out his hand, which I accepted, and said, *"Mi' we`:lu:ṭakmu."* Which I took to mean thank you.

They then left, driving the six head of cattle back from where they came. Buck took his hat off and said, "Sorry about what I said, boss. But I still think you're crazy. Them injuns are taking advantage of you."

"Maybe. But it's better than them stealing cows." I said.

After all of the excitement, we continued on to the main house. Queequeg barked as we approached, his tail was wagging, and he ran around the yard as if I had been gone for days instead of hours. When Jane stepped off the buckboard Queequeg started to jump on her.

"Queequeg! Down. Sit." I snapped.

Queequeg did as he was ordered. He sat reluctantly looking at me as if he'd been punished.

"Jane, this is Queequeg. You'll have to excuse his enthusiasm." I said.

"No. He's fine." She said as she knelt down next to the old hound and began to shower him with affection. Queequeg proceeded to lay on his side and raise his back leg inviting her to rub his stomach, which she did until I took her luggage out from the buckboard.

"Let's go see, Sarah," I said.

"Jane! Oh, it is so good to see you." Sarah cried as she held out her arms. Jane rushed to her and hugged her. She sat at her bedside.

"How are you feeling, dear sister?" Jane asked.

"I'm good. Just feel tired all the time. And with Ishmael working during the day. Plus, there are times he has to be gone for days at a time, I get so lonely being bound to this bed."

"Well, I'm here now. We have a lot of catching up to do."

"Dear sister, it's been too long. I can't tell you how much it means to me that you are here."

After I placed Jane's luggage in the spare bedroom, I came back to find Queequeg sitting by Sarah's bed with his head laying on Jane's lap.

"If'n he becomes a bother, just tell him to go lay down," I said.

"He's fine, really."

I walked over, leaned down, gave Sarah a kiss, and said, "Well, I'll let you two catch up. Gotta see what's going on with Buck and the boys."

When I went back outside, the buckboard had been put back into the barn. *Chapawee* had been saddled, Buck, Gus McCall, Jed Cartwright, and Cody Walker were waiting, mounted. They even had Bill "Cookie" Winter there with the chuckwagon.

"What's up?" I asked.

"We've got some cattle down in the south field," Buck announced.

"Jed. Ride into town and get Doc. Hebert, the Vet. And bring him out here right away," I shouted.

"Right boss," Jed said as he sprinted off into town.

"Okay, Buck lead the way," I said.

When we reached the south field, there was nine head of cattle lying down separate from the main herd. We dismounted and tried to get the cattle back up on their feet. But no go.

I had the men drive the main herd away from the down cattle, but not too far in case Doc. Hebert needed to examine them. We sat out there around the chuckwagon drinking cups of coffee, strong, scalding hot, and barefooted (black). Buck named it dehorned bellywash, but I liked what Gus called it, brown gargle.

Eventually, Doc. Hebert and Jed come riding up. The Doc climbs out of his buggy with his little black bag. I met him on his way to check out the livestock.

"Hey, Doc. Thanks for coming out," I greeted.

"Howdy, Ishmael. Is this all of them?" He asked.

"As far as we know. I've had a couple of the boys go and check the other herds," I replied.

Hebert got down on his hands and knees and began to examine the downed cows. After a few minutes, he came over to me and Buck and announced, "Looks like you have a case of Leptospirosis."

"What the Hell is that and is it infectious to the others?" I asked.

"It is infectious. You should keep them segregated from the others. These I can treat with antibiotics," Hebert said.

I had him go and examine random cattle for the main herd. Luckily, he didn't find any evidence that the infection had spread.

"So, Doc. How did they get infected?" I asked.

"Leptospirosis is caused by bacteria. If I were you, I would move the herd to another pasture and burn this field down to the ground. Once the bacteria is killed off the new growth should be free of them."

"Okay, thanks, Doc."

I had Jed escort the good Doctor back into town while me and the boys moved this herd up to the north field to join the main herd. Buck stayed behind and burnt the south field like Doc. Hebert suggested. You could see the black smoke for miles around filling the air. It reminded me back to my days of pirating when we would set ships ablaze that we had conquered. Argh, they were good times.

Jane was still sitting with Sarah when I returned later that night. Jane was reading the book that Samuel Clemens had given me in San Francisco, *The Innocents Abroad*.

"How is she?" I whispered.

"She says she's fine. But I know she's scared," Jane uttered softly.

"I know and so am I."

"Isn't there anything we can do?"

"Not really. Doctor Hamilton said that what she needs is plenty of bed rest and just to take it easy."

"I feel so helpless."

"Me too. But the doctor says it's only another five or six weeks. Jane, I really appreciate your being here. I know she's glad to have you here by her side."

"Well, now that you're back, I think I'll retire for the night. It's been quite a day," Jane said.

"I'm sorry about the incident with the *Miwok* warriors. They are a peaceful people who have been pushed around, taken advantage of, and persecuted just for being Indians. All of this used to be their lands, until the white settlers drove them off onto the reservations. Oh, I'm sorry to go off on a rant. Let me know if there is anything that you need. Good night," I said.

"That's quite all right. Good night, Ishmael," She said with a grin.

I closed the bedroom door and got out of my work clothes and into my night-shirt then slipped into bed, turning down the kerosene lamp to a hint of a glowing ember. It seemed like I dropped off to sleep as soon as my head hit the pillow. The next thing I know the roosters are crowing and I am finally brought around to consciousness by the aroma of eggs, bacon, coffee, and fresh-baked biscuits.

I gave Sarah a wake-up kiss before getting dressed and heading downstairs.

"Mmmm, good morning, my love," Sarah said as she put her arms around my neck.

"Good morning, dear. How did you sleep?" I asked.

"Wonderful. It's so nice to have Jane here. Thank you," She said.

"For what?" I feigned.

"For bring Jane here, silly."

"I'm glad she's here, too."

"Oh!"

"What is there something wrong?"

"Quick give me your hand," She said as she placed my hand on her stomach.

"There. Did you feel him kicking?"

"I did. I had never felt anything so amazing in all my life. Frisky little rascal," I said grinning from ear to ear.

"He going to take after his father," Sarah said with a smile.

"We really haven't talked about names. Any thoughts?" I asked.

"Jonah, if it's a boy. And Esther after my mother if it's a girl."

"Jonah. I like it. Esther, I like, too," I said as I kissed her.

There was a soft knock on the door. "It's me, Jane. May I come in?"

"Of course," Sarah answered.

"Good morning. I brought a breakfast tray for Sarah," She brightly said.

"Oh, that's so sweet of you," Sarah replied smiling.

"That cook, Gretchen is preparing yours now,

Ishmael. She said that you should come down and eat before it gets cold," Jane exclaimed.

"Yeah, Gretchen, she one tough old bird, but don't be too hard on her she's had a rough life. Besides she's one Hell of a cook. Well, I better get down there before I get scolded. I shouldn't be too long today. Love you," I said as I headed downstairs.

"Good morning, Gretchen."

"*Ya, Ya, guten morgen*," Frau Schmidt answered indifferently with her back to me as I entered the dining room. I sat down to a plate of four slices of bacon, three eggs, over easy, and two biscuits smothered in gravy.

"Gretchen, this looks wonderful."

"*Ya, Ya, wunderbar.*"

Gretchen Müller was a sixty-four-year-old German immigrant whose family left Düsseldorf in 1816 when she was ten years old due to the upheaval of the Industrial Revolution that was sweeping through the country. They originally moved to the Midwestern "German triangle," which was between Missouri, Ohio, and Wisconsin. They settled in Milwaukee.

When Gretchen Müller was 21 she married a young tavern owner, Hans Schmidt. Hans and his two brothers, Ernst and Otto owned the very successful Hofbräuhaus. Life was good for them in Milwaukee. The business was good, they purchased a modest home, and they were blessed with three children. They were happy and believed that they would spend the rest of their lives in Milwaukee. Until a series of three tragedies occurred.

In 1847, a Cholera pandemic ran rampant throughout the Midwest. Thousands died, including Gretchen and Hans three young children all died within hours of each other. Gretchen and Hans were gutted. Gretchen walked around like a zombie. She was unresponsive, she didn't get out of bed for days on end, she didn't eat, and she stayed inside their house never venturing out. It was almost three years before she slowly came back to life. All the time Hans stayed steadfast and stood by her side.

In 1850 the second of three tragedies happened, late one evening during a terrible storm, lightning struck the Hofbräuhaus causing a fire that burnt the tavern down to the ground. Ernst and Otto decided that they would rebuild; Hans and Gretchen decided that he would go out to California and try their hand at gold mining.

They sold their house and belongings and bought two first-class tickets on the Western Pacific Railroad to San Francisco. The trip would take four days. At first, Gretchen was sad about leaving their family and friends behind. But after the first day, she began to get excited about the new chapter of their lives. The next three days were like the honeymoon that they had never had. The other passengers seldom saw them during the trip. They stayed hours on end making love in their Pullman compartment, coming out only for meals.

Once they arrived at the Mission Depot in the heart of San Francisco, they took a carriage to the Niantic Hotel. The Niantic Hotel was the most talked-about in San Francisco at the time. The Niantic was an actual ship built in Connecticut in 1832 and was used in whaling. It brought a load of 248 passengers from Panama to San Francisco in 1849. After that, it was abandoned by crew and passengers alike, all heading out to the goldfields. It was eventually sold and converted into a hotel.

Soon Hans had purchased a horse, wagon, supplies, tools, and camping gear that they would need to make their way northeast to begin their quest. The one thing that Hans didn't think to buy was a gun for protection.

On the fifth day, they were camping on the Bear River about thirty miles north of Sacramento when three men rode into their campsite. The leader was a man called Walter Hitchcock, who on his wanted for murder poster was described as shifty-eyed with a prominent nose. The other two men were C. J. "Black Bart" Bolton, and Joaquin Salinas, are both wanted for murder, robbery, and rape.

Hans was tending to the campfire while Gretchen was cooking a pot full of beans and hardtack when the three desperados rode upon him. Hans stood to greet them, "*Hallo.*"

Walter Hitchcock dismounted, smiled, and said, "Howdy, Pard."

Black Bart and Joaquin walked up to the fire. Bart took a deep breath and asked, "Them beans ya cooking?"

"They smell mighty good," Joaquin smirked as he slowly walked behind Hans.

Hans thought that they would eat and ride on if he offered them something to eat. But deep down, he knew that wasn't about to happen. He walked over to where Gretchen was standing, put his arm around her, and said, "We got plenty. If'n you like to have some beans. We'd be happy to share."

Hitchcock smiled; his teeth were brown, stained from chaw tobacco; he laughed then spit out a large plug of tobacco and said, "Well, that's right neighborly of you, Pard. And how bout sharing the woman?"

Before Hans had a chance to react, Walter Hitchcock pulled his colt pistol and shot the German in the chest, sending him tumbling backward.

KAPOW

Gretchen started to run to Hans' body when Hitchcock grabbed her, punched her in the face, and threw her to the ground. She fell on her back next to her husband, who was still alive, moaning. Hitchcock threw Gretchen over on her stomach and began ripping off her clothes.

She was screaming, "*Hans! Nein! Nein! Nein!*"

Hitchcock, cursing, hit her in the head with the barrel of his gun as he was mounting her.

"Shut up, bitch," Hitchcock demanded.

As he was trying to penetrate her, Hans continued to groan in pain; frustrated he shouted to Joaquin, "Fer, God's sake will you shoot the bastard. I can't stay hard while he's grousing like that."

KAPOW

Joaquin shot Hans in the head, killing him instantly, spraying Gretchen's face with her lover's brains and blood. That was the last thing she remembered. After all, three of the killers had raped her multiple times; they rifled through the campsite stealing anything they felt had any value, then setting anything they had no use for they set afire.

"Hey, Hitch, what about the bitch?" Black Bart asked.

"Leave her for the next horny bastard," Hitchcock snickered.

Gretchen lay naked and unconscious for two days until, by chance US Marshall Jackson Boone happened upon her. Marshall Boone was on his way to Stockton, escorting a prisoner who was wanted for cattle rustling, Kidd Dooley.

Dooley was mounted on his horse and was restrained with his hands shackled behind his back. Boone had Dooley's horse's reins tied to the back of his saddle, pulling the prisoner and his stead along behind him.

As they approached the carnage, Boone turned back to Dooley and said, "Don't try anything stupid. You're wanted dead or alive. Understand?"

Dooley said nothing; he was trying to work out in his mind how this might work out to his advantage. Boone dismounted, tied his horse's reins to one of the burnt-out wagon's wheels, and walked over first to the blowfly and maggot-covered body of the man.

"Poor bastard," Boone said under his breath. He then knelt down to see if the woman was dead. He was surprised to see that she was alive, but just barely. He searched through the burnt-out wreckage and found bits and pieces of clothing to be able to dress her. He brought over his canteen off his saddle and gave her some water. She was all bloody from being beaten and from her husband having been shot. He could tell that she had been badly raped and battered.

He picked up a shovel lying on the ground and dug a shallow grave, dragged the lifeless body of Hans Schmidt where he placed him face up and covered him up.

"Hey Marshall, how about letting me have a go had her?" Dooley laughed.

"Shut your mouth before I come over there and stomp the shit out of you!" Boone barked.

When Gretchen finally realized that she had

survived the ordeal and was having her face gently washed off. She began to sob uncontrollably. She looked up at the compassionate face of an older man wearing a Marshall's badge. She asked, "Where's my husband, Hans?"

"Ma'am, if'n that fellow who was over there was your husband, he's dead. I done buried him."

"*Mein lieber Hans,*" She wept.

"Are you able to tell me what happened, ma'am?"

"Three men."

"Had you ever seen them before?"

"*Nein,*" She said, shaking her head.

"No, but I remember a couple of names. Joaquin and Hitch, I think."

"Joaquin and Hitch? If'n they are the ones I'm thing of, you're lucky to still be alive." Boone said.

"Lucky?" Gretchen whispered, looking around.

"Ma'am, I'm heading down to Stockton. I think you should come with us."

"How's she going to come with us. We only got two horses," Dooley quipped.

"She'll ride your horse."

"All right, Marshall! That's mighty kind of you," Dooley grinned.

"She'll ride your horse. You'll walk, Dooley."

"Fuck you, Marshall! I ain't walking nowhere!"

The Marshall strode over to Dooley astride his horse, grabbed him by his belt, and threw him to the ground. Dooley lay on the ground, looking up at Boone. He scrambled to get to his feet and sneered, "I'll kill you for that, you bastard!"

"Sure, you will," Boone answered. He walked to his horse, took his lariat off the saddle, walked back to

Dooley, and placed a noose around his neck.

"You walk ahead of me, try anything funny, and you'll be arriving in Stockton straddled over a saddle. Don't matter to me."

Marshall Boone got Gretchen and helped her up on Dooley's horse.

"Are you all right?" He asked.

She said nothing, just nodded.

"If'n you need anything, just holler."

Boone walked to his horse, mounted it, snapped the lariat, and ordered, "Okay, Dooley, head out."

The rest of the trip to Stockton was uneventful. When they arrived at the Marshall's office, Dooley was formally arrested and placed in a jail cell. Boone took Gretchen to Saint Mary's Catholic Church after Gretchen revealed that she was a Catholic.

The nuns had offered her passage back to Milwaukee, but she felt that she couldn't face her family after such a traumatic incident. To repay the church, she began to cook and clean for them. She stayed with Saint Mary's for ten years until Ishmael offered her a position at the Devil Fish Ranch as a cook for him and Sarah. They met, talked for several hours, and he finally brought her home to meet Sarah. Gretchen started the next day.

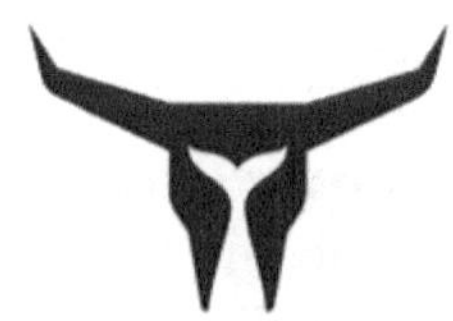

Once Marshall Boone had taken Gretchen to Saint Mary's Catholic Church, he returned to the US Marshall's office and swore out warrants for the capture of Walter Hitchcock and Joaquin Salinas, dead or alive, for the crimes of robbery, rape, and murder.

The bounty was set at 5000 dollars each. Within the week, wanted posters were sent out throughout the territory and neighboring states. The hunt for Hitchcock and Joaquin Salinas was on. As for Kidd Dooley, he was found guilty of cattle rustling and hanged by the neck until dead.

"That was a wonderful breakfast, Gretchen," I said as I stood up from the dining room table.

"*Gut*, I'm glad you liked it. How is *Freulin* Sarah today?"

"She's doing well. She's enjoying having her sister, Jane, here."

"*Ya, ya, ist gut.*" She said as she collected the breakfast dishes and walked into the kitchen.

Queequeg was lying on the porch waiting for me. I kept the screen door open and said, "Queequeg, go see Sarah. Go on."

He reluctantly meandered into the house, stood at the bottom of the stairs, and looked defiantly at me.

"Go on."

He gave a short growl and went upstairs. I had decided that he couldn't continue to go out riding with me to tend the herd anymore; he was almost fourteen years old. We had been through a lot together, the gold mining days, the war, and now the cattle ranching. I know he wants to come with me, but I think it better that he stays at the farmhouse with Sarah.

It was later that day when me and the boys were out

herding the cattle from the east pasture to the west field and checking the fences when the three strangers rode into the Devil Fish Ranch. The only ranch hand not out with the cattle was Gus McCall, a retired gunfighter who had changed his name in order to avoid his reputation. Back in his gunslinging days, he went by the name of "Handsome Jack" Reeves. Gus mostly roamed the Montana and Wyoming territories with the occasional journey down into New Mexico. He was known to have killed sixteen men in "fair" gunfights.

When he realized that he wasn't as fast on the draw as he used to be, he decided to hang up his six-shooters while he still could and became a cowboy. To avoid reprisals from friends or family of those he killed, he headed west to California.

Gus was working in the barn repairing the stirrups on his saddle when he became aware of the three men riding up to the farmhouse. He had seen his share of desperados and outlaws to know that these men were ne'er-do-wells looking to do evil. He snuck back to the bunkhouse and collected his Buscadero tooled gun belt with two matching side holsters that held two Colt .45 pistols. He strapped the gun belt on his waist, tied the thigh laced ties, checked to ensure the pistols were loaded, and headed back to the barn.

By the time he got back, the three men were dismounted and were preparing to walk into the house.

"Can I help you, boys?" Gus shouted as he approached the house, hands down by his sides, ready to draw at the first sign of trouble.

"Mister, we're looking to see if'n you might be hiring on?" Walter Hitchcock said.

As they stepped off of the porch, Gus could tell right

away that they were beginning to position themselves for a gunfight, spreading out to gain an advantage. Gus was no stranger to such tactics. He stood his ground; in fact, he felt he had the edge as the sun was behind him, so the ruffians were facing into the bright morning light.

Meanwhile, Gretchen had heard the voices outside and went to the screen door and recognized the men who had killed her Hans and raped her all those years ago. No amount of time could erase those three from her memory. She silently went upstairs and alerted Jane and Sarah.

"Lock *das* door," Gretchen whispered as she grabbed the double-barreled 12-gauge Remington shotgun sitting in the bedroom corner.

"Look, Pard, we ain't looking for no trouble. So, why don't you just unbuckle that gun belt before someone gets hurt." Hitchcock said, laughing.

"Oh, it's way too late for that, *Pard*," Gus said condescendingly.

Hitchcock and the two others looked at each other as if they had never run across such unafraid opposition. All of a sudden, uncertainty and doubt of this stranger had them slightly hesitant.

"Well, are you going to pull those pistols or play with yourselves?" Gus taunted.

He had sized up the three of them up and what the order of his kill shots would be. The mouthy leader would be his first target; the Mexican would be the second, and the weasely scared-looking one would be the last to die. Of course, with any battle plan, once the fighting starts, you can just throw the plan out the window because there is usually something unexpected that will happen that will throw a wrench into the plan.

Hitchcock's eyes narrowed; he curled his lip in anger, sneered, then spit out a large plug of tobacco before yelling, "Eat lead."

Gus had begun to draw his pistols the second Hitchcock spit out the plug tobacco. He had seen that distraction once before in Bozeman; it didn't work then, and it sure as Hell wasn't going to work now.

Just as Gus fired his first and second shots, killing Hitchcock with a bullet in his forehead, blowing out the back of his skull, spewing his brains and cartilage all over his saddle, and hitting Joaquin in the shoulder, spinning him around, Gretchen came bursting out of the front porch door blasting both barrels from the Remington shotgun, hitting Joaquin Salinas, who was facing her in the lower torso blasting a hole the size of a dinner platter where his guts used to be.

KAPOW

BLAM BLAM

Leaving Gus to finish off C. J. "Black Bart" Bolton with three bullets that formed a perfect triangle grouping in the middle of his chest, killing him instantly.

KAPOW KAPOW KAPOW

Gus stood surveying the carnage, replaying the whole scenario in his head. The only unexpected variable he hadn't counted on was the German cook bursting out from the house and firing the shotgun. Luckily, the unexpected worked into Gus' hand.

Gretchen dropped the shotgun, collapsed onto the porch, and began sob uncontrollably. After reassuring Sarah, Jane, who had witnessed the whole incident from the bedroom window, came running downstairs to console Gretchen.

While Jane was comforting the grief-stricken Gretchen, Gus McCall went about carrying the bodies out of sight into the barn. He laid the three bandits side-by-side, covering them with a canvas tarp, only their boots exposed.

He was walking their horses into the barn when me and all the ranch hands came galloping to the ranch. I saw Gus walking toward the barn with three saddled horses and Jane and Gretchen sitting on the porch.

"Gus, what's happened? We heard gunshots," I said.

"Three gunmen came to do villainy. I would not abide it," Gus proclaimed.

"You took all three of them yourself?" I asked.

"Nay, I dropped two of them, the German cook kilt one with the shotgun."

"Gretchen?"

"Yes. I suggest you send someone to fetch the Marshall, boss," Gus said as he continued bringing the three mounts into the barn and began to unsaddle them.

Buck pulled up next to me and asked, "Shall I send Josh into town and fetch the Marshall?"

"Yeah, and have him bring Doc Hamilton, too."

"I don't think they'll be needing a doctor, boss."

"No. The Doc is to check on Gretchen and Sarah," I replied.

I dismounted *Chapawee* and stepped into the barn to gaze upon the three brigands lying dead in the barn. I folded back the tarp and peered upon them, but I did not recognize nor recall ever seeing them.

"Gretchen, are you all right?" I asked, who was still crying and in a state of shock.

Jane, holding her said, "From what I can gather,

these are the men who attacked her and killed her husband."

"If they are them, Gretchen, you did the right thing."

She peered up from Jane's embrace and sobbed, "Vengeance is mine saith the Lord."

"Gretchen, you did good. Thanks to you and Gus, you not only saved your lives but that of Jane, Sarah, and the baby. Thank you," I said.

"Come on. Let's get you inside," Jane said, cradling Gretchen in her arms. Jane walked into the house, helped her to her room, and put her to bed. I went upstairs and checked in on Sarah, who was visibly shaken by the ordeal. I sat by her on the bed and held her tightly.

"Sarah, my dearest, everything is fine now. No need to worry."

"Oh, Ishmael, I was so scared. What if those men…"

"It's all over. You're safe. I've sent for Doctor Hamilton. He should be here soon. Now, you lie back and try to relax."

"Don't leave me!" She begged.

"I'm not going anywhere. I'm staying right here. Now, lie back, dear."

"What about Gretchen? Is she all right?"

"Gretchen is fine. Jane is with her," I assured her.

Sarah laid back in bed and eventually fell asleep. It wasn't too long after that Doctor Hamilton arrived. His first visit was to see Gretchen, who was in a state of shock. After giving her a though examination, he reached into his black medical bag and held up a small brown bottle.

"Gretchen, I want you to take two spoonfuls of this elixir every four hours for the next three days,"

Hamilton said as he handed Jane the bottle. Be sure to contact me if there's no improvement.

"Yes, Doctor," Jane answered.

"Now, I'll go up and see Sarah."

"Oh, Doctor, what's in this?" Jane asked as she held up the bottle.

"Mostly water, alcohol, and a touch of morphine. I mix it up myself. It should calm her nerves down after a couple of doses," He said as he left the room.

When Hamilton entered our bedroom, I was still sitting by her side; Sarah was in a fitful sleep, tossing and moaning softly.

"How is she?"

"She had quite a scare. But she's fine," I said as I was about to wake her.

"No need to disturb her," Doctor Hamilton said as he pulled his stethoscope from his bag and listened to her heart. He then took out another small brown bottle of elixir and gave me the same instructions as he did Gretchen.

"Will do, Doc," I said.

I then walked the doctor downstairs and as he was leaving, Marshall Boone galloped up to the house with his deputy, Bob Collins.

"Hey, Ishmael," Boone called out.

"Marshal."

"I hear you had a bit of excitement."

"Yeah. We got three dead marauders out in the barn."

"Who is responsible?"

"One of my hands, Gus McCall."

"McCall dropped the three of them all by himself?"

"No. Gretchen shot one of them with my shotgun."

"Gretchen?"

"Yeah, she says that they are the ones who killed her husband and raped her."

"Jesus Christ!" Boone said as he pushed his hat back.

"I know."

"Where are the bodies now?"

"In the barn."

"And this McCall?"

"He's in the barn waiting to talk to you."

"Gus McCall?" Marshall Boone asked.

"Yup."

"Where are the bodies?"

Gus walked the Marshall over to where he had laid the corpses side-by-side. He flipped back the canvas tarp to reveal the mutilated bodies of the villains.

Marshall Boone knew who exactly who he was looking at. He uttered, "Well, I'll be God Damned. It's Walter Hitchcock, Joaquin Salinas, and C. J. "Black Bart" Bolton!" Boone uttered.

"The Five Aces Gang. There's a big reward for these hombres," Deputy Collins' proclaimed.

"Tell me what happened here," Boone asked.

"Well, I was working in the barn when I noticed these three shady ravagers ride up. I see them dismount and start looking around to see if there is anyone about. They then head towards the main house. I decided to confront them to see what sort of chicanery they might be up to.

They state they are just looking to see if there are any ranch jobs to be had. When I tell them that there aren't any, that's when they tipped their hand by trying to gain position over me. They spread out as if to intimidate me. I knew that I had a slight advantage in having the sun behind me. I could see that they were squinting as the sun was bothering them. I played the whole scenario out in my head, so when the leader made his move, I drew hitting this one in the head," Gus said, pointing to Walter Hitchcock.

"I glimpsed the German cook burst out of the house just as I was taking aim at that one." He said, indicating to Joaquin.

"Go on," Marshall Boone requested.

"Well, I just winged him because the old woman distracted me, and besides I saw she had a shotgun. So, I turned my attention to that one there and laid him down," Gus added, pointing to the victim.

"That is some mighty fine shooting Mister McCall," Boone admitted.

"Where did you learn to shoot like that?" Deputy Collins' asked.

Gus lied, "Arizona."

"I'll need you to come into town at some point and write out a statement and sign it. Then we'll see about getting you that reward." Boone stated.

Collins noted, "The reward is over five thousand dollars."

"I think the German cook should get half," Gus said.

"Whatever you say," Boone affirmed.

"That's mighty Christian of you, Gus," I said.

"Seems only fair," Gus replied with a smile.

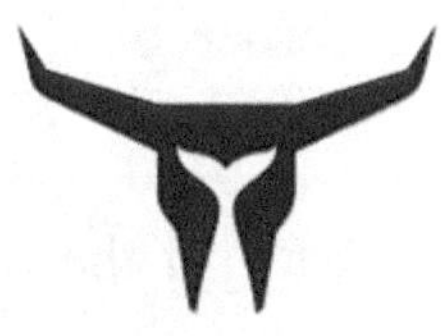

In the weeks that followed, once the word of the shootout spread throughout the area, people began to show up at the ranch looking to see if they could catch a glimpse of Gus McCall, "the gunslinger" and the "German Belle Starr." The local paper even sent out a reporter and photographer. The story made the front page with photographs of the three dead desperados. Both Gus and Gretchen declined to have their photographs taken, but crude sketches were used in their stead.

It got so bad that I had to post a man at the entrance to the ranch to keep the gawkers away and even had to post signs telling folks that they risked being shot if found trespassing. Eventually, things died down, and life on the ranch got back to normal.

It was three weeks before Sarah was due to have the baby when I got word that Eugene Darcey, my partner in the Devil Fish Gold Mine and my banker, needed to see me in the next day or so. I was planning to go into Stockton anyway to purchase some much-needed supplies.

I rode the thirteen miles to Stockton to the Wells Fargo Bank at the corner of El Dorado and Weber Streets. I went through Jones & Hewlett Groceries, Provisions & Hardware, Purveyors of Agricultural and Mining tools to the back of the building to the Wells

Fargo Bank offices.

I went up to the teller's window and said, "I'm here to see Mister Darcey. He's expecting me."

"And you are?"

"Ishmael."

"One moment, please, sir," The young man said as he scampered off.

Moments later, Darcey appeared with a large grin on his face.

"Ishmael! It's so good to see you. It's been ages. Please come on back to my office; there's someone who has traveled all the way from San Francisco to meet with you," He said with an air of excitement.

"It's nice to see you as well," I replied as I followed him to his office.

When I entered, I was surprised to see Charles Sutton, my stockbroker from San Francisco, whom I hadn't seen since before Sarah was with child.

"Ishmael! I hear congratulations are in order. You're going to become a father," He said elatedly.

"Yes, thank you."

"When is the blessed event?" Sutton asked.

"Well, the doctor expects anytime within the next couple of weeks."

"That's wonderful! That's wonderful!"

"What brings you down to Stockton?" I inquired.

"Oh. I'm just passing through. Heading up to Sacramento for business," He stated.

"You sure are taking the roundabout way of getting there," I said.

"Actually, I just came from Modesto. I was there for a couple of days, and I'll be here until tomorrow and then off to Sacramento. So, while I was here, I thought

I'd come and give you an update on your portfolio."

"I should leave you two alone," Darcey said.

"No, it's all right, you can stay," I elected.

"Well, Ishmael, I am happy to report that your portfolio has almost doubled to a grand total of one hundred thirty-three thousand dollars and some odd cents."

"Why, that's excellent, Mister Sutton. Thank you for stopping by to see me; I know what a busy man you are."

"I'm happy to have been a service to you all these years. And I understand that Mister Darcey has some good news as well."

"Oh?"

"Ishmael, I, too am happy to report good news. Three days ago, I got word from Bob Grant that the Devil Fish Mine has struck the motherlode. According to Bob, they uncovered an enormous gold vein that could be worth millions!" Darcey jubilantly declared.

"Say, that is good news," I said.

"We're millionaires, Ishmael! Millionaires!" Darcey exclaimed, jumping for joy.

Now, don't get me wrong, I was as excited as Old Darcey, but I was carrying a huge weight on my mind. The health of Sarah and the baby, who was due any day now.

"Mister Sutton, Eugene, thank you both for such astonishing news, but I have errands to tend to and must get back to Sarah and the ranch."

"We understand, Ishmael. I wish you all the best with the baby. Send Sarah all my best wishes. I'm sure everything will be all right," Sutton said.

"You go on, Ishmael. We'll talk soon. Love to

Sarah," Darcy added.

"Thank you, gentlemen," I said as I made my way out of the office. I made all of my purchases at Jones & Hewlett. I loaded up the buckboard with foodstuffs and other miscellaneous items, and for the gear that was too cumbersome, such as rolls of barbed wire, fence posts, and two new wheels for the chuck wagon, they would deliver.

When I got back to the ranch, I saw Doctor Hamilton's buggy out front of the house; Gretchen was pacing back and forth on the porch.

"Gretchen, What's happening?"

"Miss Sarah, she is in bad way."

As I bolted up the stairs, taking two and three at a time, I heard Sarah moaning and screaming in pain. By the time I reached our bedroom, it had become deadly silent. Then the sound of a crying newborn filled the house; what a joyous sound it was. I opened the door just in time to see Doctor Hamilton placing the bedsheet over Sarah's face.

"Sarah!" I screamed as I rushed to her.

"I'm so sorry, Ishmael. I couldn't save her," Doctor Hamilton muttered.

I drew the sheet from her face; she looked so peaceful, like she was asleep. She had what I perceived to be a slight smile on her face. I leaned over and kissed her and whispered, "I love you, my love. I always will."

I covered her again and began to cry until Jane, who was standing in the corner holding the baby, staring out the window, tears streaming down her face, said, "Ishmael, come meet your son."

Doctor Hamilton said, "Ishmael, You have a perfectly healthy boy."

I left Sarah and went to where Jane was standing. There, wrapped in a blue cotton baby blanket, was my son; his green eyes were open, looking up at me. He held his tiny arms out as if asking me to hold him. Jane offered him to me, I took him and held him close to me, and he smiled.

Jane whispered, "What are you going to call him?"

"Call him Jonah."

After Sarah's death, Jane decided to stay on and help me raise Jonah. Being that she had been a schoolmarm and had years of experience being with children, which I did not, was truly appreciated.

Jonah was a typical boy; he love playing with the animals around the ranch and could ride a horse almost before he could walk. He was smart and good at book learning. By the time he was six, he could read and write. From a young age he worked the ranch, at first he'd collect eggs from the hen house, help with the milking of the cows, and groom and curry *Chapawee*. I couldn't be prouder of him.

I wanted the best in the world for my son. When he turned ten years old, I began to take him whenever I had to travel, to Sacramento, San Francisco, Denver, Chicago, and New York. I would take him to museums, the theater, symphonies, and even operas. Back home, on the ranch, he would participate in the occasional rodeo. He was a Hell of a roper and a fairly decent bronco buster. As much as he was privileged to have he never considered himself entitled.

When Jonah was fourteen, I thought it would be good for him when me and a bunch of the ranch hands along with Cookie would take a couple of days and ride the perimeter to check and mend the fences. We had been gone two days when we noticed that someone had cut out a large portion of the barbed wire fence. We figured that several hundred head of cattle had been rustled.

I sent Clint Cassidy, one of our hands back into town to alert Marshall Boone while the rest of us would give chase. Buck determined by the freshness of the tracks that the culprits might have a six-hour head start on us. I had Cookie give us each three days of hardtack and jerky, then sent him back to the ranch with the chuckwagon. We left Shane Dillion and Reno Stoddard to stay behind to repair the fence while the rest of us began to dog the trail of the cattle rustlers and our herd.

Moving a herd of cattle is slow going, the bigger the herd the slower you go. If you try to move too fast, you run the risk of cattle dying, or becoming too tired and collapsing. And a fast-moving herd is harder to control unless you have a lot of men which we could tell by the tracks that there were only four or five men.

By late afternoon we could see the trail dust that the herd was kicking up. We were only an hour away. I sent my foremen Buck, Josh Randall, and Jed Cartwright to swing off to their right flank to see if they could get ahead of them. Me, Jonah, Cody Walker, Gil Favor, and Gus McCall would catch them from behind. Hopefully, between Buck and his men and me and the boys, will be able to put the squeeze on them.

It was an hour later when we finally caught up with

the first of the rustlers who spied us coming and hightailed without warning any of his accomplices. I sent Cody Walker to fetch him back. It was shortly thereafter that Buck and his boys intercepted the front of the herd. Shots were fired. That's when we made our presence known. There were only five men now since the first man we encountered absconded.

The total intervention took only minutes once the bandits realized that they were outnumbered. Even though shots were fired, no one had been shot. We restrained the rascals and began to turn the herd around to head back to the Devil Fish. As we were driving the herd we could see Cody bringing the escapee back.

Marshall Boone, Deputy Collins, and Clint Cassidy came across us bringing the herd back.

"Hey, Marshall."

"Howdy, Ishmael. What do we have here?" He asked eyeing the six men hand-tied.

"Rustlers," I replied.

Boone had them dismount. He replaced the rope restraints with iron shackles. The oldest of the rustlers apparently had heard the Marshall speak my name, he cried out, "Oye! Are you the Ishmael that once sailed with Captain Black Dog Billy Twigg?"

"I am," I said.

"Ishmael, it is I, Billy Buckets!"

I looked at him but wasn't recalling the name nor the face.

"You remember me, "Greybeard."

"Greybeard! Aye, I remember now. How the Hell are you?" I asked but soon realized that it was a foolish thing to say.

"Well, matey, I've been better."

"Ishmael, do you know this man?" Boone asked.

"Long time ago, in another life."

"Is there anything you can do fer an old shipmate?" Buckets pleaded.

Marshall Boone said, "Ishmael, I think it best that we take these hombres into custody at this time, and you can come into town later and we can discuss things at that time."

"Greybeard, I'll stop the Marshall's office in a day or two."

"I sure appreciate it." Buckets said as he and the five other rustlers were led away back to the Stockton jail.

While I was talking to the Marshall, Buck and the boys were driving the herd back to the ranch. Jonah had stayed behind with me during my conversation with Boone and Billy Buckets.

"Pa, who was that man?"

"That was a man I knew a long time ago."

"During your whaling days?"

"After."

"Who was Captain Black Dog Billy Twigg?"

"Come on, son. Let's head on back to the ranch and I'll tell you all about my days as a pirate, but this is just between you and me, you can't tell anyone, especially your Aunt Jane. Understand?"

Jonah nodded with excitement.

"Okay, then I'll tell you all about my days sailing with Captain Black Dog Billy Twigg, Calico Jack, and One-Eyed Willie."

Jonah's jaw dropped and stammered, "One…One…One-Eyed Willie?"

So, on the ride back to the ranch I regaled my son with my exploits during my pirating years. I must admit there were times when I may have embellished a tale or two, not so as to make me a hero, but to spare the child from details that I deemed to be too gruesome. I reminded him of my reasoning for becoming a pirate was in large part of my guilt and have been the sole survivor of our encounter with the Devil Fish, Moby Dick.

We rode in silence for a spell before Jonah asked, "So, Pa, what are you going to do about Billy Buckets?"

"Well, seeing how we were shipmates, I will go into town tomorrow and talk to Marshall Boone. I'll see what I might be able to for the poor wretch."

By the time Jonah and I reached the farmhouse, Buck and the boys had the stolen herd back on the ranch and the fence repaired.

"Boss, I was thinking maybe we should start staggering our fence patrols for that we don't keep a scheduled pattern," Buck said as Jonah and I were bringing our horses into the barn where all the boys were.

"Great idea Buck. I'll leave it to you. And to all you boys, I'm giving ya'll a twenty-five-dollar bonus for all of your help today," I announced.

An echoed chorus of hoorahs, yippees, and cheers filled the cavernous barn.

"Night boys, again great job," I said as Jonah and I headed into the house for some Gretchen's fried chicken, mashed potatoes with gravy, hot rolls, and apple pie.

Jane greeted us as we came into the house, "Is everything all right? We heard that there was trouble with rustlers."

"Aunt Jane, you should have seen it, we saved the herd and caught the rustlers! Marshal Boone and Deputy Collins showed up and arrested them," Jonah exclaimed.

"Well, that's enough excitement for one day. Go wash up and come and have some dinner," Jane said.

"Yes, ma'am."

As hard as she tried to steer the conversation elsewhere, she couldn't get Jonah to stop talking about the day's adventures. I finally asked, "Jonah have you seen Queequeg tonight?"

"No, Pa I haven't."

"That's odd he's usually underfoot at dinner time. If you're done with your dinner would you go see where he is?"

He took his plate and silverware into the kitchen and went about looking for Queequeg. He looked all around the house, then he went outside. It was shortly after he went outside that I heard, "Pa! Come quick! It's Queequeg!"

I ran outside to the barn where my old friend was lying there just inside the barn, softly whimpering.

"Pa, what's wrong with Queequeg ?"

"I don't know son. Help me hitch up the wagon, we're going into town to see Doc. Herbert."

Jonah sat crying in the back of the buckboard holding Queequeg's head in his lap talking to him. By the time we arrived at the vet's home, Queequeg couldn't stand much less walk. I scooped him up and as I carried him into the office around the back of Herbert's house Jonah was knocking on the front door. I could hear Jonah explaining to the vet why we were waking him up.

Just as I reached the office door, Doc. Herbert opened the door.

"Sorry to wake you Doc. It's Queequeg," I said.

Holding a kerosine lamp that illuminated the room he said, "Bring him in and lay him on the table."

He gave a box of matches to Jonah and told him to light the other three lamps scattered around the office. He looked into Queequeg's eyes, put a stethoscope to listen to his heart and lungs, and felt around his body.

He removed the stethoscope from his ears, looked at Jonah, and then to me, "Ishmael, how old is Queequeg?"

"Not sure, Doc," I replied.

"He's old, he's tired, and he's dying."

"Isn't there anything that you can do for him Doctor Herbert?" Jonah pleaded.

"Jonah, look at him. He's suffering. You don't want him to suffer, do you?"

"No, sir," Jonah wept.

"Come here and hold him and talk to him. Tell him

how much you love him and that he's a good boy."

"Can he hear me?" Jonah asked.

"Of course. Now, you hold him while I give him a shot, so he'll go to sleep. It won't hurt a bit. I promise."

Jonah cradled Queequeg in his arms and softly whispered in his ear, "Queequeg, you a good boy. You're the best pup. I love you. Just go to sleep. I love you, boy. Whadda good boy."

As Jonah was consoling Queequeg, Doctor Herbert discreetly gave the injection. Within minutes my longtime companion slipped away. I found myself crying like I did when my dearest Sarah passed away.

"Stay with him as long as you like," Herbert said to Jonah, but I know he was talking to me as well.

We put Queequeg in the back of the buckboard with Jonah again holding his head in his lap. The ride back to the ranch was a somber one. I don't think we spoke more the ten words between us. When we got back to the ranch Jonah asked, "Can we bury him now, Pa?"

"All right. Where would you like to lay him to rest?"

"Under the big oak outback. That was his favorite tree."

As Jonah carried the lifeless body of Queequeg around to the back, I went into the barn and brought back two shovels and a blanket. While I began to dig, Jonah wrapped our dear friend carefully in the blanket, then he took the other shovel, and we dug the final resting place for old Queequeg.

After we finished, Jonah asked, "Pa, would you say a prayer?"

"All right," I said as I thought about saying a prayer for a dog. But Queequeg wasn't a dog, he was my good friend. Maybe my best friend.

I bowed my head, "Lord, deliver Queequeg from any pain and suffering. Grant Queequeg Your peace as we place him into Your capable hands. We ask for healing, we ask for strength, we ask O Lord that You welcome Queequeg into Heaven. In Your name, we pray. Amen."

Jonah softly muttered, "Amen."

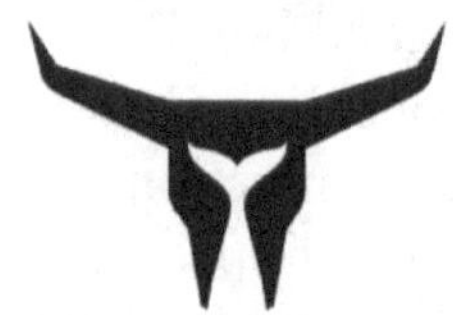

The next day I saddled up *Chapawee* and rode into Stockton to meet with Marshall Boone. When I arrived Deputy Collins informed me that he was in a meeting with the city council and wouldn't be back for a couple of hours.

So, I thought that I'd stop in Wells Fargo and see what's the latest with Darcey.

"Ishmael! What brings you by?" Darcey asked.

"I have some business with Marshall Boone, who's in a council meeting."

"Oh yes, I heard about the rustling."

"News travels fast," I remarked.

"Is it true that you knew one of the rustlers?"

"A long time ago. Anyway, I had some time, I figured that I'd stop by and see what's new with the mine," I said to get the subject changed. I know that the gold mine is his favorite subject to talk about. A topic he can ramble on for hours about.

"Oh, did I tell you that they found a major vein in one of the tunnels?"

"Yeah, you said that we were going to be

millionaires. Is that true, Eugene?"

He got a smile from ear to ear, walked over to the door, and said, "Wilcox, bring in Ishmael's statement when you can."

He returned to his desk, leaned back in his overstuffed chair, placed his hands behind his head, and said, "Just wait and see. I think you're going to be pleasantly surprised."

A short balding, puggy man wearing an eyeshade, and thick spectacles stuck his head in the door and said, "Here's the statement you asked for, Mister Darcey."

"Come in Wilcox. Come in." Darcey barked.

Wilcox did as he was ordered.

"Give Ishmael the statement. Now go!"

Wilcox handed me the printed page and quickly scooted out of Darcey's office.

I read the numbers at the bottom of the tally sheet, at the bottom of the page where the total was, it read a total of 2.5 million. I looked up at Darcey sitting in his chair smiling like the cat that ate the canary.

"I told you," He said laughing.

"Is this true?"

"Of course, it's true. And this is just the beginning. There's plenty more where that came from, my boy."

"Unbelievable. I started that mine thinking it might be worth a couple thousand," I uttered to myself in disbelief.

"Boy, were you wrong!" Darcey chortled.

I glanced up at the mahogany regulator clock hanging behind Darcey and noticed that it was time for me to go see if Boone was available.

"Eugene, I must be going. I have to see Marshall Boone."

"It was good seeing you, partner. Stop by anytime and say hello to Jonah for me."

"I will. Good seeing you, too. Goodbye."

By the time I got to the Marshall's office, he had returned from the city council meeting. Deputy Collins was busy filling out paperwork when I walked in.

"Oh, hi, Ishmael, Marshall Boone is expecting you. Go on in."

I knocked on the Marshall's door before stepping in. "Afternoon, Marshall."

"Afternoon, Ishmael. I assume you're here to talk about Billy Buckets?"

"I've given it a lot of thought and I've decided to…"

"Let me stop you right there. I did some checking on Billy Buckets. He has quite an extensive history of cattle rustling, as well as two charges of bank robbery. So, even if you wanted to drop the charges, I couldn't let him go. He's wanted in three states including right here in California."

"Sorry, I didn't know. Can I go see him?"

"Sure. Follow me," Boone said as he grabbed the keys for the cells. He led me from his office to the back of the building where the jail cells were located. There was a row of four man twelve cells. Eight of them were occupied. I recognized the five men who rustled my cattle. Boone had the five of them in two cells and Billy was in a cell by himself.

"You got ten minutes, Ishmael," Marshall Boone announced.

Billy was lying on a cot reading a copy of the National Police Gazette. I stood outside his cell unnoticed for about a minute, then I said, "Looking to see if they spelled your name right?"

"Ishmael! Thank you for coming."

"Hey, how you doing Billy?"

"Can you help me out, Ishmael?" Buckets asked.

"I came down here to not press charges."

"Oye, that's great matey. So, when are they going to let me out?"

"There's just one little problem, Billy."

"What's that?"

"It seems that you're wanted in three states and here in California. So, you see, even if I dropped the charges you'll still be arrested. I'm sorry."

"Are you the foreman on that ranch?"

"Not exactly. That's my ranch."

"The Hell you say!"

"What about you, Billy? How'd you end up here?"

"Once I got on dry land I went from one lousy job to another. Then I got caught up in the wrong crowd."

"What did you do with all the money that we left the ship with?"

"I went through it pretty quick. Whores. Gambling. Drinking."

"I'm sorry, I can't do anything for you, Billy."

"That's all right matey. I guess I chartered my own course, and I ran afoul," Billy said with a crooked smile.

From down the hall, Boone gave a short whistle and waved that time was up.

"Billy, I've got to go. But I can come back to see you if you'd like," I offered.

"Nay, matey, it appears that me and the boys are being taken to Nevada to stand trial for a bank robbery in the morning."

I held my hand out. Billy took it, and I said, "Good

luck to you. And may the wind be at your back, Billy Buckets."

"Fair winds and following seas to you, matey."

Life on the ranch returned back to the daily routine of cattle ranching. Jonah continued with his education, he transferred from his Aunt Jane's homeschooling to attend Stockton's St. Mary's High School. It was decided that it would be better for Jonah if he were to go to college to have a formal education rather than be homeschooled. And because it proved too time-consuming to have him travel back and forth every day from school back to the ranch, I moved him and his Aunt Jane into town to live in the house Sarah had as the boarding house where we first met. They would come out to the ranch on weekends and during holidays.

As time went on I noticed that Jonah's interest wasn't leaning towards ranching. His interests seemed to be more in the science fields. He talked about going into law and possibly becoming a lawyer.

Of course, not all of his interests were of an academic nature. At the ripe old age of sixteen Jonah discovered girls. And as a wiser fella than myself once said, "In the spring a young man's fancy lightly turns to thoughts of love." And Jonah's thoughts turned to Becky Hamilton, Doctor Hamilton's daughter. Becky was tall, blonde, with blue eyes, cute, smart, and a year older than Jonah. He fell hard for her, but Becky, although she liked Jonah, she liked other boys as well. It's true that you always remember your first love, but equally, you always remember your first broken heart.

When he turned seventeen, Jonah, his Aunt Jane,

and I took a trip back east to investigate potential colleges. We looked at Harvard, Columbia, Duke, and New York University. His first choice was Harvard Law, and when he applied he was accepted.

So, in the fall of 1880, Jonah went off to study law at Harvard University. Jane, Gretchen, and I took him to the train station to see him off.

"Jonah, I have prepared some fried chicken, potato salad, and apple pie for you. So, you won't get hungry." Gretchen said weeping.

"Thank you, Gretchen. I know I'm going to miss your cooking," Jonah said as he gave her a big hug.

He hugged his Aunt Jane and he kissed her on the cheek. "You take care of yourself, study, and be sure to write."

"I promise I will, Aunt Jane," He said as he too started to weep.

"Son, I want you to study hard, but it's also important that you enjoy these times. All I ask is to use your common sense and think before you act. You're not a little boy anymore, you're a man now, so be responsible, treat others like you want to be treated, always do the right thing."

"Yes, Pa," He said.

We shook hands and then I pulled him close to me and gave him a big hug and whispered, "We'll see you for Christmas."

And so, it went, I would see Jonah for summer

breaks and on Christmas for the first two years at Harvard. Then he wrote me asking if he could stay in Cambridge and work at some law firms during the summer. We only saw each other at Christmas for the remainder of his college life. There were a couple of occasions that Jane and I would make a trip to specifically get together with him during the holidays. We would sometimes take short trips to New York City, and Philadelphia. Once we made a journey to the island of Nantucket, where I shipped out on that fateful day over thirty years ago with Captain Ahab on the *Pequod*.

One night after Jonah and Jane turned in for the night, I took advantage to step out and go down to the seaport. I got an eerie sensation walking the streets around the port and seeing the new steam-powered whaling ships. It was amazing how it seemed that everything had changed and yet nothing had changed. Most of the whaling ships were out to sea. There were only two ships in dock, the *Aurora* and the *Grasshopper*. Both were undergoing extensive ship maintenance.

I stood and watched for an hour or so, then I went down to the Brotherhood of Thieves Tavern on Broad Street not far from the docks for a pint of Ale. The Brotherhood of Thieves Tavern had been the tavern of whalers for over a hundred years. As soon as I opened the door the warmth from the roaring fireplace, the smell of pipe tobacco, and the stale odor of beer smacked me in the face. It hadn't changed a bit in the thirty years since I was last there, with the exception of there being gas lamps instead of lanterns.

I strolled to the bar and asked the innkeeper for a

pint of Ale. As I was drinking, I heard a boisterous bellow from behind me, "Ishmael?!"

I turned around to spy Thomas Fogg the gunner from our days sailing as pirates on the *Hornet's Nest*. I will always remember Thomas standing in a whore house refusing to pay for services rendered when Madam Emilla rushed to him, grabbed him by the testicles, and placed the blade of a sharp kitchen knife to his manhood. Thomas did relent and not only paid for the girl but gave Madam Emilla a sizeable tip.

"Thomas? What are you doing here?" I asked.

Thomas took me by the arm and led me over to a table in the corner where two other men were seated. As I sat down, Thomas introduced me to his shipmates.

"Ishmael, this is Isaac and Patrick, me shipmates. And this here is an old mate of mine, Ishmael. We served alongside each other on the *Hornet's Nest*. Had us many a adventure back in the day. Didn't we Ishmael?"

"Aye, that we did. So, tell me, Thomas, what misadventures have you been up to low these many years?" I asked.

"Well, I did set sail with Mister Turner and Captain Black Dog Billy Twigg on the *Hornet's Nest*. We terrorized many a ship in the South Pacific and took much booty. It was when we sailed into the Sea of Japan that we ran into trouble with the American fleet. They pursued us day and night for two weeks. We were finally able to elude them when Black Dog Billy Twigg gave them the slip one night when we sailed up the Kampar River. The big warships couldn't follow as the river were too shallow. So, we just waited them out until they were forced to leave.

Well, after that encounter we knew we had pressed our luck one too many times. So, we set sail south to Australia, gave up pirating, and turned our fortunes to whaling. We whaled in Perth for seven years until I got passage back here to Nantucket. And I've been whaling ever since, I'm the head harpooner on the *Aurora*.

I have a wife and three young'uns, and my house is not too far from here, over on Rose Lane. Me life is good. And I have good friends." Thomas said as he patted his mates on their shoulders.

"Whatever became of Mister Turner and Captain Black Dog Billy Twigg?" I queried.

"The last time I laid eyes on them they were still in Perth, whaling. And what about you, Ishmael, what have you been doing all these many years? The last time I saw you, you were walking off the gangplank heading into San Francisco."

"Thomas, I must tell you that my life has taken many twists and turns, none of which I ever could have ever foreseen. I have been for the most part fortunate over the years. I went prospecting for gold, I fought in the Civil War, I married and have a wonderful son, and now I'm a rancher. That's not to say that my life hasn't had its tragedies, I was shot in the back while looking for gold, I was wounded in the war, and my dear wife passed away giving birth to our son. Like you, I've had my ups and downs. Can I buy you, boys, another round?" I asked.

"Aye, that would be most hospitable of you," Thomas said as he waved for the barmaid's attention.

As she sauntered over, I requested, "Another round, if you please."

When she returned I foolishly revealed my wallet

and the money there within as I paid for the drinks. I did not see that Thomas's friends had observed my negligence. After quickly finishing their Ales, Isaac and Patrick excused themselves leaving Thomas and me alone. We chatted for another hour or so and as the night grew on I was beginning to feel fatigued, I too decided to take my leave.

"Thomas, my friend it was good to see you after all these years. Fare thee well and fair winds," I said as I stood and shook his hand.

"And may the wind be always at your back, Ishmael."

Outside the tavern, the streets were covered in fog. You could not see one's hand in front of your face. If I had not been familiar with the streets I surely would have been lost. As I was walking back to the boarding house I noticed two sets of footsteps following me. When I stopped they stopped. I had an ominous feeling of foreboding that something dastardly was about to happen. I eased my right hand into my coat pocket where my .38 Smith & Wesson pistol lay hidden. When I found a clothing shop, I leaned my back against the door, so no one would be able to sneak up from behind, and I waited.

Through the fog, two figures began to take shape, as they came closer I could make out that it was Thomas Fogg's two mates, Isaac and Patrick.

"Good evening, gentlemen," I said, my hand still posed nonchalantly in my coat pocket.

"We're sorry to bother you, Ishmael, but if you would be so kind as to hand over that wallet no harm shall befall you." Isaac sneered as he displayed an eight-inch boning knife.

"We're not fooling. It's your money or your life." Patrick snarled as he too produced a weapon, a wooden belaying pin.

"And if I refuse?"

"Then we'll kill you, take your money, and throw your carcass in the sea." Isaac laughed.

"What's it going to be?" Patrick jeered taking a step toward me.

I pulled the pistol out from my pocket and calmly said, "Put your weapons on the ground and walk away."

Patrick did as he was told, but Isaac lunged at me, and I fired one shot striking him in the right shoulder. He fell to the ground moaning. Patrick ran off leaving his partner withering on the ground.

The shop owner who lived above the shop opened the window and shouted, "What is going on down there?"

"I just shot a would-be robber. I need a constable." I replied.

Moments later the shop owner and his son came down to investigate. I explained what had just occurred. The shop owner's son ran off to fetch a patrolman.

We waited until a police officer arrived. I relayed the story of the attempted robbery, Isaac was taken into custody and treated for the gunshot wound.

I had to go down to the police precinct that night and file an affidavit. My understanding is that both Isaac and his accomplice will stand trial for attempted armed robbery.

On the ferry ride back to Boston, Jonah and Jane were both proud and aghast at reading about my exploitations in the Nantucket Inquirer and Mirror. Jonah was proud and bragged all over Harvard about his Pa, while Jane was aghast and too ashamed to ever bring up the subject again.

When I returned to the ranch I had decided that I needed something more in my life now that Jonah was graduating from Harvard and was going to start a life back east as a lawyer. I discussed my feeling with Jane and asked her what is it that she would like for her life going forward. I owed her so much for giving up her career as a schoolteacher, uprooting her life in St. Louis to stay and help raise Jonah after Sarah passed away.

"What would make you happy, Jane?"

"I'm happy staying on here, Ishmael. I've grown to love the life I have here on the ranch."

"I am going into town to visit with my attorney J.R. Lazarus to see about transferring the deed to the ranch to you and Jonah, as well as my half of the Devil Fish mine. I have enough money to last twenty lifetimes. I am feeling the need to travel and see the world. I'm almost sixty now and there is still so much I want to see and do."

I rode into town slowly on *Chapawee* who just celebrated her thirtieth birthday last week. I keep wanting to put her out to pasture, but she'll have none of it. Whenever I go into the barn to fetch my saddle, she begins to whinny and bray until I saddle her up. She seems happy and proud when we ride together. I am preparing myself for the end, which I know I will take hard.

J.R. Lazarus was sitting behind her large wooden desk, she didn't look up from what she was doing, she just said, "Take a seat, I'll be with you in a minute."

I did as I was told. I sat there an article in the Stockton Times, under the heading of Yesterday's Tragedy. The article headline was "Three men hurled into eternity in the duration of a moment." I was just started getting into the story when I heard, "Ishmael. So good to see you. How have you been?"

"I'm well and you?"

"I'm well. Won't you please come in? What can I do for you, today?"

"I'm going to be doing a lot of traveling and I want to amend my will and draw up documents turning my mine and my ranch over to my sister-in-law Jane and my son Jonah as sole owners and sole beneficiaries to my estate upon my death."

"That shouldn't be any problem. How soon are you planning on leaving?"

"Oh, not for a couple of months."

"Well, I should have these drawn up for you within a fortnight. Is that sufficient?"

"That will be fine."

"So, where are you thinking of traveling?"

"I'm not sure at the moment. I'm thinking of Europe, of course, Africa, India, and possibly the Far East."

"How exciting for you. Will you be traveling

alone?"

"Yes, alone."

"Well, I'm sure that you'll make friends very quickly."

"Ah, I best go, I want to tell Mister Darcey of my intentions."

"I'll have these documents finished for you, soon. And please do stop by before leaving on your adventure."

"Good day."

"Good day, Ishmael."

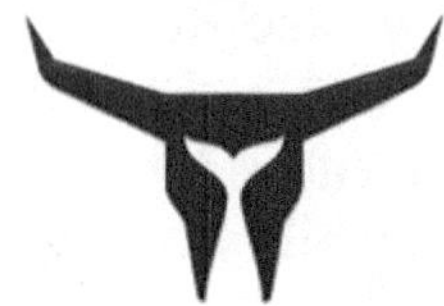

I ran into Darcey as I was tying *Chapawee* to the hitching post. He was returning to the bank from having lunch.

"Ishmael, what brings you here?"

"I wanted to talk to you. If you have a few minutes."

"Here, let's go into my office," He said as he led the way through the Jones & Hewlett Groceries, Provisions & Hardware store to the Wells Fargo Bank. Inside his office, he proceeded to sit in his 'seat of power'.

"Now, what can I do for you, partner?"

"I wanted to stop by and tell you that I am going to be going out of town and I don't know for how long. I plan on doing some traveling. I just stopped by my attorney, and I am having my share of the ownership of our gold mine to be divided between Jane and Jonah. As well as ownership of the ranch."

"How long are you going to be gone?"

"I don't know."

"When will you leave?"

"In a couple of weeks."

"This is kind of sudden. Isn't it?"

"Not really. With Jonah living back east, I think I'm in need of an adventure."

"Well, I must say, I'm going to miss you."

"Thank you, Eugene that's kind of you to say."

"If there is anything that you need, you will let me know."

"I would like to open two checking accounts, one for my sister-in-law Jane Rogers and the other for my son Jonah. The opening balance should be one hundred thousand dollars for each. Also, I will on occasion need access to my funds while I'm overseas."

"Oh, that should be no problem. I will set up the accounts today and I will have the proper documentation that will permit you access to your funds anywhere in the civilized world."

"That's excellent."

"You are only going to the civilized world, aren't you?"

"Well, Eugene, you just never know," I said with a smile.

I had been back at the ranch for a week when *Chapawee* stopped eating and became very lethargic. I don't know if she sensed that something was about to happen, or that I was going to be leaving. But it seemed that she gave up the ghost. Four days before I planned on leaving she laid down in her stall and refused to get up. I spent her last conscious hours cradling her head in my lap until she finally closed her eyes and passed.

Again, I suffered the loss of a loved one. It seems

that the older I get death comes into my life more
frequently

For the next couple of weeks, I was busy getting my
affairs in order. Arranging my travel itinerary, booking
rail tickets to New York City, and then boat passage to
England. I thought that I would start my adventure in
England before tackling countries that speak languages
that I do not totally understand.

The train ride to New York was long, although it did
give me plenty of time to read several travel books on
what to do and see while in England, but primarily in
London. When I arrived at Grand Central Station I was
met by Jonah and a lovely young lady called, Martha
Astor, niece of John Jacob Astor IV.

"Hello, Pa," Jonah said as he gave me a big bear hug.

"Jonah, you're looking well, son. How have you
been?"

"I'm doing really well. I started my new job as a law
clerk at Bernkopf Goodman last week."

"And who is this young lady?"

"Pa, this is my girlfriend, Martha Astor."

"Martha, it's a pleasure to meet you," I said.

"Hello, sir, it's a pleasure to meet you. Jonah has
told me so much about you."

"All good I hope."

"Oh, yes sir."

"Let's not be formal, please call me Ishmael."

"All right, Ishmael."

"Where are you staying, Pa?"

"I have a room at the Cosmopolitan Hotel."

"The Cosmopolitan Hotel. That's where my uncle is staying."

"Oh, really. Maybe we should all try and get together. Maybe for dinner," I suggested.

"I think that would be wonderful. I'll ask him," She said.

"Good. I'll just go and collect my luggage and we'll be off."

Jonah said, "I'll hail us a carriage. We'll see you out front, Pa."

"Very good," I replied as I collected a red cap to take my luggage out to the street, where Jonah and Martha were waiting with the carriage.

Once the luggage was on board, Jonah shouted, "95 West Broadway. The Cosmopolitan Hotel."

"So, you're into ranching, Ishmael? How long have you been doing that?" Martha asked.

"Oh, let's see, now. Over twenty years."

"Do you like it?"

"I do. It's a hard life. It isn't suited for everyone, right, Jonah?"

"That's right, Pa," Jonah said laughing.

"Jonah says you also were a prospector, fought in the war, and went whaling when you were a boy."

"That's right. A little younger than Jonah is now."

"Gosh. You've led such an interesting life."

"I guess looking back. Although at the time it didn't seem all that interesting."

"What does your father do? If you don't mind my asking?"

"My father passed away many years ago. He was a

real estate developer with my Uncle John.”

"I'm sorry to hear that. So, your uncle is a real estate developer?”

"Yes. In fact, he reminds me a little of you.”

"Really? How so?”

"Well, like you, he has done a lot of different things. He's a real estate developer, an inventor, investor, and a writer.”

"Now, he sounds like he has led an interesting life. Makes mine sound rather tame.”

"Nonsense. I'm sure you two shall hit it off swimmingly. I can't wait for you to meet him.”

Jonah changing the subject boasted, “Pa, Martha graduated from Harvard's Radcliffe College.”

"Really? What was your major?”

"Literature. I'm thinking of becoming a teacher,” She said.

"That's wonderful. Just like your Aunt Jane.”

"She has also written several short stories that have been published,” Jonah proudly added.

"Ah, a writer, like your uncle.”

A voice from outside and above announced, “Here we are. The Cosmopolitan Hotel.”

"Listen, I'm going to check-in and get settled. Jonah, I'm sure you two have things to do, so, why don't you run along and let's plan on having dinner around seven. Of course, Martha, you are most welcome to join us.”

"Thank you, sir…I mean Ishmael, that's most kind. I would love to,” Martha replied.

"Excellent. I'll see you both at seven.”

Jonah offered his hand, but I instead gave him a hug, which I'm sure must have embarrassed him in front of

Martha, who had a broad smile on her face as they walked off.

After checking in at the front desk, the bell boy was called to carry my bags up to my suite. The room was situated on the sixth floor looking out onto Broadway. Even though my room was up on the sixth floor the street noise was considerable, especially noticeable at night. Once I had settled in, I decided that I would go out for a walk and do some exploring. I must admit I was surprised by all the motor cars, double-decker buses, and the horse-drawn trolleys on the streets.

I walked east on Chambers Street and turned left on Broadway heading north. I walked for a long time until I got to Washington Square Park. It felt good to stretch my legs after spending so many days cooped up on the train. I sat on a park bench for an hour or so watching people walk by it was quite entertaining. While sitting there I purchased a hot frankfurter from a man pushing what he referred to as a dog wagon. I must say it was very good, I ate two.

On the way back to the hotel I walked west to the Hudson River where all the ocean liners were all lined up. Some were preparing to leave, others had just arrived. There were the *SS Germanic*, *SS Lydia*, *RMS Majestic*, *SS Columbia*, and the ship that I will be sailing on the *RMS Britannic*.

These magnificent floating palaces were truly ocean greyhounds, being able to cross the Atlantic in a mere two weeks.

I am looking forward to setting sail once again. This time as a passenger and not crew.

When I came down to the lobby at seven Jonah and Martha were waiting. Jonah was wearing a blue pinstriped three-piece suit. I couldn't get over how grown-up my little boy looked standing there next to this beautiful young woman, whom I believe was very much in love.

I am by no means an expert on ladies' fashions, but with her hair worn up with curls at the front topped off with a navy-blue hat that matched her dress, decorated with stylized bluebirds. She was quite fetching and turned many a man's heads.

"Good evening. I must say you look quite lovely tonight, my dear," I said.

"Thank you," Martha said, blushing.

"Jonah, you're looking rather dashing, I must say."

"As are you, Pa."

"I confess, I haven't fully become accustomed and comfortable wearing city duds. I prefer my denim jeans and work shirts."

"Well, I think you look very stylish," Martha said smiling.

"You're too kind," I replied giving a tuck at my collar.

"I agree with Martha. You look like you fit right in, Pa."

"Thanks, son. So, what do you say we go get something to eat? I've made a reservation at the Fraunces Tavern. The man at the front desk highly recommended it.”

“I love that place,” Martha said.

“I’ll have the doorman fetch us a carriage,” Jonah declared.

Fraunces Tavern has been around since 1762, located in what I’m told is the financial district. It sits on the corner of Pearl and Broad Streets. The building is a stately three-story red and yellow brick with numerous windows on each floor that gives the interior a light and airy feel. The interior is a step back in time with its 1700s New England style furniture. I found it to take me back to my youth.

We were promptly seated upon our arrival on the second floor. Our waiter came by and asked if we’d prefer wine or beer. Martha and Jonah preferred to have red wine, while I ordered a Yuengling Lager. For dinner, we all ordered the roast prime ribs with roasted potatoes and mushroom sauce. Then to top off the meal we each had a slice of the Georgia Pecan Pie.

“Before we leave, I need to powder my nose,” Martha said.

Once she left, I asked, “Martha seems like a very nice girl. Are you two serious?”

“I love her, Pa. Now that I have a job and a nice place to live, I’m going to ask her to marry me.”

“I’m very happy for you, son. When do you think you’ll ask her?”

“Since her father has passed away, I was going to ask her Uncle John for permission.”

“Isn’t he in town and staying at the Cosmopolitan?”

“Yes. I was hoping to ask him tomorrow.”

“Have you ever met him?”

“No. Martha is planning for the three of us to have

dinner with him tomorrow night if that's all right with you."

"Of course, son. Oh, here she comes." I warned.

As she approached I stood indicating that we should be leaving. Jonah helped her with her wrap, and they followed me out onto the street.

"Care for a carriage, sir?" The doorman asked me.

"Yes, please."

As we were getting into the carriage Jonah informed the driver, "Two stops. The first the Cosmopolitan Hotel and then the Hotel Victoria."

John Jacob Astor IV opened the door and welcomed in his niece Martha and the young man escorting her into room 614.

"Martha, my dear, it's so good to see you again. It's been too long. You look wonderful," He said as he greeted her with a kiss on the cheek.

"Oh, Uncle John, it's good to see you, too."

"And who is this?"

"Uncle John, this is Jonah." She said joyfully.

"Jonah. It's very nice to meet you."

"It's a pleasure to meet you, sir."

"Please won't you both come in?"

John Jacob Astor IV was tall, slender, good-looking, and sported a handlebar mustache. He was the great-grandson of German-American fur-trader John Jacob Astor, one of the wealthiest families in the United States.

He was an American business magnate, real estate developer, investor, and writer, and eight later would become a lieutenant colonel in the Spanish–American War.

"So, how have you been, Martha?"

"I'm doing really well. I've written several articles and had them published. I'm thinking of possibly teaching literature, but I haven't decided."

"Well, you're still young. You have plenty of time. And you, Jonah what is it that you do?" Astor asked.

"I have recently graduated from Harvard Law, and I've started clerking at Bernkopf Goodman."

"Excellent law firm, the best. I'm impressed. I don't know if you know this, but I, too am a Crimson."

"Yes, sir, Martha told me."

"Can I get you two something to drink? I have champagne," Astor asked holding up a bottle of Dom *Ruinart* Blanc de Blancs Brut Millesime.

"Yes, thank you," Jonah replied holding Martha's hand.

Astor poured three chilled glasses, handed everyone a glass, and asked, "What shall we drink to?"

Jonah stood, held up his glass, and said, "If you don't mind, sir? I would humbly ask your permission for the hand of your niece in marriage, sir."

John Astor's expression turned stern, he looked at Jonah sharply, then gazed at Martha whose face looked overcome with delight.

"Martha?" Her uncle asked.

"Oh, Uncle John, yes. Yes. Yes."

John Astor held up his glass and toasted, "To Jonah and Martha. I wish you a happy and healthy life."

Jonah smiling, turned to Martha, clinked their

glasses together, gave her a passionate kiss, entwined their arms, and they took a sip of champagne.

"Thank you, sir. I promise I will love her forever."

There was a knock on the door that seem to have broken the atmosphere in the room.

"Excuse me," Astor said.

When he opened the door, I said, "I'm sorry I'm Jonah's father, Ishmael. He and Martha asked that I meet them here at six-thirty."

"Pleased to meet you, Ishmael. I'm John, won't you please come in. We were just getting ready to celebrate the engagement of your son and my niece, Martha."

I entered the suite which was exactly like mine to find Jonah and Martha standing in the living room holding glasses of champagne. John Astor scurried by me to fill a glass of champagne for me.

"Jonah, Martha, I hear congratulations are in order," I said as I raised my glass.

"To health and happiness," I toasted.

"Please, let's all sit down and talk before we go out to dinner," John said.

The four of us sat in John Astor's hotel suite and had a most harmonious evening discussing the engagement and many thoughts about the wedding. Jonah and Martha decided upon a traditional June Wedding to be held in one year's time at the Old North Church in Boston.

I never raised my son in any particular religious sect, although I was brought up in the Anglican church. The Astors were originally members of the German Reformed Church, but Martha held no allegiance to any organized faith, so because the status of having an Astor marry in Boston's Old North Church would be a society coup, it was decided that it would be the Old North Church.

Once that was settled, John announced, after looking at the wall clock that it was time for us to depart for dinner.

"I've gone ahead and arranged for us to eat at a charming restaurant, Delmonico's on Beaver Street. I highly recommend the Lobster Newburg and they have created a fabulous dessert they call baked Alaska." Astor exulted.

"Can't wait," I replied.

John Astor's private carriage was waiting for us when we exited the hotel.

"Good evening, sir," The coachman said.

"Good evening, James. Delmonico's."

"Yes, sir," James said as he helped everyone into the coach and latched the door.

The conversation in the coach was again, primarily about Jonah and Martha's wedding. During dinner, the discussion turned to John Astor, his business affairs, writings, basically all things John Astor. It wasn't until Martha embarrassingly began to tout some of my achievements and adventures that Astor started to show some interest in me. I am not one who feels compelled nor comfortable bragging about myself and was not interested in trying to impress anyone.

"Now, Martha, I'm sure your uncle isn't interested in hearing about such trivial stories."

"On the contrary. I am very much interested, and I apologize for my rambling on. So, I understand that you have a cattle ranch in California. Is it a big ranch?" Astor asked.

"It's a fair-sized ranch. Thirty-thousand acres."

"How many cattle?"

"Close to six thousand head of cattle."

"Hmmm, sounds rather substantial. What is the name of your ranch?"

"The Devil Fish Ranch."

"A very exotic moniker."

"It's derived from something that occurred in my past."

"Have you always been a rancher, Ishmael?"

"Uncle John, I told you that he founded a very successful gold mine," Martha lauded.

"Ah, that's right. I remember you telling me that. You're quite the entrepreneur as am I, with the exception that I do my exploring in the urban jungles while you do yours in the wild."

"I think yours is more dangerous." I quipped.

"You may be right. So, Ishmael, what's next for you?"

"Well, in two days' time, I'll be sailing on the *RMS Britannic* to England for a couple of months and then over to the Continent."

"Ah, the *Britannic*, I know her well. I've made quite a few voyages on her myself. She's an excellent choice, old man. Do you have any contacts in London?"

"No, not really."

"Well, let me drop off a list before you leave of people that you must meet. I guarantee they will show you London as it should be seen."

"That's very kind of you, but…"

"Now, now, I insist."

I felt obliged to accept his offer, so I acquiesced, "Thank you, John that's very gracious of you."

"Nonsense we're practically family."

He held up his champagne glass, smiled, and toasted, "Bon Voyage."

BRITS, BETH, AND BERTIE

Jonah and Martha came to see me off at Pier 52 at 5:40 pm. John Astor was true to his word and gave me an extensive list of notable influential people. He was also kind enough to arrange to upgrade my suite to a deluxe outside cabin. Because of that, I was to be seated at the captain's table for meals.

During our first formal dinner, we were introduced to our captain, Captain Charles Bartlett. Captain Bartlett was an old-line merchant seaman, who later would garner the nickname "Iceberg Charlie" due to his alleged ability to detect icebergs miles away.

"Greetings, everyone, I'm Captain Bartlett. I want to thank you all for choosing to sail with the White Star Line. We're currently expecting a smooth voyage and I want to assure to that we will do everything we can to make your trip as enjoyable as we possibly can."

Now, why don't we go around the table and introduce yourselves and tell a little bit about you? Sir, why don't we start with you."

"Good evening, my name is Booker T. Washington. I am an educator, author, and presidential advisor. And this is Margaret, my wife."

"It's an honor to meet you both," Captain Bartlett said.

"My name is Henry Ibbotson, and I'm a botanist."

"It's a pleasure to meet you Mister Ibbotson, welcome aboard," Bartlett said.

"Thank you, Captain."

"Mister Ibbotson, I want to say that I am quite an admirer of your work. In particular with your work on *A Catalogue of the Phœnogamous Plants of Great*

Britain." Mister Washington complimented.

"Thank you, sir. Coming from you that is quite an honor indeed."

"Good evening, Captain Bartlett. So good to see you again. To those of you who don't know me, I am Anthony Fane, the thirteenth Earl of Westmorland. And this is my wife, Lady Sybil St. Clair-Erskine."

"Welcome back, Lord and Lady Westmorland, it's always a pleasure to see you again," Captain Bartlett said.

Finally, it was my turn to announce myself to all these notable people.

"I am Ishmael and I fear that I am not all that interesting as the rest of you."

"Nonsense. John Astor assured me that you are a true man of the world. Founder of a successful gold mine, a decorated Captain in the War Between the States, and now a cattle rancher in California. Do not sell yourself short, sir," Captain Bartlell stated.

"Ishmael, I too am impressed with what you have achieved for such a young man," Mister Washington said in agreement. As the whole table nodded in agreement.

"Thank you, all. You're too kind," I said.

"I for one would like to hear more about your service in the American Civil War. Were you in any battles that I may be aware of?" Lord Westmorland asked.

"The only major battle that you might be familiar with would be the Battle of Gettysburg. All the others were small battles and skirmishes in the New Mexico / Arizona Territories."

"I say, Gettysburg. Over fifty-thousand dead in three

days. My God, sir. I can't imagine," Westmorland professed.

"I would be happy to discuss the battle with you, but this may not be a conversation to have at the dinner table."

"Quite right, old man. Quite right." Westmorland agreed, showing embarrassment.

The rest of the dinner conversation was the sort of subjects that could be discussed in polite society. Theodore Roosevelt became the 26th President, the death of the artist, Vincent Van Gogh, and the first modern Olympic games held in Athens, Greece.

During the crossing, I was fortunate to be able to have conversations with everyone from the Captain's table during the voyage.

I have to admit, it felt good to be back out on the ocean once again after being away so long. The salt air, the spray on my face, by God I'm a seafaring man. But after two weeks of smooth sailing, we arrived in Southampton where I was met by a personal friend of John Astor, Sir John Ainsworth, a fellow industrialist.

"Welcome to England, Ishmael. I'm John Ainsworth, John Astor asked that I welcome you upon your arrival."

"That is very thoughtful of you, taking time away from your busy schedule to come all this way."

"Nonsense, I always enjoy meeting people from the colonies," Ainsworth said joking.

After the ship's porter gathered my luggage, Ainsworth's driver placed the baggage into the back of the red Clement-Talbot CT4K motor car.

"Where are you staying in London, Ishmael?"

"The Savoy."

"Jolly good. I would say that it is without a doubt the finest hotel in all of London."

Ainsworth leaned forward in his seat and spoke to his driver, "James, the Savoy Hotel."

"Very good, sir," James replied.

"So, what is that you do, Sir Ainsworth?" I asked.

"I have an interest in iron mines, railways, and banking. I understand that you have an interest in gold mines," He said.

"Actually, just the one gold mine that I discovered. I am now into cattle ranching."

"So, you're a cowboy?"

"Well, I guess you could say that."

"I say, I've never met a real-life cowboy. Do you carry a pistol?"

"Not usually. Although, I did bring my Colt 45 along with me. I have heard that you Brits can get a bit rambunctious," I said with a grin.

"Oh, good show, old man. I would love to see your Colt sometime."

"Anytime, Sir."

"Now, we'll have none of that, it's John."

"Anytime, John."

"Ah, listen, would you mind terribly if we were to stop off at my estate I would really like to see that Colt of yours."

"If you'd like. I'll be happy to show it to you and have you fire it."

"Excellent."

He then tapped James on the shoulder, "Slight change of plans James. We'll be stopping by Ainsworth Manor first."

"Very good, sir."

As we approached Sir Ainsworth's manor I couldn't believe that the building that stood before me was built for one family. It looked like the size of the Cosmopolitan Hotel in New York.

"Welcome to my humble adobe."

"This is your home?"

'Well, one of them. Come let me show you around."

"Before you do, let me unpack my holster and pistol," I said as I retrieved the weapon from my valise.

Sir Ainsworth's eyes got as big as saucers when I handed the pistol to him. He carefully inspected the piece, turning it over and looking at every detail.

"Would you like to try it out?" I asked.

"Jolly good. Let's go around to the back of the manor to the skeet range."

"Lead the way," I said as I strapped on the holster and began to load the Colt.

By the time we arrived at the backyard skeet range, a couple of the servants had set up a faux target range complete with bottles and pieces of cut logs with bullseyes painted on them.

"Would you like to have a go?" I offered.

"I rather not. I prefer to see you in action before I try my hand at it."

"Now, I am not a gunfighter, so don't expect to see a Wild Bill Hickok or a Wyatt Earp."

I tied on my holster, checked my gun, and drew the Colt.

POW POW POW POW POW POW

When the smoke cleared, I had hit three bottles, split two logs, and missed the third log completely.

"Bravo! Bravo!" Ainsworth shouted clapping.

I walked over to my host, unstrapped the holster,

loaded the six-shooter, and held out the holster to Ainsworth, who was as giddy as a schoolgirl.

"Now, It's not drawing the gun faster than your opponent that will always win the duel. It's having a steady hand, nerves of steel, and taking aim. Shooting wildly usually ends up you killing innocent bystanders and getting yourself killed as well.

So, wear the holster so the gun is resting slightly below the wrist, once it's where it feels comfortable, tie the leather strap around your leg, and try a couple of draws. Slowly at first, when the Colt has cleared the holster aim for your target and fire," I explained.

"I'm rather nervous."

"There's no need. You're not facing a dangerous desperado. Try a couple of draws without firing, just to get the feel," I said with a grin.

Ainsworth's first attempts were less than perfect. He had a hard time clearing the holster. So, I lowered the holster, and it became easier. After an hour he was able to draw the Colt and fire at the targets in one motion. He never was able to hit any of the targets, and finally gave up.

"Drat. I don't think that I will ever get the knack."

"Nonsense, all you need is practice. Here I gift this to you," I said as I handed him the holster and Colt.

"No sir, I cannot accept such a generous gift."

"Sir Ainsworth it would be an honor if you would. Besides, me being a cowboy, this is not my only outfit. So, please."

"Ishmael, you sir are a true gentleman and friend. If there is ever anything that I can do for you, do not hesitate to ask."

After our shooting exposition, Ainsworth had his

culinary staff prepare a most delightful lunch consisting of Beef Wellington, green beans, potato Dauphinoise, honey-balsamic glazed carrots, and roasted asparagus. And for dessert, we had Banoffee pie with such a heavenly combination of Bananas, caramel, biscuit, and cream.

"John, I must confess that this was by far the best meal that I've ever had…in England," I said laughing.

It took Ainsworth a few seconds before he got my little joke, but he too broke out laughing.

"Jolly good, Ishmael."

"But seriously, this meal was fantastic."

"Well, I'm so glad that you liked it, old man. Now, I think it best that we get you to London."

He walked me out to the motor car, where James the chauffeur stood at the ready.

"James, be a good chap and take Ishmael into London. He's staying at the Savoy Hotel," Ainsworth ordered.

"Very good, sir."

"Ishmael, I say old bean I had the most enjoyable time with you today. What say we do it again? And I warn you; I am going to practice my drawing and shooting."

"I look forward to it. And thanks again for your kind hospitality."

"So long, cheerio."

Once we arrived at the Savoy, six bellmen rushed

out to see if they could be of service. When I reached my room after checking in, there must have been a dozen baskets from friends of John Astor welcoming me to London with requests and invitations to lunches, dinners, and galas. There was even an invitation from King Edward VII to attend a tea at the Savoy the following week.

I spent my first week in London just roaming the streets and getting familiar with the lay of the land. I was fascinated with the London Underground. I would just ride for hours on different subway lines observing people, and occasionally, I would disembark and wander around, stopping in shops and pubs.

One evening as I was passing the front desk at the Savoy, the young desk clerk called me over.

"Sir, I have an envelope for you."

"Thank you," I said as I handed him a one-pound note.

"Oh, thank you, Guv."

The thick cream-colored envelope had the crest of the King of England printed in gold. It was a royal invitation to a tea hosted by King Edward VII.

Below the royal crest, it read, *"The Lord Chamberlain is commanded by the King to Invite You to a Tea Party in the Main Ballroom of the Savoy Hotel on Tuesday, 16th May 1896 from 4 to 6 pm. Black Tie Required."*

This being the Friday before the event and me not owning a tuxedo, I went back to the front desk.

"Excuse me. Any idea where I might procure a tuxedo, young man?"

"I would have to say, Ede &Ravenscroft."

"And where might they be?"

"93 Chancery Lane, sir."

"Thanks, son," I said, giving the lad another one-pound note.

"Gee, thanks, Governor."

I headed out the lobby entrance and hailed a cab, "93 Chancery Lane."

" Ede &Ravenscroft, right you are, Guv."

The cabbie drove by the River Thames, past the Waterloo Bridge, and the Royal Courts of Justice to Chancery Lane. It took all of ten minutes before we arrived.

"Here you go, Guv. That'll be one pound, six shillings. Want I should wait?"

"No, thank you. I don't think that will be necessary."

The small shop was very tasteful, as soon as I entered I was approached by a very proper Brutish man dressed impeccably.

"Good day, sir. My name is Reginald. May I be of service?" He asked.

"I hope so. I need a tuxedo for a royal tea that is happening next Tuesday," I said.

"Well, then, let's get to it. Shall we?" He said as he whipped out a measuring tape from his suit coat pocket and began to measure me from top to bottom and all points in between.

"Do you think it will be ready in time?"

"Well, there will be a small surcharge for having it ready in time. I will need you to be prepared to come back for a fitting Monday."

"Just tell me when."

"Monday at eleven o'clock."

"All right."

"Now, you'll need the proper shoes, a white

Marcella Waistcoat, Marcella bow tie, at least two Delaney stiff bib tunic collar shirts, a pair of white tie cotton dress gloves, and if I might, an Ivory herringbone silk scarf."

"Whatever you say."

"Very good. Oh, and just one more thing."

"Yes?"

"A Hetherington top hat."

"Really?"

"Whom are you going to be seeing?"

"King Edward VII," I confessed.

"Oh, then it is a must, sir."

"If you say so. I trust your judgment."

"Very good. Shall I send these items to your hotel?"

"Yes, please. I'm staying at the Savoy Hotel, room 666."

I arrived at Ede &Ravenscroft at precisely eleven o'clock and was greeted at the door by Reginald.

"Good morning, sir."

"And a good morning to you, Reginald," I said.

"If you would step this way. We are ready for your fitting."

I followed Reginald to the back of the shop, where an old man stood stooped over from too many years bending over, taking customer measurements. He peered up at me with a tape measure wrapped around his neck, tailor's chalk in one hand, and a mouthful of straight pins.

"Gof mawnin," He mumbled.

"Good morning," I replied.

Reginald held out his hand and asked, "May I take your coat, sir? So, Willian can make the alterations."

I took off my coat and trousers and was asked to step up onto a small platform. I was handed my new tuxedo jacket and pants, which I promptly put on and stood there while William proceeded to chalk, fold, and pin areas that he felt needed to be altered. The old man moved around me like a whirling dervish; his hands moved with the procession of a highly trained surgeon.

It took Williams less than fifteen minutes to complete the fitting. Afterward, Reginald said, "Shall we have the garment sent to your hotel, sir?"

"That would be most appreciative, Reginald."

"Very good, sir. It was a pleasure making your acquaintance."

I smiled and said, "Cheers."

Instead of taking a cab, I decided to walk back to the Savoy along the River Thames.

I stood in front of the full-length mirror in my room, looking at myself all duded up in my tuxedo, sporting my top hat and tails. I felt the fool.

I rode the elevator down to the lobby. When the doors opened, there were dozens of similarly dressed men, all looking as foolish as I was. However, there were many beautifully dressed women in their evening gowns.

As we entered the ballroom, there were half a dozen attendants checking our invitations. Once I was allowed in, I found myself standing all alone until I heard a familiar voice call out from behind, "Ishmael!"

It was Sir Ainsworth walking towards me with two other men.

"This is the chap I was telling you about," He told his two companions.

"So, you the American?" One of the men asked.

"I don't know if I'm *the* American. But I am an American." I countered.

Sir Ainsworth laughed as he put his arm around my shoulder, "Ishmael, here is one Hell of a shot, gentlemen."

"Have you been practicing, John?" I asked.

"I have. I would love for you to return to the manor and give me some more lessons."

"I would love to. Anytime."

"Ishmael, I'd like you to meet James Cecil, the 4th Marquess of Salisbury and this and Frederick Hamilton-Temple-Blackwood, 1st Marquess of Dufferin and Madeleine," John said.

I gave a small quick bow, "Gentlemen."

"We understand from John that you're quick on the draw. Is that the phrase?" Frederick Hamilton-Temple-Blackwood asked.

"That is the phrase, I may be quick, but I'm hardly gunfighter quick," I said.

"Come. Come. Don't be modest; John here said that not only were you fast but had a deadly aim as well," James Cecil professed.

"Gentlemen, I will modestly admit that I am a good

to fair shot. But I am no Wild Bill Hickok."

"Well, I would like to see a demonstration of western shooting, if you don't mind? Next time you go out to see Ainsworth." James Cecil asked.

Sir Ainsworth chuckled and said, "I promise to inform you both once a date is procured."

From the back of the ballroom, a booming voice hollered, "His Royal Highness, King Edward VII."

The room got deadly quiet as everyone turned to the back of the room. I was located about in the middle of the ballroom. Sir Ainsworth took my arm and led me into the greeting line for the King.

The King would stop and carry on a brief conversation with every person in line after the men would bow their heads, and the women would give a curtsy.

Sir Ainsworth whispered, "Ishmael, just bow and say, Your Majesty when he gets to you. Just follow my lead."

Sir Ainsworth gave a bow as the King approached and said, "*Your Majesty.* This gentleman to my left is the man I spoke to you about. Ishmael."

"Ah, very good.," King Edward uttered.

As he stood before me, I gave the proper head nod and said, "*Your Majesty.*"

"Sir Ainsworth informs me that you are quite the adventurer. I would love for you to come by Buckingham Palace so you could tell me about some of your exploits, Ishmael. May I call you Ishmael?"

"By all means, *Your Majesty.*"

The King gave a nod and a smile, then moved on to James Cecil, the 4th Marquess of Salisbury, who was standing next to me. Edward didn't stop and converse with any of the others in the line after me.

I must admit, I found it to be all too amusing. Here I am, a lowly American of no notable fame having a conversation with the King of England and being invited to meet with him in Buckingham Palace while the hordes of nobility are standing around staring and wondering who the Hell is this Yank.

At the other end of the ballroom, the orchestra began to play a Waltz. I, who never considered myself a dancer, decided to go to the bar and see about getting myself a drink. I was surprised to be surrounded by a group of British elites, men and women trying to find out just who the Hell I am, that would have His Royal Highness, King Edward VII, stop and take the time to speak to me.

As I was being bombarded with questions from all sides, luckily, Sir Ainsworth came to my rescue and began to fend off many of the questions. At one point, I saw him signaling to a rather beautiful woman, who worked her way through the crowd until she reached Sir Ainsworth and myself.

"Ishmael, I'd like you to meet my niece Elizabeth Ainsworth. Elizabeth, this is Ishmael, the gentleman I spoke to you about," Ainsworth said.

She held out her hand. I took it, bowed, and kissed it as I had seen many others do that night, "It's a pleasure to meet you, Miss Ainsworth."

"Beth," She said.

"All right, Beth."

"Would you care to dance, Ishmael?"

"I'm afraid I don't dance. Not like you folks, anyway."

"Come, we'll wait until they do something slow. It

will be fun, I promise," She said as she led me away from the group.

"Can I bring you something to drink?" I asked.

"Champagne."

"I'll be right back," I said as I made my way to the bar. I got the bartender's attention, "One champagne and one whiskey, please."

I then made my back to the other side of the ballroom, where I found her waiting, talking to Sir Ainsworth, who had a smile on his face like he had just swallowed the canary.

"Ishmael, I have my car waiting outside. Why don't you two go out someplace for dinner? You look like a fish out of water." Sir Ainsworth said with a wink.

"But what about the King?" I asked.

"Don't worry, old chap, I think he was his hands full," He said, looking around at all the people.

"Cheerio," I said, holding out my arm to see if Beth was game. She was, and off we went.

"Good evening, James," I said to Sir Ainsworth's driver.

"Evening, Guv. Where to?"

I looked to Beth for an answer, "Beth, this is your town."

"The Savoy Grill," She said to James with a coquettish smile.

"But madam, you're at then Savoy all ready."

In an embarrassing giggle, she laughed and said, "Oh, so we are. That will be all, James."

Beth took my arm and walked me into the grand lobby. She sidled up next to me, smiled, and whispered, "I'm starving. Let's go up to your room and order room service."

The bellman prepared the table in the suite, set the silverware, and arranged and placed the plated food in position. As he gently set the meal in front of each of us, he announced the courses, "Poached oysters, oscietra caviar, roasted cod loin, Dover sole Grenobloise, and for dessert, a selection of British and Irish cheese with cherry sourdough bread. Bon appetite."

He then poured a small amount of Dom Pérignon into my glass to sample. I can assure you that I am anything but a connoisseur of fine champagne, but it tasted good to me, so I gave the nod of approval.

"Will there be anything else, sir?"

"No. I think we're good. Just put on the room and give yourself a good tip."

"Oh, thank you, sir. Thank you very much."

We sat opposite each other, looking at each other. I don't remember which one of us started to eat in a seductive manner. But I began to observe Beth playing with her oysters, slowly caressing them with her tongue and pursing her lips while sucking the juice from the shells. It wasn't too long before we stood naked in front of each other, passionately kissing each other deeply.

I picked her up and carried her to the bedroom, where I gently laid her down and placed a pillow under the small of her back. I laid on top of her slipping my hand down from her breast to the soft silky down between her legs. My fingers lightly spread her Honeypot as I felt her warm naked flesh against me as I thrust my white staff deep inside her. Each time I lunged deep inside, she would utter wild little cries until, at the moment of climax, we both called out God's name, then collapsed into each other's arms and fell into a deep sleep.

The following day when I awoke, Beth had dressed and gone. On the mantle, I found a note that she had left.

"Dearest Ishmael,

Thank you for last night. I regret to say that I must travel to Paris for a few weeks. I look forward to seeing you when I get back. Until then...

B. "

A nondescript black car was waiting for me in front of the Savoy, sent from Buckingham Place. Standing by the rear of the vehicle, the driver was wearing an olive-green chauffer's uniform, black boots, black gloves, and a matching cap. He looked to be in his fifties, with grey hair, trim built, and sporting a handlebar mustache.

He said not a word as I approached; he closed the rear passenger door once I was seated. He was silent on the drive to the palace until I spoke, "Good morning."

"Good morning, sir," He said in a monotone voice,

staring straight ahead, not looking in the rear-view mirror.

"Have you been doing this long?" I asked.

"Going on twenty-two years now."

"Do you like it?"

"I do, sir. Very much."

"Say, I like your mustache."

He perked up, smiled, glanced in the rear-view, and gave the end of his handlebar a slight twirl.

"Thank you, Guv," He said with a toothy grin.

As we were approaching the palace driving head-on from the Mall, the Victoria Memorial loomed large as we veered left onto Spur Road and into the grounds of the palace, where we were met by two Guardsmen. The driver handed one of the guards a pass, who, after inspecting the pass, peered into the car to inspect me.

Seeming satisfied, the guard waved his hand and muttered, "Enter."

Once inside the palace grounds, the car pulled up to the main entrance, where I was greeted by a young gentleman in a black suit.

"Follow me," He ordered as I exited the car.

As we were walking through a maze of hallways, all decorated with magnificent works of art, he was walking slightly ahead of me, speaking over his shoulder.

"When you are presented to the King, you call him "Your Majesty" and "Sir" on subsequent mentions. For other members of the Royal Family, it is "Your Royal Highness" at first mention, then "Sir" or "Ma'am." It is important to bow when you first meet him; a simple nodding of your head will suffice. Is that clear?" The man spoke as if he had given this speech a thousand times, which I'm sure he had.

"Crystal," I replied.

We stopped in front of two enormous golden doors; he turned and charged, "Wait here!"

I stood outside those massive doors until he stuck his head out and said, "You may come in." as he opened the doors.

I walked into a room decorated in gold. There were four grand gold and crystal chandeliers hanging from the four corners of the room, French golden silk chairs with matching sofas, huge mirrors and paintings framed in gold, portraits by Van Dyck and Canaletto, sculptures by Canova, and wall-to-wall carpet, woven red and gold. The walls and ceiling were white with golden fillagree. It appeared to me what heaven might look like.

As I walked in, I spied a lone figure at the other end of the room; it was His Royal Highness, King Edward VII, sitting on a sofa reading a copy of the London Times.

"Ishmael, please come in. You may go, Farnsworth," He bellowed.

I walked towards him alone, and as I stood in front of him and was prepared to bow, he said, "Now, now, we'll have none of those formalities. Please have a seat."

"Thank you, Your Majesty."

"Bertie. Call me Bertie. That's what my friends call me."

"Bertie?"

"It's the nickname my mother gave me when I was a child."

"So, Ishmael, I've heard many tales about you. Tell

me all about yourself."

"Why on earth would you be interested in me, Bertie?" I asked.

"Why? Because I enjoy talking to fellow adventurers. For me, my adventures have been well orchestrated and nonspontaneous. But you, on the other hand, Ishmael, have had what I believe is an extraordinary lifetime of adventures. If you would, please indulge me."

So, I told him of my days as a whaler and of my encounter with Moby Dick. Then, how my survivor's guilt and need to experience living life on the edge of death and danger drove me to a life of piracy. After many years of swashbuckling, I told him I had had my fill; I wanted to seek my fortune in the goldfields of California, which led to my near-death experience with being shot in the back by some claim jumper. All the while, King Edward VII sat with his mouth agape and eyes wide open.

I recounted my Civil War battles and my encounters with the likes of Kit Carson, whom I found to be a master scout who possessed a brilliant military mind, but with whom I disagreed on the value and worthiness of Native American Indian's lives. And finally, my becoming one of the largest cattle ranchers in all of California.

"You, sir, are one of the most remarkable men that I have ever had the pleasure to encounter. What a life you have lived," Bertie said with a hardy laugh.

"Thank you, Your Hig…" I stopped as the King held up his finger as a reminder.

I corrected myself, "Bertie."

"Say, Ishmael, I'm going hunting next week at

Gwern Borter Manor near Rowen and would love it if you were to come along. What say you?"

"I'm sorry, Bertie, but I must get back to the States. My son, Jonah, is getting married in a couple of weeks."

"Ah, quite right. Quite right. Well, promise me that when you get back to jolly old England that we must get away to Gwern Borter Manor and go hunting."

"I promise," I said.

London, thanks to my relationship with John Jacob Astor, Sir Ainsworth, and of course Bertie, all doors were opened to me that never would have if it were not for them. People invited me into their homes and into their inner circle of friends with just a drop of a name.

For one shining moment, I was the toast of London town.

BACK TO AMERICA

I arrived at the Old North Church an hour before my son Jonah and his bride-to-be, Martha Astor, were to be wed. Jonah was waiting in the South portal with his best man, Jonathan Wilcox, a fellow lawyer at the law firm of Bernkopf Goodman.

"Good morning Jonathan. It's good to see you again."

"And you, sir."

"Well, son, this is a big day for you. How are you doing?"

"To tell you the truth, Pa. I'm a little nervous."

"No need to be; Martha is a wonderful girl. I just hope that you'll be as happy as your mother and I were. I'm sure you will be."

"Any fatherly advice?"

"Always be truthful to each other, treat each other as your equal, and be kind to each other."

"I will," Jonah said.

A few moments later, John Jacob Astor stopped by to give his good wishes to Jonah. I could tell that he was surprised to see me.

"Ishmael! It's so good to see. It's been a long time. I don't think you've had the pleasure to meet my wife, Ava."

"No, I have not. It's my pleasure to meet you, Ava, on such a blessed occasion."

"It's so nice to meet you, too. I have heard so much about you, Ishmael. Now I see where Jonah gets his good looks," She said with a grin.

"You're too kind. I think that he probably gets his good looks from his mother."

"John, I want to thank you for introducing me to so many of your English friends. It meant a lot," I said.

"It was my pleasure. I understand you were quite the man about town. King Edward VII?"

"Pa? What about King Edward VII?" Jonah inquired.

"Rumor has it that your father and King Edward VII are tight friends," Astor remarked, half-joking.

"Really!" Jonah exclaimed.

"Mister Astor is exaggerating. I just happened to meet the King a couple of times. That's all."

"The tongues are wagging all over London. Your father is the most sought out man in all of London. The men want to be seen with him, and the women just want him," Astor said, laughing.

"Enough. This is Jonah's wedding day. It's not about me."

The priest that was going to perform the wedding, Father Newman, came into the room and announced that it was time to take our places.

Unlike many churches, the Old North Church has box pews; each box pew was owned by an individual or family that was decorated by their owners. The closer the box pew was to the Altar, the wealthier and more important person you were.

The concept of the box pew resulted from the fact that the early meeting houses were not heated, and the walls of the box pews would minimize drafts, thus keeping the occupants relatively warmer in the winter. But as time went on, the box pew became a status symbol. In fact, if one didn't own a pew box, you had no place to sit, and you were not allowed into the services.

Since this was a private event, we were allowed to sit in any box pew we desired. I sat in one of the bow pews in the very front with Jonah's Aunt Jane, whom I had come out for the wedding, unbeknownst to him as a surprise. The look on his face was priceless when he saw her sitting next to me.

The church was packed with people, mostly a large contingency of the Astor family and dozens of business acquaintances of John Astor. Once everyone was seated, the pipe organ in the sanctuary began to play Felix Mendelssohn's "Wedding March" in C major.

John Astor walked Martha, his niece, down the aisle to where Jonah, his best man, and Father Newman were standing at the altar. Martha wore a white high-waisted empire line dress with sleeves worn to the elbow, gloves, and a veiled hat. She carried in her arms a sheath bouquet of white roses, orchids, lilies of the valley, and orange blossoms.

When John and Martha reached the alter, Father Newman, said, "Who giveth this woman to be married be married to this man?"

Astor announced, "I do."

Martha stood alongside Jonah and turned toward the priest. Father Newman, holding the Bible, said, "We have gathered to celebrate the joining of Jonah and Martha in a covenant of love. This covenant is the promise of hope between two people who love each other, who understand their love as a gift of God, who trust that love, and who wish to share the future together.

It enables two separate people to share their desires, longings, dreams, and memories and to help each other through their uncertainties. It provides the encouragement to risk more and thus to gain more. In this covenant, these two people belong together, providing mutual support and stability, and if it is God's will, a place in which their children may grow.

Here in the presence of God, we recognize and bless their relationship as they begin their married life together in the community."

Jonah turned and faced Martha taking her right hand, said, "*In the Name of God, I, Jonah, take you, Martha, to be my faithful wife, to have and to hold from this day forward, for better for worse, for richer for poorer, in sickness and in health, to love and to cherish, until we are parted by death/until death parts us. This is my solemn vow.*"

Martha facing Jonah, took his right hand and said, "*In the Name of God, I, Martha, take you, Jonah, to be my faithful husband, to have and to hold from this day forward, for better for worse, for richer for poorer, in sickness and in health, to love and to cherish, until we are parted by death/until death parts us. This is my solemn vow.*"

Father Newman held up the wedding rings high above his head, saying, "*Bless, O Lord, this ring to be a sign of the vows by which this man and this woman/these persons have bound themselves to each other; through Jesus Christ our Lord. Amen.*"

He then handed the rings back to Jonah and Martha. Jonah slipped the ring onto Martha's hand and said, "*Martha, I give you this ring as a symbol of my vow, and with all that I am, and all that I have, I honor you, in the Name of God.*"

Martha took Jonah's hand, slipped the ring upon his finger, and said, "*Jonah, I give you this ring as a symbol of my vow, and with all that I am, and all that I have, I honor you, in the Name of God."*

Father Newman held his arms up towards heaven. He declared, *"Now that Jonah and Martha have given themselves to each other by solemn vows, with the joining of hands and the giving and receiving of a ring, I pronounce that they are husband and wife, in the Name of the Father, and of the Son, and of the Holy Spirit.*

Those whom God has joined together, let no one put asunder."

The whole congregation called out in unison, *"Amen."*

The wedding reception was held at the Boston Athenaeum, one of the most distinguished independent libraries and cultural institutions in the U.S. It's home to over half a million volumes on everything from Boston history to the fine and decorative arts. Its five galleried floors overlook the sacred Granary Burying Ground.

The reception lasted for over eight hours. When Jonah and Martha finally left for their honeymoon, it was well past midnight. Since Astor insisted on paying for the wedding and reception, I thought it only fair to pay for the honeymoon, three weeks in the Greek Isles.

That night would be the last time I ever saw my son Jonah.

THE DARK CONTINENT

After Jonah and Martha's wedding, John Astor invited me to his estate, Ferncliff, outside of Rhinebeck, New York, in the Lower Hudson River Valley. Ferncliff is a working farm with dairy and poultry operations and stables where he bred horses. The Victorian mansion included turrets, sprawling porches, and enviable views of both the Hudson River below and the Catskill Mountains in the distance.

John met me as the car pulled up to the front entrance around 6 pm. James, the chauffeur, opened the door for me as we arrived.

"Thank you, James," I said.

"Very good, sir," He answered with a smile and a tip of his cap.

"Ishmael, so good of you to come. Welcome to Ferncliff."

"What a lovely home you have."

"Thank you. Come let me show you to your room," Astor said as he led me into the mansion.

The interior looked like some of the museums I had visited in New York, Boston, and London, with dozens of paintings and sculptures. My room was on the second floor, which had a spectacular view of the Hudson River.

"I hope you'll be comfortable; if there is anything you need, let me know."

"Thank you, John. I'm sure I'll be fine."

"Oh, later on after you get settled in. We're having a small dinner party; I have some people I'd like you to meet. Dinner is at eight, and we dress for dinner. So,

I'll see you then," He said as he left the room.

All the while, two manservants were unpacking my luggage and taking my evening clothes downstairs to be pressed in time for dinner.

Later that evening, as I came downstairs, I was greeted by a maid and informed that drinks were being served in the salon.

"Right this way, sir. If you would follow me," She said.

The salon had pale green flocked wallpaper with matching curtains trimmed with gold leaf. Overhead was a giant crystal and gold chandelier. The paintings on the walls were primarily the Astor ancestry going back to Johann Jakob Astor, who immigrated to America from Germany in the 1700s. In one corner of the room was a string quartet playing chamber music while a dozen or so people stood in the middle of the room near the fireplace where a small fire was burning for effect. Once inside, a butler approached with a tray of glasses of champagne. He said nothing; he just held out the tray. I took a glasses and moved into the center of the room where I saw John talking to a stocky man of medium height, wearing wire-rim spectacles.

When John spotted me, he called out, "Ah, there you are. Teddy, this is the chap I thought you'd like to meet. Ishmael, I'd like you to meet Teddy Roosevelt, a good friend of mine."

I extended my hand and said, "Mister Roosevelt. I've heard so much about you. It's an honor to meet you, sir."

"And I have heard much about you as well, Ishmael. Please call me Teddy. All my friends do."

"Ishmael told me several months ago that he wanted

to do some exploring on the Dark Continent. And Teddy, I understand that you're going to head up an expedition outfitted by the Smithsonian Institute sometime next April."

"That's right. Ishmael, do you think it is something you'd be interested in doing?"

"Maybe. How long are you planning on being away?" I asked.

"Probably a year," Roosevelt said.

"I'm in," I said.

"Bully! A fellow adventurer," He roared as he slapped me on the back.

"Excellent. I knew you two would hit it off." Astor said, smiling.

"Dinner is now served," Announced the majordomo standing in the doorway, dressed in a smart black and white livery.

We were ushered into the grand dining room, where the servants were standing at attention against the walls at the ready to help the ladies with the chairs. There were place cards set up on the table, alerting the guests where to sit and whom to sit next to. I was seated next to Benjamin Guggenheim, a businessman whose family made their fortune in copper mining. I found him to be a true gentleman with a great sense of humor. On my left side, seated next to me, was a fascinating young woman, Helen Churchill Candee, an American author, journalist, feminist, and one of the country's first female interior decorators.

For dinner, we started with Mulligatawny Soup and Stewed Eels. Our main course was a choice of Curried Lobster with Rice or Fricandeau of Veal with Spinach. And for dessert we had Blancmange. Each course was more delightful than the next. It was eleven o'clock when John stood and announced that the gentlemen would be retiring to the library for brandy and cigars. It wasn't long before the conversation went from politics and women to exploration being led by none other than Theodore Roosevelt. He began talking about his days riding with the Rough Riders of the 1st United States Volunteer Cavalry and his charge up San Juan Hill.

"Has anyone else experienced war?" He asked.

"I said that I had fought with the California Brigade at Gettysburg and many a battle in New Mexico Territory alongside Kit Carson."

"By God, sir, I knew I liked you from the first time I set eyes on you," Roosevelt roared.

John Astor stood holding his snifter of brandy and said, "Gentlemen, I'd like to propose a toast to our two intrepid warriors."

"Cheers! Cheers! Cheers!"

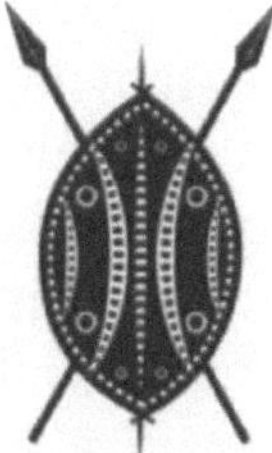

I met Roosevelt and the expedition party in Naples, Italy. I decided to spend some time in Boston visiting Jonah and Martha before going off to Africa, not knowing what to expect and if and when I might return.

I joined them on board the *Admiral*, a German-flagged ship that the expedition leader legendary hunter-tracker R. J. Cunninghame had chosen because the ship's owners permitted us to load large amounts of ammunition.

R. J. Cunninghame and Leslie Tarlton had gone on ahead to arrange for our travel arrangements and rendezvous with Cherry Keaton, a wildlife filmmaker. The latter was going to document the expedition for Smithsonian.

Once everyone had time to stow their gear and get acclimated, we met as a group in the ship's galley to get acquainted with each other.

Aside from our leader R. J. Cunninghame, the expedition included Australian sharpshooter Leslie Tarlton; three American naturalists, Edgar Alexander Mearns, Edmund Heller, and John Alden Loring, Roosevelt's nineteen-year-old son Kermit who would act as official photographer, and myself. Once we arrived in Mombasa, British East Africa, we would travel by the Uganda Railway to the Kapiti Plains. The safari would hire a large number of porters, gunbearers, horse boys, tent men, and askari guards.

The expedition's equipment included material for preserving animal hides, including powdered borax, cotton batting, and four tons of salt, as well as a variety of tools, weapons, and everything ranging from lanterns to sewing needles. We had a full collection of firearms, ranging from several Springfield M1903 .03-03 caliber rifles. And for larger game, we brought along five Six Winchester 1895 rifles and eight.405 Winchesters.

Teddy kept reminding us that since the Smithsonian Institute funded the expedition, capturing, collecting, and cataloging of wild and unknown species was to be the main objective of the safari.

The planned route that we were to take had us

traveling from Mombasa into the Belgian Congo to Nairobi, the vicinity of Mt. Kenja, the Loita Plains, Lake Victoria, Lake Albert, and up the Nile to Khartoum.

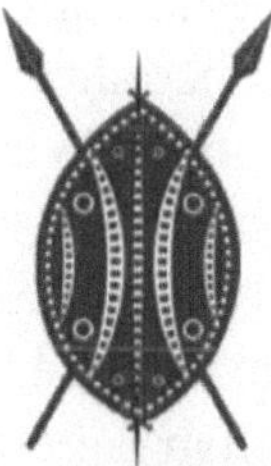

What follows is my account and recollections of the Smithsonian-Roosevelt African Expedition. Please read Teddy's book African Game Trails for a more accurate account.

After almost a month at sea, we landed in Mombasa in the late morning. We make our way to the Uganda Railroad Depot for the two-day train ride to the Kapiti Plains.

As the train porters were placing our personal luggage in our cabins, we all met in the club car for drinks and to discuss the upcoming expedition. While we were enjoying our libations, the conductor stopped by to inform us that the Uganda Railway had mounted a special observation platform at the front of the locomotive, especially for Teddy Roosevelt and three of his friends. Teddy asked if I would be interested in joining him on the platform, and I declined, "Teddy, I think for the first time it should be you, Uganda Governor Frederick Jackson, Frederick Selous, and Doctor Mearns."

When the train finally pulled out of Mombasa, Teddy Roosevelt and the others sat in front of the locomotive dressed in their coats and ties, all wearing pith helmets, looking very esteemed.

Later that night, Roosevelt wrote in his journal titled African Game Trails, "our safari was awaiting us. The goal of the safari is to collect birds, mammals, reptiles, and plants for the Smithsonian, and big game animals for the National Museum in Washington D.C."

On the first leg of our safari, we enjoyed the hospitality of Sir Alfred Pease's 6000-acre ranch, which was located nearby the Uganda Railway. Pease, 2nd Baronet, was a British Liberal Party politician who sat in the House of Commons between 1885 and 1902 and became a pioneer settler of British East Africa. He, along with Frederick Selous, founded the Shikar Club, an international sporting and big game hunting club. It was at the Pease's ranch that we acquired the rest of the hunting party and our 250 local guides and porters.

On our first day on the hunt, we rode out on horseback, looking for lions. We rode out to an area called Killima (Hill) Ugami, where seven Kukuyu ostrich boys ran ahead of us, beating the tall grass to roust the lions out into the open so we could shoot them. We dismounted and walked in teams of two; I was teamed up with R. J. Cunninghame, known to the Swahilis as "Bwana Medivu," the Master with the Beard. That day we got two and one small lion. I did not claim any kills on our first hunt on this day. Teddy was the one to claim the two large beasts; Sir Alfred Pease bagged the smaller one. The natives skinned the three lions where they fell and left the carcasses out for the buzzards and other scavengers.

On the way back to the ranch, one of our porters was attacked and mauled by a large male leopard; Kermit chased it down on horseback, treed it, and shot it dead, making Teddy extremely proud of his son.

We spend the next three months collecting live specimens of fauna, as well as mammals. Our hunting party kills and mounts numerous varieties of animals like rhinos, lions, cheetahs, wildebeest, spotted hyenas, and impala for museums. We also killed and skinned, and beheaded dozens of species for our own trophies.

In August, we traveled up into Nairobi and Mt. Kenia, where Teddy and Kermit were to be the guests of honor at a public banquet by Governor Jackson in Nairobi. We would take the opportunity to hunt elephants.

I was to be teamed up with Frederick Selous, explorer, and professional hunter. Selous has laid claim to killing over four hundred lions, elephants, buffaloes, and rhinos. I am glad that he is my teammate when hunting elephants, as I have never seen one except in a circus. We camped next to a Kikuyu village as the tribesmen were skilled at locating the massive beasts.

The following day after arriving and setting up camp, we trekked through a heavily wooded area with thick brush. Off in the distance, we could hear what the natives told us was a large elephant herd of bulls, cows, and babies heading towards us. We stood behind a grove of Fever Trees, waiting for the herd to appear.

At last, we saw the mighty game slowly meandering in our direction. Teddy and R. J. Cunninghame were off to our left. We each were holding a weapon at the ready, and our gun-bearers each held a loaded Winchester 1895 rifle and a .405 Winchester as a backup. Suddenly, three bulls, with good ivory, must have gotten wind of us because they began to charge in our direction. Teddy saw that the bull closest to him had turned its head, exposing the side of its face. Teddy aimed behind the eye, thinking that the bullet would travel up into the brain, But the elephant's skull was too thick and massive, so it just stunned the beast. He stumbles forward, half falling, and as he recovered, Teddy fired a second shot; this time, the bullet sped true. The great lord of the jungle came crashing to the ground.

The bull that charged me came so close that I could have reached out and touched him as he came rushing by. I leaped to my right and hid behind a tree trunk. As he twirled around to come back for another charge, I wheeled around and fired two shots. Both shots struck the bull near the heart. It stopped his charge, but he juked to the left and disappeared into the forest, the thick vegetation closed over his path like the wake of a ship. We heard crying trumpeting for several minutes, and then nothing.

While Teddy and R. J. Cunninghame had the porters begin to skin the dead elephant to preserve it for mounting in a museum, Frederick Selous and our gun-bearers went in search of my quarry. We tracked the great tusker for over three hours until we found him dead in an open field, with two cows and a baby standing nearby, mourning him. Being that it was too far to try and skin the beast and carry it back to the camp, it was decided just to remove the tusks. When they were weighed, they tipped the scale at one hundred and twenty pounds the pair.

After two months of hunting elephants, Teddy thought it was time to move onto Lake Naivasha to collect several hippopotami, crocodiles, and numerous waterfowl. In October, we caught the train to the Uasin Gishun Plateau. It has been an arduous seven months. Many of our horses had died, and it looked like we might have had to travel on foot. Luckily we did not. We were able to make it to the railway and take it to Lake Victoria Nyanza, and from there, we traveled on the Uganda Railroad to Uganda's capital Kampala.

In Kampala, we were finally able to travel by motorized vehicle. Every day in Kampala, there were thunderstorms. The rumor is that three men have been killed by lightning. Nonetheless, Teddy and Kermit arrange to go on a Situtanga hunt. The Situtanga is a swamp-dwelling Antelope. Luck seemed to be with father and son Roosevelt. By the time they reached the swamp, the weather had cleared, and they were able to bag a pair of the Situtanga.

To start the new year off right, we marched on foot to Buitaba, on the shores of Lake Albert Nyanza. It took us ten days to march 160 miles from Lake Victoria to Lake Albert Nyanza. On the march, we occasionally got the opportunity to hunt, on one night after Christmas Day, Teddy and Kermit were able to bring down a giant bull elephant. The look on Teddy's face when they stood to have their picture taken next to their trophy was one of fatherly pride.

We were greeted by Captain H. Hutchinson of the Royal Navy Reserve, who will take charge of the flotilla down the River Nile, where the rare White Rhinoceros lives. If he can bag one, it will be one of Teddy's prized trophies of the whole safari. Even though the White Rhino is considered scarce in the territory, Teddy believes that it's his duty to science to collect a specimen. He is successful; he kills three.

Teddy says, "It's a good day for science."

The hunting party boards the steamer Dal at the end of February and continues our journey down the White Nile, making dozens of stops to hunt. On March 14th, 1910, we reach Khartum. The Roosevelt African Expedition is officially over.

The party gathers at the train station. Teddy reunites with his wife and daughter, where the train will carry us all to Cairo. When we arrive in Cairo, Teddy and his family are returning to the States. I have decided to go to London before heading back to retire on the Devil Fish Ranch.

"Ishmael, I am so glad that you could join us on this adventure," Teddy said as he gave me a pat on the back.

"Teddy, I wouldn't have missed it for the world."

"I don't know what my next undertaking will be. But I would love to have you alongside me."

"Oh, I think that this was probably my last true enterprise. I think I'm getting too old for these ventures."

"Nonsense!" He bellowed.

"Teddy, promise me that next time you are anywhere near Stockton, you'll take some time and come visit the Devil Fish Ranch."

"I promise."

"Bully!" I said.

The look on his face was priceless when I said, bully. I thought he'd bust a gut laughing. He looked around, gave me a big bear hug, and whispered, "You take care of yourself."

The result of our expedition was that the United States National Museum acquired approximately 1,000 skins of large mammals, 4,000 small mammals, and other specimens totaling approximately 11,400 items. About 10,000 plant specimens were also obtained, and a small collection of ethnological objects.

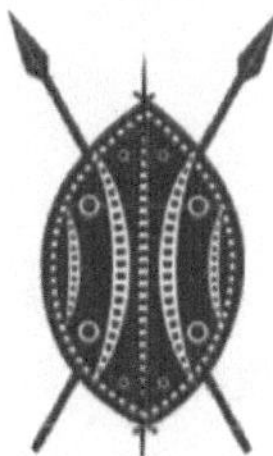

On the day I arrived in London, it was overcast, foggy, and rainy. The streets were filled with men dressed in black and grey overcoats holding their bumbershoots high over their heads. The scene reminded me of a painting by famed British painter J.M.W. Turner.

"Good day, sir. And welcome back to the Savoy," The receptionist behind the counter greeted.

Behind the reception desk hung a picture of the recently departed King Edward VII; his portrait was draped in black.

"Thank you, Charles. It's good to be back. I'm sorry to hear about the King," I said.

"Thank you, sir. He will be missed. The King is dead. Long live the King," The young man said.

"Did they say what he passed away from?" I asked.

"Heart attack."

I wasn't surprised; Edward was known to smoke twenty cigarettes and twelve cigars a day, every day.

"Here you go, Gov. I have your old room, 666. If there's anything you might need, just give me a call. Oh, and you have a message," He said as he handed me a personal-sized envelope with my name handwritten in script.

"Thank you, Charles; I'll do that."

After settling into my room, I read the note from John Astor.

Dear Ishmael,

I am glad to hear that you had a successful expedition with Teddy. I am currently in London on business with Ava and am staying with our good friend Sir Ainsworth.

We would love to get together at your convivence to hear all about your adventures in the Dark Continent. Sir Ainsworth has a dinner planned for this upcoming Friday. Please let us know if you can attend.

We are all looking forward to seeing you then.
Regards,
JJA

THE FINAL VOYAGE

Sir Ainsworth greeted me at the door when I arrived for the dinner party.

"Ishmael, it's so good to see you, old chap. You're looking well. I guess going on safari agrees with you," Ainsworth said, half-joking.

"You as well. Have you been practicing your draw? You never know when you might get into a gunfight."

He looked around to see that no one was listening and softly said, "I have, actually. Maybe later we can slip away, and I can show you."

"I would look forward to it, pardner," I whispered, smiling.

Ainsworth directed me into the salon where a group of people was standing together talking, laughing, and sipping champagne, with the exception of John Astor and his lovely wife, Ava. I didn't know any of them.

"Ishmael, good to see you. It's been too long," Astor said.

"Good to see you. And you, Ava. How are you enjoying London?" I asked lady Astor.

She smiled and said, "I love London, but I hate the weather. It's always so gloomy."

Sir Ainsworth stepped up and said, "Ishmael, I would like to introduce you to some friends of mine and Johns."

We walked over to the group, "Everybody, I'd like you all to meet a very good friend of mine, Ishmael.

Ishmael, I'd like to introduce you to George Widener and his wife, Eleanor. George is head of the Philadelphia Traction Company. They're involved in the development of cable and electric streetcars."

"Mister and Mrs. Widener, it's my pleasure to meet you," I said.

"The pleasure is ours," Widener replied.

"Have you ever been to Philadelphia?" Mrs. Widener asked.

"No, ma'am, I've never had. But I've always wanted to see the Liberty Bell."

"Well, you have an open invitation to Lynnewood Hall whenever you have the time," Mrs. Widener offered.

"Thank you. That's very kind of you."

"And Ishmael, I'd like you to meet my very good friends, Sir Cosmo and Lady Duff Gordon, a prominent Scottish landowner, sportsman, and Baronet. Lady Duff Gordon is one of the World's most celebrated fashion designers," Ainsworth said.

"Would the dress you're wearing tonight be one of your designs? Because it's quite lovely," I asked.

"Why yes, thank you. It is," She said, seeming pride and yet a bit embarrassed.

As we were spread out having drinks in the salon, I noticed that one of Sir Ainsworth's border collies silently went about the room, gently touching and rubbing against the guest's legs. Causing people to unconsciously take a tiny step toward the center of the room. Eventually, we became aware that the dog had managed to herd us into a tight group, where we were all standing next to each other.

Sir Ainsworth began to scold the dog, "Ranger! Sit!"

"Don't scold the pup. He's only doing his job," I said.

Lady Duff Gordon and several other guests came to Ranger's defense. "That's right; the poor thing is just doing what comes naturally."

"Ladies and gentlemen, dinner is served," The head steward announced.

Sir Ainsworth went to the salon doorway and said, "Right this way, please."

I was seated next to John Astor and Sir Cosmo Duff Gordon. I spent most if not all of dinner talking about my time on the expedition with Teddy Roosevelt and my teaching in Sir Ainsworth the fine art of quick-draw shooting.

Towards the end of dinner, John asked when I might be going back to the States. I decided that I was ready to go back to the Devil Fish Ranch after stopping in Boston to visit Jonah and Martha.

"Ishmael, everyone here is planning on taking the White Star's newest liner back to New York City on April 10th. If you'd like, I could arrange your passage when I have my secretary book mine?" Astor asked.

"April 10th, that would work for me. Thank you, John, that's very kind of you," I said.

"What the Hell, you're family," He said with a grin.

"Lady Duff Gordon and I are booked to sail, too. As are the Wideners," Sir Cosmo disclosed.

Sir Ainsworth stood away from the table, "Shall we retire to the salon for some brandy and cigars?"

"Later. Let's go out back and have Ishmael demonstrate the art of quick-draw," Sir Cosmo demanded.

"And you can show how much you've improved since the last time we practiced," I said to Sir Ainsworth.

Sir Ainsworth had a western-style shooting range specially built. There were several bullseye targets and painted figures of gunfighters and Indians. Sir Ainsworth and I strapped on our holsters as the guests crowed around to watch.

"You go first," I said to my host.

Sir Ainsworth took off his evening jacket and tied off his holster's leg tie. He pulled out the Colt, opened the cylinder to ensure it was loaded, and slid the pistol back into the holster. He took his stance, drew the pistol, and fired.

POW POW POW POW POW

"Oh, Sir Ainsworth, that was quite impressive. Very good. I can see that you've been practicing," I exclaimed.

The shots didn't get close to the bullseye, and he would have only winged the painted figures, but at least he didn't miss. The audience gave Sir Ainsworth a polite round of applause. He graciously took a slight bow, turned to me, and said, "Thank you, thank you. Ishmael, now you."

I also went through the same ritual as Sir Ainsworth, taking off my evening jacket and tying off the holster's leg tie. I checked the Colt's cylinder to make sure it was fully loaded. I took my stance, drew the pistol, and fired.

POW POW POW POW POW

When the smoke had cleared, I had scored three bullseyes and two kill shots to the painted gunslingers.

The onlookers gave me a somewhat larger round of applause. I walked over to Sir Ainsworth, put my arm around him, and said, "I would feel comfortable going into a gunfight with Sir Ainsworth by my side. Right pard?"

"Right."

"Any of you would like to give it a go?" Sir Ainsworth asked.

No one stepped forward; all the men looked down at the shoes. I finally got John and Sir Cosmo to strap on the gun belt and fire off a few rounds. They both were terrible, which brought great joy to Sir Ainsworth, who had taken much ribbing in the past. As the evening came to an end, I said goodbye to Sir Ainsworth, "Goodbye, Sir Ainsworth, thank you for everything."

"It was my great pleasure, Ishmael. Come back anytime."

"Why don't you come out West. I can always use a good shot on the ranch."

"I'll think about it. Can I bring Ranger?"

"You bet. Once Queequeg passed, we haven't had a good working dog on the ranch since. So long, pard," I said.

"Goodbye and bon voyage, buckaroo." Sir Ainsworth called out as I joined John Astor and Ava in their car.

On April 10th, hours before we were to set sail, I sent a telegraph to Jonah,

DEAR JONAH AND MARTHA STOP LEAVING SOUTHAMPTON APRIL 10 STOP WILL ARRIVE NEW YORK APRIL 17 PIER 59 STOP CAN'T WAIT TO SEE YOU AND MARTHA STOP LOVE DAD STOP

That night the Astors, the Duff Gordons, Benjamin

Guggenheim, the Wideners, Margaret "Molly" Brown, and I were the guest of Captain Edward Smith to sit at the Captain's table in the First-Class Dining Saloon.

I had rarely seen such elegance in a restaurant on land and never on a ship; the Dining Saloon was enormous. It could accommodate over 500 passengers. The walls were made distinctive by painting them white with beautiful leaded-glass windows covering the portholes giving the room the appearance of an elegant, land-based restaurant.

I spent most of my days taking walks on the Promenade, playing poker in the Smoking Room, and meeting other First-Class passengers such as the painter and sculptor Francis Davis Millet, noted architect Edward Austin Kent, and silent film actress Dorothy Gibson. Sometimes I would sit for hours in a deck chair on the Promenade, watching the world go by. Occasionally I would spot a pod of sperm whales off in the distance on their yearly migration. I can remember the excitement the sighting of a pod of sperm whales would have generated among the men on board the *Pequod*.

It happened on our fourth day out, on April 14th, when I swear that I spotted a white whale amongst a large pod swimming eastwardly. When I spotted it, I hurried up to the Bridge to see if I could borrow a pair of high-powered binoculars so that I could ease my mind.

While standing outside the Bridge, peering out into the ocean, I caught a brief glimpse of the white whale. I can't swear that that was Moby Dick, although I know that sperm whales can live to be 80 years old and some even longer. I got a shiver down my spine. Could it have been him? I will never know, but deep down, I wish it were. After all these years, seeing him brought a thousand memories flooding over me like a giant tsunami.

That night after dinner, while John Astor, George Widener, Sir Cosmo, Benjamin Guggenheim, and I were playing a friendly game of five-card stud, drinking brandy, and smoking Cuban cigars when we felt a shutter that ran throughout the ship at 11:40 PM.

"What the Hell was that?" Sir Cosmo asked one of the stewards.

"I'll go find out," He said as he hurried out of the Smoking Room.

UNSINKABLE

Moments later, the steward entered the room looking a. white as snow and announced that the ship had just hit an iceberg.

"Surely it is of no consequence. The Titanic is unsinkable," Sir Cosmo chuckled.

Soon we began to hear the stampede of people running along the decks in a panic, screaming. Then we heard the order to start lowering the lifeboats. That's when everyone at the table knew that the Titanic was going to sink. John Astor and Sir Cosmo, George Widener, Benjamin Guggenheim, and I say our goodbyes knowing that the chances are that we will not survive as the abandoning of the ship is a colossal fuck up.

"Good luck to each of you, and Godspeed," I said as I went out on deck to see if I could be of some assistance.

Most of the lifeboats are being loaded well below capacity; a boat that could hold 65 is being lowered with just 27 people on board. The order is given for only women and children to board the lifeboats. I did spy Sir Cosmo Edmund Duff Gordon and his wife and seven crew members occupying one of the life rafts. I saw him bribe the crew to keep anyone else out of the lifeboat. He saw me and knew that I had seen what he had done and quickly turned away as the boat was lowered.

I was making my way to the bow of the great ship when I passed Benjamin Guggenheim and his valet, who had just put Benjamin's mistress into a lifeboat. He said, "We've dressed up in our best and are prepared to go down like gentlemen."

Benjamin Guggenheim was the last person I saw

before the ship finally went under; although I didn't see them, I did hear the Titanic orchestra playing 'Nearer. My God to thee.'

As the Titanic slowly descended into the black waters on the North Atlantic, I began to reflect on my life. I must admit I have no complaints. I have lived a rich and full life. I have no regrets; my life has had many twists and turns, as has everyone. I was lucky to have had numerous adventures, been married to a wonderful woman, and had a son, whom I am most proud of. I lived among pirates as well as kings.

This was my story. Call me Ishmael.

M. Ward Leon – Author

M. Ward Leon is a former advertising creative director who started his career at Doyle Dane Bernbach, New York, during the Madmen era. While at DDB, his writing on the Volkswagen Rabbit campaign won him inclusion into the Smithsonian Institution Advertising Archives. Recently his writing has earned him two National Emmy Awards for Public Service advertising.

His novels include *The Blood of the Beast, Revenge of the Beast, The Strange and Curious Cases of Roscoe Brown, Detective NYPD,* and *Ambush at Fig Tree Gulch.* Several novels are award winners, including the 2020 Texas Best Action-Adventure Award, Honorable Mention in the Paris Book Festival, and the New York Book Festival.

Mr. Leon is a California State University Los Angeles graduate and an Art Center College of Design alumnus.

To learn more, please go to *mwardleon.com.*